COOKING MOST DEADLY

J O A N N E   P E N C E

HarperPaperbacks
A Division of HarperCollins*Publishers*

![HarperPaperbacks logo] HarperPaperbacks
A Division of HarperCollinsPublishers
10 East 53rd Street, New York, N.Y. 10022-5299

ISBN 0-06-104395-8

HarperCollins®, ![logo]®, and HarperPaperbacks™
are trademarks of HarperCollinsPublishers Inc.

Cover illustration by Richard Rossiter

First HarperPaperbacks printing: September 1996

Printed in the United States of America

Visit HarperPaperbacks on the World Wide Web at
http://www.harpercollins.com

❖ 10 9 8 7 6

To my husband, David, for twenty-five wonderful years of love, laughter, unwavering support, and never a dull moment—here's to the next twenty-five.

ACKNOWLEDGMENTS

Thanks and gratitude go to many people for their assistance with this book. To Homicide Inspector Napolean Hendrix, SFPD, for his time and patience; to Kate Moore, Monica Sevy, Barbara Truax, Pam Collins, Tracy Grant; to Joan Grant—who I'm sure is watching over us, smiling and wise as ever; to Berta Flynn, Doris Berdahl, Helen Howard, and Meredythe Crawford; to Luke Murden; to Rose Lopez and Madeline Addiego, who know the *right* way to cook; to Robert Lopez for *his* North Beach; to my agent, Sue Yuen, for helping put the pieces together; to my editor, Carolyn Marino, for her encouragement and support in the creation of this series; and most of all, to David Pence, for his help in every way possible.

My apologies for any errors, omission, or license taken with the facts for purposes of the story.

CHAPTER

ONE

He sat in the cold, cramped, lime green Honda, his legs and spine stiff and aching.

Earlier, he had watched the fog advance from the Pacific to immerse the neighborhood and its bundled-together houses under a suffocating shroud. Shapes had become blurred and obscure in the frigid dampness, the streets slick and treacherous.

Now it was night. The thick fog had faded into a fine mist that powdered his windshield.

No one seemed to notice him sitting there. No one had paid any attention to him last evening either, or the evening before that. Alone, he kept his vigil over the homicide inspector's brown-shingled cottage. If tonight didn't work out, he'd return tomorrow. What did one day, or five, or even ten, matter? His patience would be rewarded.

He'd planned everything meticulously. Even the unexpected had been anticipated, reasoned. He'd learned that when people rush they grow careless, make mistakes. But, even taking his time, it should be over by Easter. He chuckled at the symbolism.

The low, throaty rumble of a Ferrari Testarossa engine

reverberated as it turned the corner onto the quiet street. Once, he'd have given his eyeteeth for wheels like that, but he'd cleansed his flesh of such material desires. His desires in this lifetime were far more pure, more simple.

The Ferrari stopped in front of the cottage he'd been watching. Its headlights switched off, and the door of the low-riding car swung open. He adjusted his glasses higher on his nose and leaned forward to watch, as if the few inches would matter with his nearsightedness.

A foot in a high-heeled shoe emerged, a narrow ankle, a shapely calf, then another. As the woman eased her way from the car, her cherry red skirt rode up, exposing the curves of her nyloned legs. She was petite, beautiful, and dressed to match the expensive elegance of the sports car.

Starting the Honda's engine, he waited until he was sure she was headed toward the cop's house, then made his way slowly toward her.

Angelina Amalfi turned around at the rackety pings of the approaching car and watched as it pulled up alongside hers. The driver leaned toward the passenger door and rolled down the window. The nearby streetlamp illuminated a long, narrow face with thick, black-framed glasses and a San Francisco Giants baseball cap pulled low over the brow.

"Complimentary copy of the *Chronicle* for you." The driver sidearmed a rolled-up newspaper over the hood of the Ferrari. It skidded to a stop at her feet.

She picked it up and read the date. "This morning's news. How exciting." She was tempted to fling it right back, but she'd never been too good with Frisbees.

"Wait," he called, as she tucked the paper under her arm and walked toward the house. "Are you the lady of the house? Two months for the price of one."

"Sorry, not interested." She kept going.

"Maybe your husband is?"

She glanced back over her shoulder. "He's not my husband, but I'm sure he's not interested either."

"Maybe someday, real soon."

"What?" His puzzling words caused her to stop, but he'd already lurched the car forward, the tires squealing on the wet pavement. He stopped at the next house and tossed a paper onto the front steps, and then went on to the house after that.

She'd have to tell one of her friends down at the *Chronicle* that they needed to hire a better class of salesman. There was something vaguely troubling about this late-working one.

"I thought I heard your car."

The voice startled her from her thoughts. Homicide Inspector Paavo Smith stood in his doorway, one hand against the frame, the other on the doorknob.

"What are you doing out there?" he asked. He had a just-awakened, slightly disoriented look, his blue eyes soft instead of sharp and controlled, and his wavy, dark brown hair falling onto his brow instead of neatly combed to the side. His gray sweatshirt was rumpled, and bare feet showed beneath his jeans.

"Did I wake you?" She hurried up the front steps to him, wrapped her arms around his waist, and kissed him. He was a big man, strong, hard, and tough. But not with her. "I'm sorry, Paavo."

"It's all right." Keeping his arms around her, he backed into the house and shut the door. "I fell asleep on the couch. I was having this great dream"—he returned her kiss— "and here you are."

He felt good in her arms, too good, too able to make her forget why she had come here. She broke away and walked into the living room. With its mismatched, overstuffed furniture and array of well-read books and magazines, the room was somehow comforting to her, so different from her formal, antique-laden apartment. "I thought you only dreamed about murder cases, Inspector."

"Not always," he murmured, following her. He studied her a moment. "Out with it, Angie."

"Out with it?" she asked innocently.

He tilted his head, his expression wry. "It's clearly not

my devastating charm that brought you here tonight. What's on your mind? Is anything wrong?"

She nodded.

"What is it?"

"I'm so upset!" She took a deep breath. "I've walked my feet raw trying to find an interesting restaurant to write about for *Haute Cuisine* magazine. There's nothing out there. I'm so discouraged, I don't know what to do!"

He led her toward the sofa. "Angie." Her name was a sigh of relief. "Is that all?"

"*All?*"

"I know it's important, but—"

"So it's not homicide. It's just my life, my career."

He sat on the sofa, trying not to smile, then leaned back. Long legs stretched out in front of him, and folded hands rested on his stomach. "Let's start over. Explain it to me. We both know this city's loaded with restaurants. Now, what's the problem?"

She put the newspaper down on the coffee table and placed her purse on top of it, then took off her jacket and dropped it over an easy chair. Paavo's big yellow tabby, Hercules, curled up on an afghan on the opposite side of the sofa, glowered at this disturbance to his peaceful slumber.

Angie went over to Hercules. Using her long, silk-wrapped, raspberry-colored nails, she scratched the top of his head and around his ears. He purred, contentedly shutting his eyes. "The problem is that nobody wants to read another magazine article about Chef La-di-dah's latest epicurean adventure," she said, her back to Paavo. "That's old hat. I want to write about something unique. Something that will make people sit up and take notice—of *me,* if not the restaurant. I'm tired of not having a decent job to call my own."

Paavo reached for the hand she was using to pet the cat and took it in his own. "Something will turn up for you, Angie. Give it time." His voice held comfort and assurance. "Believe me."

"I hope you're right," she said softly.

Tugging on the hand he held, he drew her toward him. This time, she didn't resist.

As the green Honda climbed California Street, its wheels spun on cable car tracks wet from the drizzling mist. Damn! If he'd been able to find a parking place, he wouldn't be having this problem. But finding parking at midnight on Nob Hill was impossible except for ridiculously expensive parking garages. He wasn't about to pay the money.

He'd waited at the cop's cottage over an hour for the broad to come out, but she didn't. He figured she'd spend the night there. That was fine with him. He had another little friend to check on.

Just past Taylor Street, a silver, boat-sized Mercedes sat in valet parking a few steps from the Coventry Hotel. It had been parked for two hours already. The Coventry seemed like pretty plush digs to be used as a by-the-hour screw parlor. But what else was it?

For those same two hours, he'd driven up and down the city streets, waiting, compelled by the need to be sure. A lesser man would have discovered the existence of a more direct target and would have stopped there. But not him. He double-checked everything. Everything had to be exact.

Two days ago he'd visited the woman's apartment up on Twin Peaks and gave her a complimentary copy of the *Chronicle*. Women were suckers for freebies like that.

She was blond and attractive, with a body that was ripe, fleshy, and well rounded; the kind that would fall to fat hips and sagging breasts in a few years, but in the meantime, made for pleasure. A man's pleasure. She was also a bit dense. He'd had to explain what he meant by a two-for-one offer.

Abruptly breaking off his thoughts, he stared hard, squinting, to see better the two figures that emerged from the hotel. He stopped the car at the first open space he could find—a garage driveway. Blocking it, he cut the Honda's headlights.

It was 11:53.

As they passed under yellow streetlights, the features of the tall, silver-haired man and the young woman beside him were illuminated. She was indeed the dull-witted blonde he'd met at the Twin Peaks apartment. But even more than the woman, his interest was directed at the man.

The man escorted her to her white LeBaron and with a smug, self-confident expression, watched her drive off, before hurrying to his Mercedes. He glanced once, dismissively, at the bespectacled man in the illegally parked Honda, then got into his car and drove off.

The next morning, the Honda cruised by the brown-shingled cottage once again. The Ferrari and the cop's car, an old Austin Healey, were both gone.

It didn't matter. They'd be back. No need to hurry. He'd planned too carefully to blow it now.

Ten years was a long time to plan. A long time to make up for.

He deserved something for those ten years. And for Heather.

This was all about Heather.

He sped through the winding, wooded paths of the Presidio to emerge at the east gate. On Baker Street, he parked directly across from the Palace of Fine Arts, the orange-hued Grecian landmark of the elegant Marina district. A half hour later, the front door of a large, stucco home opened. An elderly, shrunken man, nattily dressed in gray slacks, a gray plaid sport coat, and bowler hat, stepped out. He watched as the old man slowly walked down the long flight of stairs to the sidewalk and turned toward the Green, the popular, lawn-covered play area that ran along the north coast of the city from the Presidio to Fort Mason.

After waiting a couple of minutes, he stepped from his car and ran up the stairs to the front door, dropped a

Chronicle in front of it, rang the bell, and raced back down to the sidewalk.

Soon, an elderly woman appeared in a pink floral house-coat, her white hair in dozens of tight little ringlets across her head, as if she'd just removed her curlers and hadn't had time to brush her hair out.

He waved at her, pointed to the rolled newspapers in his arms, and then to her stoop. When she saw the paper lying at her feet, she smiled and nodded, waved back to him, then took the newspaper indoors with her.

It was going to be almost too easy, he thought.

CHAPTER

T W O

"You better button it up, Vinnie," Butch Pagozzi shouted, running halfway down the basement stairs. Over sixty years old, he was small, lightweight, and felt every bit as spry as forty years before, when he'd fought Tiny Alvarez for the bantamweight title. Butch lost. "We got a customer. A broad!"

"You gotta be kiddin'. What kinda broad would wanna eat in a joint like this?" Vinnie Freiman stood his pickax against the cement wall right beside the sledgehammer, picked up his cigar, and chewed the end as smoke billowed around his balding head. A Coleman lantern lit the area beside him. When he glanced up at Butch, the light created shadows on the layers of bags under his eyes, giving him even more of a basset hound look than usual.

"I don't know," Butch muttered. "What am I gonna do?"

"Get ridda her."

"I cooked somethin' up just in case somebody wanted to eat. But what if she don't like it?"

Vinnie, a short, stocky man, pulled a huge, rumpled handkerchief out of the back pocket of his baggy brown

trousers and mopped his brow and the back of his neck.
"Who the hell cares? We don't want her here anyway,
remember?"

"You're right. Who cares? But you never know—she
might like it." Butch wrung his hands. "I mean, nobody
ever complained about my cookin' before."

Vinnie took the cigar out of his mouth. "That's 'cause
they was too busy barfin'."

"Jesus! What am I doin' here?" Butch grumbled. He sat
down on the steps. "How'd I get into this mess?"

"Get up there and get ridda the broad," Vinnie ordered.
"I got work to do. Or maybe you think doin' this is better
than standin' over a stove? You want we should change
places?"

"But you don't cook," Butch said.

"Not a lick."

"I'll take care of the customer."

"I thought so."

Butch ran back up to the kitchen of what had once been
a small but thriving restaurant. The kitchen was fully
equipped and clean. After some of the places he'd cooked,
Butch still marveled every time he stepped into his new
quarters.

Still, the thought of a paying customer in the dining
room made his eye twitch so badly, he could barely keep it
open. He checked the seasoning in his spaghetti sauce. He
guessed it was okay. It seemed okay. Sort of.

"'Ey Butch," Earl White yelled, pushing through the
swinging doors from the dining room. Earl, the third member of the trio, had the assignment of working the dining
room since he was the only one with experience in dealing
with customers. He'd once worked as a bouncer in Vegas.
The job didn't last too long, though. Tough as he was, he
found that five-foot-five bouncers sometimes got bounced
themselves. "Da broad ain't leavin'. What am I s'posed to
do?"

"Give her a menu."

"A menu? But you only cooked spaghetti an' meatballs."

"So?"

"But I t'ought I was s'posed to get ridda her," Earl said quietly, not wanting to press the obvious. He didn't want Butch to get mad at him.

Butch eyed the door to the basement. Vinnie's cracks about his cooking still smarted. "Well, maybe she wants to eat somethin' first. This is a restaurant, you know."

Heaving a sigh, Earl searched for a menu.

Angie glanced over her shoulder at the sign in the window. It definitely said "OPEN." Too bad no one connected with the restaurant knew it. When she walked in, the waiter had stared at her without a word and then run into the kitchen.

As she waited at the entrance, she looked over the empty dining area, a small, cozy room, with wood-stained walls and big, round, white lighting fixtures. It might have had some charm except that the tables were topped with gray Formica, had aluminum legs, and were surrounded by aluminum chairs with padded gray vinyl seats. Glass salt and pepper shakers completed the decor. This was hardly the accoutrement she expected in a restaurant with the ethereal, whimsical name of The Wings Of An Angel.

Then it struck her. This had to be one of those fifties nostalgia places. That's why it looked so tacky. It was supposed to. She felt a little slow, but then, she was a nineties kind of gal.

The chubby little man who'd run away earlier peered at her from the kitchen and then stepped through the swinging doors into the dining room. He wore a yellow shirt and brown polyester slacks—the sartorial equivalent of gray Formica and vinyl, she guessed.

"You wanna eat?" he asked. His thick, curly brown toupee looked almost shellacked, reminding her of those fifties dolls with plugs of shiny vinyl hair stuck into their scalps. She was impressed. This place really went all out for authenticity.

"The restaurant is open, isn't it?" she asked, still staring at his hair.

"I guess." He didn't move. When she didn't move either, he waved an arm toward the empty tables and said, "Have a seat."

"Thanks." She was growing more dubious about staying. But maybe the waiter had a weird sense of humor. He certainly had a weird accent. He had to be from either San Francisco's North Beach or Mission districts—or Brooklyn. The accents were amazingly similar.

She chose a spot by the window overlooking Columbus Avenue. This part of the avenue was fairly quiet. A drugstore, card shop, jewelers, locksmith, and small corner grocery served the people who lived and worked nearby.

The waiter dropped an old, greasy menu on the table in front of her. The name across the top, Columbus Avenue Café, had been lined through with a ballpoint pen. The new name hadn't been written in.

"I understand this restaurant just opened," she said.

"Couple days ago."

"How's business?"

He shrugged. "Okay."

Why didn't she believe him?

"Good," she said, eyeing the menu again. She'd always thought preparing a menu and seeing the restaurant's name printed on it would be one of the biggest thrills a new owner could have. For the owner to still be using the former café's menu made no sense to her at all.

As the waiter walked away, she turned her attention to the dinner entrees. Pasta Primavera. Ravioli. Veal Parmigiana. All the regulars. It was a surprisingly complete menu, and the smells coming from the kitchen were inviting.

This place had been closed for months, ever since the Columbus Avenue Café, a well-respected but unprofitable establishment, had gone under. The building's owners had been desperate, she'd heard, and willing to rent out the restaurant space for a song. The problem was the location. A little too far north of fashionable North Beach restaurants to pick up the trendy crowd, yet too far south of Fisherman's Wharf to get its trade. The location ended up serving only people who unknowingly wandered away from the other restaurants and grew desperate. A tough way to make a living.

She beckoned the waiter over.

"I'll try your manicotti. With it, I'd like a small salad with Italian dressing served with the main course, not before, and the house red."

He squinted as if in pain. She noticed that his face was heavily lined under the toupee. "Uh, we don't have no manicotti today."

"Oh. That's too bad. How's the lasagna?"

"Same as da manicotti."

She wasn't sure she'd heard right. "Veal Parmigiana?"

He shook his head.

She shut the menu. "What *do* you have?"

"Spaghetti an' meatballs."

She handed him back the menu. "Fine."

He half waddled, half ran back to the kitchen. Maybe she'd be smart just to leave without waiting for dinner. But she was hungry, and this was a new restaurant in town. Leaning back wearily, she ran her fingers through her hair, brushing it back off her forehead. Being a freelance restaurant reviewer meant she had to be adventurous, despite the occasional disastrous meal. On the other hand, if the food here was especially good, this would be regarded as her personal find. A feather in her cap.

Right now, though, she had the sinking feeling her cap would soon resemble a plucked turkey.

Somehow, she was going to have to come up with a job that paid a decent salary. She lived in a beautiful apartment in a building owned by her parents, and her Ferrari had been a gift from them. But it was time to become independent, self-sufficient—especially if she planned to give serious thought to marriage.

She was a person used to knowing her own mind and acting on that knowledge with conviction. Great conviction, in fact. Marriage, though, had her baffled. The thought of it was scary.

The sight of Curly-locks heading her way juggling a heaping plate of spaghetti and meatballs, plus a basket of French bread and butter, broke her out of her reverie. As he placed it on the table, he stared at her forehead.

"Thank you," she said, trying unsuccessfully to make eye contact. "It looks wonderful."

"Yeah." He continued to stare.

"This restaurant has a beautiful name," she said uneasily. Was there such a thing as a forehead fetish? "The Wings Of An Angel. I was expecting gossamer curtains on the windows and warm wooden furnishings."

"Yeah? Well, dis ain't so classy. Maybe you wanna leave now?"

"Leave? I haven't eaten yet."

"You got some doit."

"Doit?"

"On your forehead. Doit."

She tugged at her bangs, pulling a few strands of hair back onto her forehead. "Not dirt, it's ash. Today's Ash Wednesday. I was at Ss. Peter and Paul's Church up the street. That's how I found you."

"We was wonderin' how you found us."

"I guess that makes me God's gift to you," she said, and then grinned. "Not only that, your restaurant has the word Angel in its name, and my name's Angelina. Sounds like fate to me."

The waiter blanched and started to back away. He couldn't possibly think she was being serious, could he? "Just leave da money on da table," he said.

"I'm joking," she called, but he didn't stop. "How much is it?"

Over his shoulder he shouted, "Two bucks."

Two bucks? Nothing cost two dollars anymore, except maybe a cup of espresso. Caffe latte and cappuccino were usually more. This place was too strange. She twisted some spaghetti around her fork and took a bite. Hmm . . .

She took another bite, shut her eyes, and chewed. The sauce was delicious. Different, she had to admit. A little odd. But still, delicious. She tasted the meatballs. They'd been cooked in the red sauce, and the combination of flavors had merged in a mysteriously heavenly way. There were all the regular meatball and spaghetti sauce flavors— ground beef, tomato paste, garlic, onion, basil, oregano, fennel, a touch of ground pork . . . and something else as well. What? It was a trifle salty, whatever it was, but quite good.

She kept eating, trying to figure out the mix of ingredients, but couldn't. "Waiter!" she called. "Waiter!"

He stuck his head out between the swinging doors. "You ain't chokin', are you?" he asked.

"No. I was wondering if I could have a word with your cook."

"He don't talk to nobody." His head disappeared.

She listened to the sound of hammering coming from the kitchen. Maybe they were still doing some construction, and that's why things were so out of kilter here. She took another bite. Delicious.

That did it. She was going to find out what was in those meatballs if it killed her.

CHAPTER

THREE

Paavo sat at his gray metal desk in the tightly crammed office of the Homicide detail and reached for his phone. Around him, stacks of books and papers balanced precariously, the only clear space being a small area in front of his computer. For the sixth time in the past three hours, he punched out Angie's number. For as many times, he'd listened to her answering machine.

He hung up in disgust. Last night, she'd told him she'd be home this evening. He'd planned to surprise her by taking her out to dinner. Too often after making plans for an evening out, he'd get involved in a case and have to cancel. This time he'd decided not to call her until he was sure he'd be free—and she wasn't home.

Homicide was practically empty. Most of the inspectors had gone home or were out in the field.

He finished his report on a suicide out on Castro Street—the third this month. This city was known for its high suicide rate, but despite all the psychological rot about why they happened here—two centuries of "go west, young man," the end of the trail, and so forth—three deaths within thirty days was too many. Homicide had to check out each one to be sure it wasn't a cleverly disguised murder. But in this case, his gut reaction was that the dying man didn't want to wait for the full ravages of the disease that would soon claim him.

He leaned back in his chair and glared at the telephone. Where had Angie gone? Between doting parents, four older sisters, all married and with kids, cousins, and friends, she could be anywhere.

He phoned her neighbor, Stanfield Bonnette. Paavo could barely stomach Bonnette, but Angie seemed to like the guy, and sometimes she dropped in over there. Bonnette lived in a small one-bedroom place across the hall from Angie's larger apartment.

"Hello! Stan the man, here."

Paavo nearly hung up the phone right then. "This is Paavo Smith. I'm trying to locate Angie. Have you seen her?"

"Ah, the good inspector! Well, well, what a surprise." Paavo hated the smug sound of Bonnette's voice. "I'm sorry to admit I haven't seen Angelina today. She usually tells me where she's going, too. I'm surprised she didn't this time. I guess she doesn't tell you her whereabouts anymore at all, does she?"

Paavo didn't know what Bonnette meant by that crack, but he knew what was being implied, and he didn't like it. "Thanks for your help," he said, then hung up. Hell, Bonnette was just trying to get his goat, and—dammit— he'd succeeded.

Paavo considered calling Angie's mother and asking if Angie was there, but immediately dismissed that thought. Once Serefina got him on the phone she'd say that if they'd just get married, he wouldn't have the problem of not knowing where Angie was. They wouldn't have to arrange dates—they'd see each other at home every night. Angie hadn't said anything yet, but he had the feeling her thoughts were traveling along much the same route.

"No luck, Paav?" his partner, Toshiro Yoshiwara, asked.

Yosh had transferred down to the San Francisco department a couple of months ago from Seattle, where he had been highly regarded. He was a big man, tall as Paavo, broad-shouldered, with huge, strong hands and a small head that bore only a stubble of black hair from his buzz cut. He had been teamed with Paavo after Paavo's long-time partner was killed by gun smugglers. Yosh was as boisterous and outgoing as Paavo was quiet and reserved.

"She's been out all afternoon."

"Tell you what," Yosh said. "Let's go down to the Court House and have a beer. You can phone her from there."

"If she goes home."

"It's worth a try." As he spoke, he swung around in his swivel chair. "Hey, look who's here. It's Mr. Jolly!"

Luis Calderon had just entered the room. Frowning, without a word to anyone, he walked straight to his desk.

"Hey there, Luis," Yosh called out. "How ya doing?"

Calderon's expression grew more dyspeptic. "Lousy."

"Lousy?" Yosh repeated, acting shocked. "What's wrong?"

"I hate this time of year. It's the worst. When I was a kid I was supposed to give up something for Lent. But we were so poor I didn't have anything to give up."

Paavo gave a quick shake of his head, hoping to stop Yosh. Everyone who'd ever worked with Calderon had heard this before. Every year, every season, a litany of Calderon complaints. Even before his wife, Carlota, left him, the guy viewed life through misery-colored glasses.

Instead of stopping, though, Yosh winked. "And soon," he said, in a mock-soothing tone, "all that changes with the beauty of Easter."

"Sure. All that candy making kids sick. Easter bunnies. You know what my family used to do with Easter bunnies? Eat them. I grew up scarfing down Peter Rabbit."

Yosh got up from his chair and plunked his bulky, well-muscled body on the edge of his desk. "I thought you said Christmas was the worst time of year?"

"Yeah." Calderon sighed. "It stinks, too. Holidays stink.

I hate 'em. So, you two supposed to stick around and cheer me up tonight, or what?"

"I'm heading for the Court House," Yosh said, then turned to Paavo. "You coming?"

"Paavo doesn't go for that stuff," Calderon said. "Anyway, I could use a little help here."

Paavo wasn't one to stop at the neighborhood watering hole, and everyone in Homicide knew it. Usually he'd just go home when work quieted down. Tonight, though, he felt antsy, and the thought of staying with Calderon had less than zero appeal.

He grabbed his jacket. "Okay, Yosh," he said. "Lead the way."

Homicide was located in the Hall of Justice, an ugly, block-sized monstrosity that housed the police administration offices, coroner, office of the district attorney, courtrooms, judges' chambers, and a variety of other city government offices. Behind it stood a brand-new, scandalously expensive city jail with a twenty-two-thousand-dollar curved sofa in the waiting room, paid for out of Art Commission funds. Across from it stood a fast-food restaurant that was shut down before it ever opened to the public because it had been built on top of a former gas station site, and someone apparently "forgot" to mention that the ground was contaminated.

One block away stood the only facility that functioned well, efficiently and profitably, in the whole area—the Court House, a decent bar in a neighborhood of dives. Hall of Justice employees from bailiffs to the chief of inspectors lifted glasses in there. Lawyers for the defense rubbed shoulders with district attorneys. It was said that more pleas had been bargained in that bar than in all the offices in the Hall put together.

The smoke-filled lounge was packed when Paavo and Yosh entered.

"Hey, Paavo," called one of the assistant DAs, Hanover Judd. "Long time no see."

The DA's offices were on the third floor of the Hall, with Homicide directly above them on the fourth. Paavo had recently spent a lot of time on three working with Judd on what had become known as a reverse burning bed case—one of those typically bizarre San Francisco cases where a husband offed his wife while she slept because, he claimed, he had grown tired of her beating him. It reflected poorly on his manliness, he cried, and had the bruises to prove it. The problem was, it was all a lie.

Paavo discovered that the so-called victim had a girl-friend and had paid her brother to give him the bruises.

Judd stood at the bar, a scotch and soda in his hand. In his early thirties, he managed to maintain an exuberance and idealism about his job that Paavo found refreshing after the politics and power-mongering that usually went along with much of the work at the Hall of Justice.

Paavo went over to him and shook hands. "How's it going, H.J.?" He introduced Yosh.

"I got a call today from someone you might know," Judd said. "A retired judge, name of Lucas St. Clair. Called to report that he's being harassed by someone, wondered what we could do about it."

Paavo ordered a Dos Equis amber, and Yosh, still enthralled by the city, ordered San Francisco's own Anchor Steam. "I remember St. Clair," Paavo said. "What's going on?"

"The guy he's complaining about hasn't done anything except loiter around the neighborhood. But today, he gave the judge's wife a copy of the *Chronicle*."

"Considering that paper," Yosh said, "I'd say that's def-initely a criminal offense—misinformation or something."

"Does the judge have any idea who he might be?" Paavo asked.

"St. Clair can't give us a good description. The guy's always wearing dark glasses and a baseball cap. Thing is, the judge lives right across from the Palace of Fine Arts. He said the guy parks next to the duck pond. It's a weird town, Paavo. The guy might just have a thing for ducks."

Paavo doubted it. "Did the judge go through the news-paper? See if there were any stories that meant anything to him?"

"I didn't ask. He said he'd already read the paper that morning."

"It might be worth looking into—a message of some kind." The *Chronicle*—Angie had left a copy of her newspaper at his place the other night. Seemed a lot of people were giving away *Chronicle*s for some reason.

Yosh had been listening to this conversation with inter-est. "You know this judge, Paavo?"

"He was one of the toughest," Paavo said.

Judd chuckled. "The DAs thanked their own saints when they got St. Clair, but the defense lawyers called him the judge from hell."

"Uh-oh," Yosh said under his breath. "Speaking of DAs, I think I'd better get out of here."

"Why's that?"

"I see Lloyd Fletcher over there. He's still pissed off by the way I answered the judge at the Marlowe arraignment. But I wasn't about to perjure myself just because he had a lousy case."

"He knows that."

"He might know it, but he won't forgive it."

Paavo glanced at a silver-haired man in a corner booth, so aloof and polished in a charcoal Brooks Brothers suit that he seemed out of place here. "He used to be a reason-able guy."

"That was before he started thinking he'd like to be mayor," Judd said.

"Fletcher? He's never held any office but DA, and that's after years as an assistant DA in the city."

"You got it. That's why he thinks he's got a chance. Who can say if he'd be a good mayor or a bad one? He can run as an open-minded liberal who's also against crime and win big in this town. No one will know whether or not he's telling the truth."

As Fletcher and the man he'd been talking to, Maxim

Wainwright, a member of the Board of Supervisors, stood up to leave, he noticed Paavo and Yosh. He made his way to them.

"Well, well," Fletcher said. "What brings Homicide's finest to these shores? Hello there, H.J.," he added, then immediately turned back to the inspectors. "I thought you two never touched anything stronger than Snapple."

"We're down here seeing how the other half lives, Lloyd," Yosh said. "Buy you a drink?"

The tall man cocked an eyebrow as if unsure how to take Yosh's remark. "No, better not. I'm on my way home. By the way, Smith, you did a great job on the Barker case."

"The guy confessed," Paavo said. "That makes it easy."

"Yes, well . . ." Fletcher glanced at Yoshiwara. "You know, Yosh, I heard you were thinking about going back to Seattle. People have been saying you might be happier there. That true?"

"What a laugh," Yosh said with a big, friendly grin. "I'm having the time of my life here. You must have heard somebody's wishful thinking."

Mr. Congeniality in action, Paavo thought. He wondered if Fletcher knew Yosh was being sarcastic as all hell.

"Good, good," Fletcher said. "Hate to lose a good man in Homicide. See you boys around." With that, holding his hand aloft like the politician he hoped to become, and waving good-bye to friend and foe alike, Lloyd Fletcher left the bar.

He sat in his green Honda and watched the procession come and go from the Court House. A couple of beat cops strolled out, then a sheriff's deputy. Three women went in, dressed to kill. They were probably receptionists or secretaries for some bigwigs. They didn't look old enough or tired enough to be any of the professional women who seemed to be taking over the running of this city.

Lloyd Fletcher had stood outside the door for a long while, waving and smiling at everyone who came out or went in. And, like the sycophants they were, they bowed, scraped, and fawned over the powerful DA.

It made him want to throw up. No one had ever fawned over him. Quite the opposite, in fact. Ten years ago they kept saying he had to have been crazy to do what he'd done. He wouldn't tell them the real reason. He wouldn't tell them that he did it for Heather.

Everything was for Heather.

He leaned forward to watch as the cop and his Jap partner parted company. Now, if only Smith would go to his girlfriend's house . . .

He hadn't been able to track down where she lived yet.

But he would.

The cop went into the parking lot and in a while reappeared in the old Austin Healey. He let him go ahead, then pulled into traffic two cars behind him. Once he found out where the girlfriend lived, he'd have all the information he needed. Then, life would be perfect.

CHAPTER

FOUR

"Is she still eatin'?" Butch asked, stirring the spaghetti sauce so that chunks of the canned tomato he'd used wouldn't stick to the bottom of the aluminum kettle.

"Looks like she likes it," Earl said.

"You think so?" Butch's eyes lit up. "Maybe I oughta cook up a couple more things?" He walked to the kitchen door and took a peek at their only customer. Wearing a self-satisfied grin, he turned to Earl. "Tell Vinnie to pipe down in the cellar. What kinda joint will she think this is?"

"You tell him." Earl was no fool.

"Nobody's gotta tell me," Vinnie announced, just emerging from the cellar steps. He stomped to the middle of the kitchen floor and glared from Butch to Earl and back again. Despite the slump age had put in his back, his black eyes were still piercing under thick eyebrows.

"What the hell you two bozos doin' feedin' people?" he asked. "What do you think this is? A goddamn restaurant? We got work to do. We gotta be fast. In and out, before anyone asks questions. Or maybe you two think everybody's as dumb as you are?"

"Look, Vinnie, we can't go throwin' out customers,"

Butch said, going back to stir his sauce. "What if she complains to somebody? We gotta look legitimate."

Vinnie's face turned fiery red. "You ain't looked legitimate since the day you was born."

"Hey! You don't talk like that about my mother, hear?"

"What mother? You was hatched."

Butch crossed the room and stuck his face close to Vinnie's. "Just remember, I was a contender for boxing champion of the world."

Vinnie didn't look impressed. "Yeah, yeah."

"Besides"—Butch folded his arms and lifted his chin—"if I quit, you wouldn't have nobody to cook. Then what would you do?"

"Ever hear of TV dinners? They probably taste better than your slop anyway."

"Okay, I *will* quit!"

"You can't." Vinnie turned his back on Butch. "Earl, hurry her up. Get her out. Give her the bill or somethin'."

"She ain't done eatin' yet," Earl said meekly.

"So? What do you think this is, the Ritz? Give her the bill and make sure she takes the hint."

Earl swallowed hard. "I don't t'ink she takes no hints, Vinnie."

"Oh, waiter," Angie called out gaily. She waited a second. No answer. "Waiter?" Nothing but muffled voices from the kitchen. What dreadful service.

Finally the waiter stuck his head through the swinging kitchen doors. "Whadya want dis time?"

"This spaghetti sauce and these meatballs are absolutely wonderful," she said, ignoring his bad manners. "I really would like to talk to your cook. I'm sort of in the business myself, you see."

"He don't wanna see you," Earl shouted.

"Why not?" The restaurant was still empty. "It can't be because he's too busy. I'm not asking that he come out here. In fact," she said as she stood, "I'll go into the kitchen to talk to him. Believe me, if he uses this sauce on just two or three more dishes, this restaurant will do wonderfully."

Earl hurried toward her, holding his arms outright the way he'd learned to do in Vegas when someone lunged for a blackjack dealer. "There ain't no way you can talk to him."

"Won't you ask him?"

"He's shy," Earl said.

"Shy?"

"Look, it's gettin' late. You want some dessert?"

Somehow, she couldn't imagine a restaurant with only one entree offering anything decent in desserts. "I've given up desserts for Lent."

"Yeah? I t'ink dis place has, too."

The waiter spoke with such a deadpan style, Angie had to laugh. She sat back down, unsure if he was serious or not. Even if she couldn't see the cook this time, she would eventually. She wasn't about to give up finding out what made the meatballs and sauce so special. If only the restaurant had a bit more to offer, it might have been a find for her—an interesting place to write about for her magazine article. Right now, though, it didn't make the grade.

The lack of a presentable menu was irritating. After all, any fool could stumble across a good high-priced restaurant in this city. It took someone clever to discover a cheap place worth going to. Someone like her, in fact.

She glanced at her wristwatch. It was eight-thirty, not late at all. If she went home now, she'd probably sit around watching TV or trying to figure out if she was ready for marriage—or both. Paavo was most likely busy as ever with his cases and would see her when he could. He was pretty good at dropping by unexpectedly for a visit—and then some—but she didn't want to get into a rut of going home to wait for him. It wasn't as if they were married. She had freedom, choice, opportunity. She just had to figure out what to do with it.

"I'll have a caffe latte," she said suddenly.

"A caffe latte?" Earl repeated.

"That's right."

"Okay."

Earl ran into the kitchen. "Now she wants a caffe latte. What's dat?"

Butch glanced toward heaven. "Didn't you learn nothin' before you went to the big house? It's half strong coffee and half milk."

"So why don't you just make da coffee weaker?"

Butch shook his head. "There's a pot of coffee all made. It's Chase and Sanborn, but I made it around noon, so it's probably strong enough to take the wax off the floor. Plug in that espresso machine, and the gizmo on the end there will make the milk all foamy. It's easy. You understand?"

Earl looked at the machine. He'd never seen anything like it before. "'Course I understand. It's easy."

"Okay. So do it. Oh, one more thing. You got to serve it in a tall glass." Butch went back down into the cellar to help Vinnie.

"Yeah. I can do it."

Earl turned on the machine before he took a half gallon of milk from the refrigerator. He poured it into a wide-mouthed pitcher and held the pitcher below the espresso machine's steam arm. He twisted the valve and a jet of steam shot some of the milk out of the pitcher onto his shirt. But it didn't look any more foamy than when he started.

He cursed and tried again. This time the milk sprayed his slacks. He gave it another try. Milk rained onto his hair.

He twisted the knob faster this time. A jet of milk shot straight into his eye, nearly blinding him as more foul language erupted.

He shoved the pitcher as high as it would go onto the steam arm and turned the valve with all his might. Milk hit the ceiling. Still no foam.

The milk that had landed on his toupee earlier seeped through it and began to trickle down onto his forehead. He wiped it away.

Rage turned to cold determination.

He moved the milk into a bowl, put it under the beaters of a big, industrial-sized mixer and turned it on.

The milk spun around in the bowl at a fantastic speed, but it still didn't get foamy. He added an egg.

That helped a little.

A bottle of blue Dawn sat on the counter by the sink. Just a splash. Who'd ever know? Like magic, bubbles appeared.

Now we're in business, he thought. Leaving the machine running, he began to search for the type of glass Butch had described. There were short, fat glasses, and tall, thin glasses, but nothing tall, yet thick enough to hold hot coffee. He didn't want the customer to burn her fingers.

Pulling up a chair, he stood on it so that he could reach into the back of the upper shelves of the cabinet where restaurant owners past had left behind mismatched cups, plates, and glasses that they didn't want to cart away with them. After several minutes searching, he found a tall, thick glass with a handle.

Perfect. He grabbed the glass, got off the chair, turned around, and to his horror saw that the milk had foamed up and out of the bowl, across the counter, and down onto the floor. It was heading for the dining room.

He carefully tiptoed through the slippery foam to turn off the mixer, then continued on to the pot of coffee. He poured the coffee into the glass. Despite the handle, it still felt hot, so he found a small, flat plate to put it on. Nice.

He then plopped a spoonful of sudsy milk on top. He'd only used a small amount, but still, a slight detergent scent wafted out of the cup, mixed with the smell of bitter coffee. Maybe she'd think they used really clean glasses.

He was headed toward the dining room when Butch came up from the basement where he'd been helping Vinnie. "What the hell! What'd you do to my kitchen?" He lunged toward Earl.

Earl tried to run, but the soles of his shoes were slick.

His feet scrambled wildly. He held the plate tightly, watching the glass as it slid from one side of the plate to the other. With each slip of the glass, he angled the plate in the opposite direction, so that, like a juggler, he managed to keep the glass upright and filled with coffee while his feet, legs, and body gyrated.

As Butch hit the slippery floor, he hydroplaned across it and smacked right into Earl's back, knocking Earl farther forward.

Earl's legs flew out from under him. He went down into the frothy muck and slid away from Butch, right through the swinging doors into the dining room.

Angie turned around to see man, foam, and caffe latte shooting toward her.

He came to a halt and somehow, miraculously, still held the coffee upright in its tall glass on its flat plate.

Angie stood as the waiter picked himself up and carried her the coffee.

"Are you all right?" she asked.

"Yeah. It's nothin'." With a deep sigh he placed the coffee on the table, but right on top of her fork. The plate made a little rocking motion, then tilted. The glass slid off the plate, hit the tabletop, tipped over, and the caffe latte rushed out of the glass, across the table, and dripped right onto Earl's shoes.

"Oh, that's too bad," Angie said. "Well, I wasn't really in the mood for coffee anyway. I think I'll take in a movie."

She opened her purse, took out two dollars, plus fifty cents for the tip, and placed them on the table. "Ciao," she said, and sauntered out of the restaurant.

CHAPTER

FIVE

"Angie, you should be talking with Paavo about marriage, not me." Bianca, the oldest of Angie's four sisters, emptied the morning's first load of wash from the dryer into a basket. She quickly refilled the dryer with another load, then picked up the basket and came back into the family room to join Angie.

"I'm not ready to yet. First, I need to understand what it would mean to us. After all, I don't want to turn into another broken marriage statistic. The problem is, though, I think about it day and night." Angie sat on the sofa, her chin in her hands. "I can't eat. I can't sleep. I can't even think about my article for *Haute Cuisine*. You've got to help me!"

"Have you talked to Mamma or Papà?" Bianca was fourteen years older than Angie and at least fourteen pounds heavier, with straight, dark brown, chin-length hair. She began to sort out underwear between husband, older, and younger sons—a chore Angie couldn't imagine herself emulating anytime soon.

"Are you kidding?" Angie said miserably.

"You're right. Mamma would have you walking down

the aisle before you're ready, and Papà would have you shipped off to a nunnery until you came to your senses—or were too old to care anymore. I've noticed that Paavo's not exactly his favorite."

"Don't remind me. That's why I've come to you. I've got to know if I'm ready for this. It's a big step. Enormous, in fact! I need you, Bianca. To tell me everything."

"The real picture?"

"The hard truth."

"The cold facts?"

"The ugly details."

"Of marriage."

"Exactly!" Angie cried. "I want the better and worse. Actually, the worse. I can handle the better."

Bianca held up a pair of jockey shorts and studied them. "Hmm, the tag with their size fell off." With a shrug, she tossed them in with her older son's clothes. "It's a tall order, Angie. Marriage, more than anything else I can think of, is in the eye of the beholder. I can give you one person's opinion, but I think you need to talk to a few other people as well."

"I will!" Angie started folding bath towels. "I mean, this is my life we're talking about. 'Look before you leap,' that's my motto. God, you've got a lot of towels here. What are you doing? Starting a bathhouse?"

"Teenage boys—when they discover girls, they discover soap and water. And since when is that your motto? I thought it was 'No time like the present.'" Bianca gave Angie a pointed, big-sisterly look.

"That aside, I need your help."

"What's marriage like . . ." Bianca said thoughtfully, matching pairs of white socks and folding them together. "Well, let's say you like opera."

"You know I love it."

"And let's suppose Paavo doesn't care for it."

"He doesn't."

"He likes, what?"

"Jazz, mostly."

"Okay, a good marriage is when you don't take him to an opera, where he'd be miserable, and he doesn't take you to a jazz concert, which you wouldn't care for."

"So what do you do?"

"You compromise. You go hear Barry Manilow."

"Oh, dear."

CHAPTER

S I X

Red-and-blue lights atop three police cars spiraled and flashed. Businessmen and professional women, shoppers, tourists, and the city's usual wide and motley crowd of street people stood eerily silent in the wake of senseless, brutal death. Beyond them, all the noise and traffic of downtown city life on a weekday morning continued as usual, oblivious to the tragedy that had struck here.

Sans Souci Jewelers was a small, exclusive jewelry shop tucked between a women's boutique and a large stationer's on Post Street. At ten o'clock that morning, someone had walked into the jeweler's, shot and killed the clerk, and escaped. The motive, most likely, was robbery.

Paavo stopped his city-issued Chevrolet behind a black-and-white. He and Yosh trained their eyes on the crime scene, already cordoned off by the patrolmen who'd first answered the call. The paramedics leaned against their ambulance, waiting patiently for the homicide team to arrive. They were in shirtsleeves, enjoying the warm, sunny spring morning, and Paavo couldn't help but notice the irony of it.

As he and Yosh walked toward the shop, a patrolman filled them in on the few details he'd learned. Pulling out their notebooks, the two inspectors began scribbling raw data. By unspoken prior agreement, Paavo would take the inside, Yosh the outside.

Yosh glanced inside the shop to get a feel for the situation, to see the victim and where he'd fallen. Then he began questioning the people who hovered around on the sidewalk—taking down their names, addresses, and initial reactions before they drifted away or said too much to each other, causing their own views and sightings to become confused or distorted by others' stories.

Inside the shop, Paavo didn't head directly toward the body, but edged along the perimeter of the store, jotting down and rough-sketching each detail noted, including the way the victim lay and the spatter from his body.

The victim, Nathan Ellis, was a white male, about age thirty, six feet tall, 180 pounds, with short blond hair and a pale complexion. He was tastefully dressed in a brown-and-gray tweed blazer, gray slacks, white shirt, and brown tie, and wore a gold watch and wedding band. He lay on his side, almost in a fetal position, in a pool of blood stemming from a gunshot wound to the chest.

None of the merchandise in the store seemed disturbed, yet the store owner, discovering Ellis's body, had called this in as a robbery. Why?

Minutes after Paavo and Yosh arrived, the coroner showed up with her team, and soon after, the photographer and Crime Scene Investigations unit. As Paavo wrote, questioned, and studied, the photographer videotaped and took stills of the inside and outside of the store, while the CSI unit began collecting trace evidence and fingerprinting. The coroner soon completed her exam, and her team waited for Paavo's okay to remove the body.

He was in no hurry. Until he was sure he'd learned everything the dead man could tell him about the way he died and by whom, he'd keep the body right where it was.

The removal team rolled their eyes at each other at the delay. Paavo saw their gesture and dismissed it. Same for the jewelry store owner, who was pacing back and forth in front of the store, anxious to get in and figure out how much was left of his money and jewels. From what Paavo could see, he didn't have anything to worry about.

"Let me go!"

Paavo whirled around at the sound of a woman's cry. A young blonde, nicely dressed in a business suit and high heels, struggled with the uniformed officer guarding the crime scene. As Paavo approached her, she stopped struggling. Fear at what she might learn filled her eyes.

"I'm Inspector Smith," he said.

Her tear-stained face would have been pretty were it not etched with worry. "I heard it on the radio," she said, her voice trembling. "On the traffic report. A shooting at a jeweler's on Post Street. I called, but it wasn't Nathan who answered the phone. It was a police officer." Her icy fingers grasped Paavo's hands. "He's going to be all right, isn't he? Tell me he'll be all right."

"Are you his wife?" Paavo asked.

She nodded.

"I'm sorry," he said gently. "He didn't make it."

"No! You're wrong!" she screamed, her grip tightening. "Let me see him."

"Mrs. Ellis—"

"He's all right!" she cried. "Please, God."

Paavo gestured at the patrolman beside her. "This is Officer Crossen. He'll take care of you, Mrs. Ellis."

"Nathan!" She sobbed hysterically as Paavo pulled his hands free of hers and backed away. The young patrolman led her slowly toward his police car. He'd take her home and find someone to stay with her.

Paavo shut his eyes a moment, running his fingers through his hair as her cries echoed in his mind. He faced the body, checking, double-checking, and all the while pondering the man who had been Nathan Ellis and all he'd lost this day.

Finally, he took a deep breath and scanned the crowd until he found a small, white-haired man. "I understand you're the owner," he said.

"Yes," the man said, his voice quivering.

Paavo drew him away from the crowd and gave the coroner's men the okay to remove the body.

"Your full name?" he asked.

"Philip Justin Pierpont."

"You're the one who discovered that Mr. Ellis had been shot?"

"Yes. I was coming back from the bank, and I heard a loud noise. I thought a car had backfired, but then I saw people running away from the shop, screaming. I hid in a doorway, I'm sorry to say. When it was quiet again, I came here and found Nathan."

"You called the police and reported a robbery."

"Yes."

In the jewelry shop, diamond rings and necklaces on black velvet had sparkled under the lights. Paavo had seen nothing broken into, nothing disturbed. The cash register was still filled with cash. "What made you think it was a robbery?"

The man's cheeks turned red, his hands moved spasmodically, as if out of control. "What reason other than robbery could anyone have been here? Why else would anyone shoot Nathan Ellis?"

At five o'clock, Paavo finally arrived at his desk to enter into his computer the lengthy notes he'd taken at the jewelry store that morning and throughout the day as he'd spoken with friends, relatives, and coworkers of the victim, as well as potential witnesses up and down the block where the jeweler's was located. It had been a frustrating day. So far, they'd found no witnesses to the crime, and no one had seen anyone go into or come out of the jeweler's that morning. The robber had to have gone out the back door into an alley, which meant he had cased the place before robbing it.

It was, in fact, a robbery. A couple of hours after he'd left the store, Philip Pierpont had phoned to tell him that three inexpensive reproductions of Russia's priceless Fabergé eggs were missing—blown crystal eggs, encrusted with gold, worth no more than a few hundred dollars apiece. The originals were in museums, but here, someone had killed a man over a set of copies. It didn't make sense.

Paavo stared grimly at the words he'd placed on his computer screen. The downtown area around Post and Grant Streets was one of San Francisco's busiest. That no one saw anything was hard to believe. He couldn't help but suspect he was dealing with the big-city problem of people not wanting to get involved in any problems that didn't affect them personally. The fact that a twenty-nine-year-old was gunned down senselessly seemed to mean little to anyone except his family and friends.

Sometimes Paavo wondered why it meant anything to him.

His phone rang. It was MasterCard's security division, giving him the home telephone numbers that matched the cards of two customers who were in Carole Anne's Dress Shoppe, next door to Sans Souci Jewelers, just minutes before the shooting occurred. There was a slight chance one or both of the women had been on the street in front of the jeweler's when the gunman entered. If so, he had to get to them fast.

Generally, eyewitnesses to murders didn't provide much help. Their memories were too easily influenced. The bigger the case, the more they tended to "remember" what was shown on TV the night before. But he wanted to find out why they'd left so quickly. Why they weren't among the people Yosh had interviewed.

He dialed the first number. No one answered. He called the second number. No answer there either. Where were they?

The unanswered telephone calls brought an eerie déjà vu from last night. Up until eleven o'clock he'd kept trying to reach Angie. He'd even checked to see if there'd been any auto accidents involving a Ferrari Testarossa. There hadn't.

After eleven, he gave up. He hadn't left a message, not wanting her to think he'd been checking up on her. She'd probably gone to visit one of her sisters. Maybe a girl-friend. It wasn't as if the words Stan had spoken about her no longer telling him where she was going or what she was doing had bothered him. He had scarcely thought about them at all except for one or two or ten times.

When he arrived at work that morning he'd skimmed the accident reports again and felt like a jerk doing it. If he didn't watch himself, he'd start calling hospital emergency rooms next.

He had no reason to expect her to tell him every time she went out in the evening. She could go where she pleased, with whomever. After all, they'd never spoken of an exclusive commitment.

He'd made some assumptions, though. Some big assumptions. Maybe even some foolish ones.

He forced himself to shove aside thoughts of where she might have gone last night. It was her business, not his. What he needed to do was to type up his notes while his scribbles still made sense. Later, he'd call. Tonight, though, with a fresh murder case to investigate, he wasn't going anywhere.

Before long, he became lost in speculation about the case and in deciphering the day's findings. Looking up from his computer, he glanced at the clock on the wall. Seven-forty. Then at his desk calendar.

His desk calendar had somehow gotten stuck on Friday. But today was Tuesday . . . Tuesday night. That seemed to mean something. He'd been too busy the last couple of days to flip the pages. Now he did.

And discovered he was in big trouble.

Angie had bought ballet tickets for the two of them for tonight. He rubbed his forehead. He'd never been to the ballet before. Had never wanted to go. Still didn't.

But she had been looking forward to it, and he'd promised to join her. He'd even told her that if he didn't call her beforehand, he'd meet her in front of the Opera

House in time for the eight o'clock performance. She was probably already there waiting.

He glanced down at his clothes. Dark gray jacket and pants, white shirt, navy tie. A day of rooting around a crime scene and hunting down witnesses hadn't done wonders for them, not to mention his way-past-five o'clock shadow, or the fact that he'd forgotten about lunch and hadn't had time for dinner.

Yosh walked into the squad room. "Here's that encyclopedia article you wanted."

Paavo took the photocopied pages.

Peter Carl Fabergé, b. May 30, 1846, d. Sept. 24, 1920, was a Russian goldsmith whose studios achieved fame for the skill exemplified in the objets d'art created by its artisans, who worked in gold, silver, enamel, and precious stones, set in ingenious designs. . . . Some of the most imaginative pieces were for the Russian courts of Alexander III and Nicholas II, including the famous series of decorated enamel Easter eggs given as presents by the tsars.

"So, what do you think, Paav? The killer have a hen fetish or something?" Yosh asked, then chuckled.

Although black humor was a big part of the way homicide inspectors dealt with the ugliness they saw every day, there were times Paavo couldn't join in. Some cases wheedled their way under even the thickest skins. Usually, they were the ones that involved kids. But today, Debbie Ellis's grief-chilled hands had made him see Nathan Ellis as a person, not just another statistic added to the city's murder rate.

"I got it!" called Inspector Bo Benson from the other side of the quiet room. Calderon's partner, he was spending most of his time lately trying to crack a gang-related teen party shooting. He walked toward them, a big smile on his face. "The guy was trying to figure out which came first, the chicken or the egg, and the clerk must have—"

Yosh grabbed Benson's arm and swung him around. "Coffee time, Bo," Yosh said, leading Benson away from Paavo's glare.

Paavo threw down the pages in disgust. Three modern Fabergé eggs. Why were they taken? Anyone would be lucky to get a fence to give a sawbuck for the lot of them. The kind of people who would be interested in that kind of decoration weren't the kind who frequented pawnshops or ran with fences.

And most puzzling, why steal eggs when there were diamonds to grab? Even a junkie desperate for a fix doesn't grab playthings when faced with diamonds.

Did Nathan Ellis spook the gunman? Maybe the killer fired in a sudden panic, snatched the nearest thing at hand, and fled.

Then again, could the gunman have come to kill Ellis and lifted the eggs to confuse everyone? But if so, wouldn't taking diamonds have been a better ploy?

Too many possibilities, too many questions only the gunman could answer—when he was caught.

Paavo glanced at the clock again. Seven-fifty-three. The ballet would last a couple of hours, he'd see Angie home, and hopefully be back here by eleven. He grabbed his jacket, and prayed a taxi would be near.

Angie stood in front of the Opera House. She should have known Paavo would be late. If she'd been thinking, she'd have left his ticket at the box office. That way she, at least, could have seen the beginning of *Romeo and Juliet*. She had so looked forward to having him see it with her, though— the beautiful dancing, Prokofiev's luscious music, and, most of all, the tragic love story—the beauty of love and commitment more important than life itself. And she couldn't even get her man to the theater on time. Where had she gone wrong?

With startling clarity, her conversation with Bianca came back to her. Was she to blame for Paavo's not being here? Was she too unwilling to compromise?

He was probably busy—and had been too busy all day to call. But he'd expressly told her that if he didn't call, he'd be here. He'd canceled out on her before, but he'd never stood her up. She didn't want to even consider him doing such a thing. Where was he?

If he'd gotten a new case, that meant someone else had been killed, another death in this city that had seen more than its share of violence. Right across Van Ness Avenue from her stood City Hall, its high, round dome lighting up the night sky, majestic and noble. That was appearance, though. Beneath the dome, battles for control of the city were legion, and not too many years before, a member of the Board of Supervisors had murdered the mayor and a fellow supervisor.

A shiver ran down her back. Maybe it was just some paperwork that was keeping him, and not a new murder at all.

She glanced up and down the street. Now that the ballet had started, the sidewalk was empty except for two street people who'd wandered over from Civic Center Plaza to ask the supposedly wealthy ballet-goers for hand-outs.

She raised the collar of her evening coat against her neck and backed up toward the tall glass doors, wanting to be inside, enjoying the warmth of the building instead of out here.

A taxi pulled ahead of a line of cars stopped at a red light, cut across two lanes, and screeched to a halt in front of the Opera House. Paavo jumped out and thrust some money at the cab driver. Angie folded her arms, lifted her nose in the air, and gazed past him. A small green car stopped behind the taxi. Something about it momentarily caught her attention.

Paavo raced up the stairs to her side. "Sorry," he said.

"It's already started," she replied matter-of-factly.

"I was afraid of that," he said guiltily. "Do you want to go in, anyway? Or just forget it this time?"

"I'd like to go in. But I suppose you'll hate it, won't you?"

"Hate it? I've never seen—"

"That's why you weren't here on time."

"No, I—"

"You could have told me. I'm able to compromise."

"Angie, what are you talking about?"

"I had orchestra seats for us, too. I thought you'd enjoy seeing the ballet."

"I hope to enjoy it," he said very quickly.

She paused. "You do?"

"Yes. I do."

Slowly, her face spread into a smile. "Oh, well, in that case, what are we waiting for?" Ignoring his puzzled expression, she took his arm and allowed him to escort her inside.

CHAPTER

S E V E N

He eased a double set of surgical gloves onto his hands, the latex like an extra layer of skin. He flexed his fingers. No more planning or preparation: it was payoff time.

After a quick glance over his surroundings—rows of apartment buildings done in postwar stark, boxlike architecture, the only thing making them at all attractive being the view of the city this Twin Peaks location provided—he scanned the name tags on the mailboxes.

There it was.

He pushed the buzzer beneath her name. His covered fingertips tingled as his tightly controlled excitement mounted.

No answer.

The silent intercom mocked his expectations. She had to be there. After all, he'd followed her all the way from City Hall earlier that evening. She couldn't have left already. What was the goddamn bitch doing?

He jabbed at the button.

More silence. He tasted the sweat that had formed on his upper lip.

"Yes?" came a hesitant voice from the intercom.

"Delivery."

"This time of night? I'm not expecting anything."

"It's a gift, ma'am. Roses. Nice, long-stemmed roses." He spoke with steady deliberation, fighting a growing impatience.

"Roses?"

"These are beautiful, ma'am. Best bouquet we have. My boss said the tall, gray-haired guy who bought them insisted on delivery tonight. Said it was special or something. I guess it's all in the card. I'll read it to you if you'd like."

"I'll read it myself. I'll buzz you in." Her pleasure was evident.

The door's lock sang with an electric hum as he pushed it open.

Inside he paused, breathing deeply. The heavy glass door swung shut behind him. He cleared his mind of all thoughts other than those of the woman in Apartment 320. Then he began his ascent up the stairs, calmly and silently.

When he reached the third floor landing he carefully placed the box of roses on the floor. He didn't want her to recognize him as the *Chronicle* salesman from the other day. With practiced efficiency, he removed his glasses and slipped them into the breast pocket of his shirt, attached a fake brown mustache to his upper lip, and put on the John Deere baseball cap he carried under his jacket. Satisfied with his transformation, he picked up the flowers, walked to Tiffany Rogers's apartment door, and knocked.

She opened the door, clutching her thin, clinging robe to her chin. With her other hand, she touched the damp hair curling around her oval face. The closeness of her barely concealed body, full, soft, and reeking of pure, raw sex, both excited and troubled him.

"I was in the shower when you rang," she said, taking a half step backward.

"Ma'am." He crossed the threshold and touched the brim of his cap.

"Oh . . . come in." Her voice was hesitant. "It is drafty out there, isn't it?"

"Yes, ma'am."

She was walking toward the purse on her living room table when he shut the door behind him. At the sound of the click she stopped, half turned, and looked at him.

"I want to tip you," she said. "I'll only be a moment."

His reply was a thin, awkward smile.

She rummaged in her purse, then turned around with the two dollars she'd taken from her wallet.

She gasped in surprise. He had silently followed her into the living room and stood close, too close. "Here," she said, and thrust the dollar bills in his direction.

He wanted to put his glasses on, to see her better. Ignoring the extended hand with the money, his eyes explored her. The robe clung and accentuated her soft curves, its V neck all but exposed her pendulous breasts to his gaze. His breath caught, and he could feel beads of perspiration at his temples.

"Here . . . the money," she said, her voice rising. "Give me the flowers."

He pushed the flower box toward her with one hand as he snatched the dollar bills with the other. The woman, clutching the box to her body with both arms, moved back, away from him. A puzzled look crossed her face. She stared at him. He could see the distaste in her gaze as she took in his sweat-streaked face, his weak, myopic eyes.

"I just wanted my flowers," she stammered with a false, fearful smile.

"And this, too," he said. In his hand, a six-inch carbon steel combat knife gleamed.

She hadn't even screamed. It figured. She was the type who took whatever a man gave her. He smiled with contempt at the bloody, seminude heap on the crimson rug. With a quick slash of the knife, he opened the box of roses and tossed them around her, then picked up the largest, fullest one. He walked to her bedroom and placed it on her bed.

Back in the living room, standing over her, he pulled a rag from his pocket and wiped off the knife with a slow, up-and-down motion. Then he slid it back into the sheath under his jacket.

This one was for Heather.

CHAPTER

E I G H T

"Actually, Angie, Charles and I never go to concerts anymore. Not rock or opera. Not even supper clubs," said Caterina, Angie's second sister. Cat, who had been called Trina and had dark brown hair when she was growing up, had somehow metamorphosed into a platinum blond Supermom with her own interior design business. Franz Kafka had nothing on her.

Angie sat in the family room of Cat's Tiburon home and watched her sister make a diorama of the Pilgrims' landing.

"So coming up with dumb compromises isn't a problem for you anymore?" Angie asked hopefully.

"Not at all. Movies are our most common entertainment now—when we can find the time. I'm always so busy!"

"Reminds me of Paavo. He's always too busy for me, it seems," Angie murmured. "Say, isn't Kenny supposed to make that diorama himself?"

"Really, Angie! Have you ever seen an eight-year-old's diorama? One of his classmate's father is in the Army Corps of Engineers. Kenny needs a fighting chance at a good grade."

Angie didn't think that was the idea of the lesson, but

she held her tongue. "So now you and Charles go to the movies."

"Not *go* to the movies. We rent them." Cat placed a big rock that had PLYMOUTH written on it in the box, then stepped back and eyed it as if she were studying the placement of a Louis XV writing desk. "Married people don't go to the movies much."

"They don't?"

"Heck, when you're newly married, who needs them?" Cat adjusted the rock about a centimeter to the left and contemplated its new position. "Then for a while, after the initial blush—so to speak—of wedded bliss, you do go to shows. But soon, quick as a wink, all that ends."

"It does?"

"That's right." Cat put some glue on the bottom of a cutout of the *Mayflower* and stuck it in the box. "Before you know it, you've got kids. Then you know what you do?"

Angie shook her head.

"You go to the video store and rent movies like *Ernest Goes to Jail*. By the time it's over and the kids are asleep, you are too. And so's your old man."

"Oh, dear."

The *Mayflower* was listing badly.

CHAPTER

NINE

Paavo picked up the insistently ringing phone on his desk. He was pulling together the last couple of bits of information before going to talk with Nathan Ellis's wife. Robbery might well have been the motive behind Ellis's murder, but he wanted to be sure that he wasn't jumping to an obvious conclusion and overlooking other possibilities. Talking to the grief-stricken Debbie Ellis about something her husband might have been involved in wasn't on his list of favorite things to do.

"Smith here."

"Paavo! I'm so glad I reached you!" Angie's voice bubbled through the phone lines. He was relieved she'd called. She'd seemed more than a little unhappy with him last night when he'd dropped her off right after the ballet. But then he realized her call might have been because something bad had happened.

"Are you all right?" he asked.

"I'm fine."

"Your family?"

"Nothing's wrong, Paavo. I can call you about good news, can't I?"

He took a deep breath. "Sure. What is it?"

"I'll give you one guess. But I warn you, it's so unbelievable, so absolutely remarkably stupendous, you'll never guess it."

"Angie, I've got a lot of—"

"Don't be such a fussbudget. Come on. One guess."

Fussbudget? "All right. You sold your article to *Haute Cuisine*."

"That would scarcely be stupendous. Besides, I haven't even figured out what to write about yet." She sounded down at that admission.

"Sorry," he said.

"It's okay. Guess again."

"Look, Yosh is waiting. I've got to—"

"All right, all right. Are you sitting?"

"I'm sitting."

"Well, I went to visit my sister, Cat, this morning, and when I got back, I had a message waiting. I didn't recognize the name, so I called back and—you won't believe it—it was a director at KROW-TV!"

"KROW? I've never heard of it."

"You haven't? It's Channel 73. They have the best Farsi shows in the Bay Area."

Paavo did sit now. "How could I have missed it?"

"Don't be sarcastic! Anyway, they're expanding their repertoire, and they've decided to add a cooking show."

"In Farsi?"

"No, not in Farsi. In English. And guess who they'd like to star in it?"

"Julia Child?"

"Paavo! Not Julia! Me!"

He laughed. "Angie, that's great news."

"Isn't it? There's just one problem. They want me to do Italian cooking, and they've come up with a terrible name—*Angelina in the Cucina*. That's Italian for kitchen."

"You're right. That *is* a terrible name."

"Maybe I can talk them out of it. But anyway, this is it,

Paavo. My big break. My big start on the way to fame. Hollywood—or is it Burbank?—here I come!"

His fingers tightened on the phone. "I guess so," he said softly, then louder, "That's great, Angie."

"I have to do an audition, of course. I've never done one before, but how much of a problem can it be, right? They said I just have to go down to the studio and cook something in front of a camera. Sounds easy to me."

"I'm sure you'll have no problem at all."

"Aren't you happy for me, Paavo?"

Why did he feel as if someone had just kicked him in the chest? "Of course, I am. It's good news, Angie. Really . . . good news."

"Let's go out and celebrate, okay?"

"I've got this investigation."

"I mean tonight."

"I'm not sure."

There was a long silence. "Right. I should have known."

He heard the hurt in her voice. "Soon, Angie. Okay?"

"Sure, Paavo. Soon."

The dial tone sounded in his ear. She hadn't even said good-bye.

Paavo put word out to all the pawnshops that if a replica of a Fabergé egg came in, he was to be contacted immediately. He silently congratulated himself on his good humor at the deluge of Easter egg and Easter bunny jokes he was hit with. It made him wonder if he was mellowing.

He went to the crime lab to see what they had learned about a couple of round, black stains the crime scene investigators had found on the jewelry store's light gray carpet. Since the cleaning crew had vacuumed and sponged off any dirt marks the night before, it was suspected that it might have come from something on the thief's shoe.

"I was just getting ready to call you, Paavo," Inspector Howard said. "We've got a match, but it's not much."

"What is it?"

"Bubblegum."

"What?"

"Looks like the thief stepped onto a big wad of bubblegum, and it stuck to the bottom of his shoe. That's it, Paav."

"You're right, Al. It's not much."

The clock on the computer screen read 3:30 P.M. After visiting her sister, Angie had spent the rest of the day trying to concentrate on her historical study of San Francisco. She figured that anyone with degrees in English and history, who'd attended some of the best universities in the world, should write at least one book. It wasn't moving far or fast, though. Maybe she wasn't cut out to be a historian. Either that, or she wasn't cut out to think about marriage. The two obviously were not compatible.

She leaned back in the new white leather ergonomic chair in her den and stretched, trying to get the kinks out of her back, neck, and shoulders. She'd never ached this way in her old, high-backed chair. It was generously padded with soft, down cushions.

Not so this one. The seat, footrests, elbow and wrist supports moved every which way but comfortable. The chair looked like something from the Starship *Enterprise*. She got up and tried adjusting it for the umpteenth time.

A shave-and-a-haircut beat rapped on her apartment door. She knew that knock. Why me, Lord?

As she crossed her living room, she gazed with renewed affection at the nonergonomic antiques collected over the past few years. If chairs like that were good enough for Chippendale . . .

Before opening the door, she looked through the peephole—a precaution Paavo had convinced her she needed to take. As expected, her neighbor, Stanfield Bonnette, stood in the hall, a dopey smile spread across his otherwise handsome face.

She opened the door a crack. "I'm busy, Stan."

He straight-armed the door, preventing her from closing it. "I haven't seen you for a while, Angie!" he said with a quiver to his lower lip. "I came by to make sure you were all right."

He was playing her for a sucker. She knew it. But how could she shut the door on someone who could make his lower lip tremble? "All right, come in. But I've only got a minute."

"Thanks!" He walked into the living room, then turned to face her with an expectant smile. "Do I smell coffee?"

She guessed Stan could seem disarmingly charming if she didn't know him so well. He was twenty-nine, tall, thin, with silky light brown hair and brown eyes, and considered himself an up-and-coming bank executive. No one else seemed to think of him as such, however. Especially not his bosses.

"The coffee's been sitting since lunchtime."

"I'm not fussy." He walked into the kitchen and went straight to the refrigerator. "Let's see what we can find here."

There was no stopping Stan in pursuit of food. "There's not much of interest except in the freezer," Angie said.

He opened the freezer door. "Oh! Looky there. Whatever it is, it looks great."

"It's called *tortoni*." As she'd suspected all along, hunger, not sympathy, was the true cause of his angst in the doorway.

"Should we split it?" he asked, lifting out the custard cup filled with Italian-style ice cream. "Though it is awfully small."

"I've given up desserts for Lent," she said. "I made that last night for Paavo, but things didn't work out I'm afraid."

Stan fished a teaspoon out of the drawer and shoved a heaping spoonful of *tortoni* into his mouth. "Delicious. That Smith is more of a fool than I thought he was."

"Sometimes I have to agree," she murmured.

"Pardon?"

"Nothing." She poured him a cup of coffee and carried it into the living room. Quickly finishing off the *tortoni*, Stan grabbed a couple of *biscotti* from the cookie jar and followed her.

"So tell me what's up," he said as he took a seat in the center of the sofa.

"Not much." Suddenly she smiled, and, with barely contained excitement, said, "I'm only going to audition for a TV show."

"Angie, that's wonderful news! What kind of show?"

Laughing, Angie sat on the Hepplewhite chair next to the sofa. "Cooking. What else?"

"Wow!" Stan jumped to his feet, pulled her from the chair, and waltzed her around in circles. "Let's go celebrate."

"What?"

"Me and you."

The thought of going out with Stan was appalling. He was a friend—and a rather annoying one at that.

"We should go dancing." He grinned roguishly. "Hot salsa, Western line, slam. Name your poison."

Stepping away from him, she sat again. "Are you joking?"

"Not at all." He also sat. "When was the last time you went to the Sound Works?"

"God . . . the Sound Works." Thoughts of the huge, raucous dance club brought a smile to her lips. "Let's see. It was before I met Paavo, that's for sure. Ah, I remember. I went with Dmitri, so it had to have been sometime last summer."

"Dmitri?"

"You met him. He was the Russian violinist. Absolutely mad. Fun, though."

"Oh, him." Stan grimaced. "Sometimes I wonder about your taste in men, Angie. Anyway, Doctor Bonnette says you need to go club dancing tonight. With him."

She stared at him. The man was actually serious. "Thanks, Stan, but I don't think so."

"What are you going to do instead? Mope around here and hope the detective gets tired of looking at corpses and decides to give you the time of day?"

"He'll come by when he can."

"Stop kidding yourself, Angie. He's not right for you. Ditch him!"

"Stan!"

"All right, don't ditch him, then. But how often does someone get asked to audition for a TV show? You deserve a celebration. And the best part is, you don't even have to dance with me if you don't want to."

She smiled, but shook her head.

"Don't say no. If he doesn't call or show up by nine tonight, that means he'll be working late, right? Then you and I can go celebrate your good fortune. Okay?"

"Well . . ." It might be interesting to take her marriage survey to the Sound Works, at that. She'd never bothered to notice how many—if any—of the couples there were married. And, if they weren't, what did that say about married life? She gazed at Stan. What did *he* think of marriage? She did want a man's opinion, and he was a friend.

He jumped to his feet. "Angie, come back! You were *way* out there. I'll see you at nine-oh-five."

"Just one thing, Stan. I want to drive by Paavo's house on the way. I don't want to call. I just want to see if he's there or not."

"Sure, Angie, whatever you say."

CHAPTER

TEN

The fourteen inspectors who made up the Homicide detail of the city and county of San Francisco were divided into seven two-man teams. From 9:00 A.M. Monday until 9:00 A.M. Friday, one team was responsible for every homicide that took place in the city, around the clock. Another team took the weekend murders—9:00 A.M. Friday through Monday morning. In the three and a half weeks between on-call time, the inspectors were expected to do all the paperwork, work with assistant DAs on cases being prepared for trial, and appear in court—grand jury, preliminary hearings, and actual trials. Oh yes, and find the murderers.

Paavo looked at the clock on the wall in Homicide. It read 8:30 P.M. He and Yosh had been the on-duty team since 9:00 A.M. Monday, and only two murders had occurred—Ellis's and one that resulted from a bar fight. The suspect, who had ten eyewitnesses to his pulling out a gun and blasting the victim, was in custody.

Ellis's murder was another matter. Early that morning Paavo had telephoned the two women who'd bought dresses the day before at Carole Anne's Dress Shoppe, next door to Sans Souci Jewelers, and this time he'd been successful reaching them. Both assured him they'd seen nothing unusual. Nonetheless, he'd asked them to come to Homicide to talk to him in person, and found that each could remember a couple of men and women loitering near the jeweler's. One in particular, a small, bearded old man, caught the attention of both women. It wasn't much, but better than nothing.

The fingerprint dusting had turned up nothing. The store owner had his cleaning service wash the glass cases each evening so that they'd sparkle the next day. The only prints found on the glass belonged to the victim, Nathan Ellis.

"You must be exhausted, Paavo." Inspector Rebecca Mayfield stopped beside his desk and smiled at him. She was Homicide's newest member, an assistant inspector. Tall, perfectly proportioned, with long blond hair that fluffed around her shoulders like cotton candy, she could almost guarantee an entire squad of patrol officers volunteering to help with any investigation she was involved with.

"You're here pretty late yourself," Paavo replied.

"I'm helping Calderon with his jumper. No note, and from all appearances, the guy had everything to live for. Anyway, my own cases seem to be running me around in circles." She pulled a chair alongside his desk and sat down. "Maybe a little breather will give me a fresh eye. Could be I'll pick up on something I'm missing now."

"Good idea."

She put her elbows on his desk and leaned closer. "It's a good idea for you, too, Paav. How about some dinner?"

"I want to finish typing up my notes." He flipped back and forth through his notebook. He and Yosh had split up the list of people whose offices overlooked the alley behind the jewelry shop. No one remembered anything strange. But putting all their statements together just might turn up something.

"Come on," she said softly. "You won't forget what you wrote that fast. You have time for one fast-food hamburger, don't you?"

Nothing about Nathan Ellis made him a likely target for a killer. He'd been married three years. His wife worked as a legal secretary at a law firm five blocks away from the jeweler's, which explained how she was able to get there so quickly after the robbery. Paavo frowned. What was he missing?

"Yoo-hoo, Paavo?" Rebecca called. "Dinner."

"Oh, sorry, Rebecca. I'm not hungry—thanks anyway."

She cocked her head. "The building's on fire."

Paavo stared at some scribbles in his notebook, trying to decipher them. He was still focusing on the most troublesome aspect of this case. Why would anyone pass up diamonds to take replicas of some museum pieces? He glanced at Rebecca. "If it was, the alarms would be going off."

"I give up," she murmured, pushing herself away from him, her back against the chair and her arms folded.

Calderon marched into Homicide. "You still here, Mayfield?"

"Just a couple minutes more, then I'm leaving."

"Any luck?"

Rebecca gazed at Paavo. "None at all....Uh, oh yes . . . your reports. They're on your desk."

Calderon grunted, the nearest he ever came to thanking anyone. Rebecca stood up. "You want to go to dinner, Luis?"

"I already ate."

"Well, then, I guess I'll go now," she said. "See you tomorrow, Paavo."

"See you," he replied, never looking up from his computer screen.

A short while later he shut the folder and put it in his desk drawer. Yosh had left for home long ago. Apparently the last couple of nights, between going to the Court House and working on the Ellis case, his wife was feeling neglected. Tonight was fence-mending time.

One more example of how marriage and homicide didn't mix. This caused him to think of Angie—and the reason why it did was so obvious it made him shudder. Every rational pore told him to give her up, that he wasn't marriage material, and it was unfair to try to be a part of her life. But another part, a more selfish part, wouldn't let her go. That part told him she was *his*—every petite, saucy, ambitious, warm-hearted, generous, maddening inch of her. They were as unlikely a pair as he'd ever come across, but when he was with her, he felt as if the whole world smiled. God, where had *that* come from?

He thought about her phone call earlier that day, about her excitement at auditioning for the TV program, and her disappointment that he couldn't celebrate with her.

He pushed his chair back from his desk, not wanting to be here anymore. Suddenly, he knew exactly where he wanted to be.

He got up, lifted his jacket from the back of his chair, and left.

The minute Angie saw Paavo's house, she knew he wasn't home. The lights were off, and his car wasn't in the driveway. Stan was in the Ferrari with her. They should continue on to the Sound Works. Why bother to stop? But then, given the off chance Yosh had given Paavo a ride home, she parked and ran up to the front door. He'd given her a key to his house for emergency use, but it didn't seem right to go barging in for no good reason. Instead, she knocked on the door and rang the bell, hoping against hope that he was there.

He wasn't.

The frustration she felt told her more than anything how much she had wanted to see him tonight. She'd put on a dynamite new black Isaac Mizrahi dress. Short, slinky, and shiny, with a flattering halter top, it fit like a layer of skin. Black silk hose and patent leather sandals with towering heels gave her the leggy look of models far taller than she. Big, bold gold earrings and a spritz of Flore completed the ensemble.

The whole time she was dressing, she'd imagined Paavo opening his door, looking surprised, pleased, and unable to bear not taking her in his arms right then and there. Of course, she'd insist they go dancing first, but soon—maybe very soon—she'd consent to going home with him and then *really* celebrate her audition request.

Now, the only man she had to show off for was Stan.

Disappointed, she turned back to her car.

A green Honda Civic pulled out of the parking space and sped to the corner. Even on city streets, the driver was probably going to have to floor the accelerator to keep up with the Ferrari he was following.

At almost the same moment, Paavo turned onto his street from the opposite end of the block. By the time he reached his house, the green Honda was no more than a distant set of taillights. He paid scant attention, though, his thoughts centered on a phone call to Angie and his hope that, after he'd had a quick shower and shave, she'd be willing to have him over. He had a lot to make up to her for.

CHAPTER

ELEVEN

As the last note sounded, Angie turned to the latest in her long line of dance partners, "Thank you," she said, smiling sweetly. "Good-bye, now."

During her pre-Paavo dating days, she'd learned how to deliver a definitive "Get lost, Buster" message without hurting a guy's feelings—or, at least, not too badly.

Tonight she'd doled out "get lost" messages by the bushel. She was tired, her feet hurt, and she wasn't having any fun. Each man who introduced himself and asked her to dance was measured against Paavo. Each came up lacking. She hadn't met a single one who, if Paavo wasn't in her life, she'd consider dating, let alone marrying. Dancing itself, while fun, didn't hold as much allure for her as it once did. She wondered if it had really been the dancing that she'd found so entertaining, or the flirting that went along with it. So far, she'd spotted only one obviously married couple. A few others were there wearing wedding rings, but they didn't appear to be married to each other.

She was ready to go home.

She tried to spot Stan from where she stood, a near-impossible task. Earlier, discussing marriage with him was just about as unrewarding as, in her heart, she should have known it would be.

"What do you think of getting married, Stan?" she had blurted. She realized as soon as she said it how the question sounded.

"Angie, this is so unexpected."

"But you know I'm mad about you," she said, then laughed. "Now, tell me what you really think."

"I accept."

"Stan, forget it." She walked away, wondering why she even bothered to try to be serious with him.

The dimly lit dance hall, hazy with smoke, was packed tighter than a can of anchovies. From the time she'd wandered away from Stan, she'd seen him a couple of times wrapped in the arms of a big redhead.

To find him now, she'd have to plow through the crowd, and even then, she'd need a considerable amount of luck. The heat and stuffiness of this room was getting to her, as was the loud, blaring music. She lifted her hair from the back of her neck and wandered toward an open window far back in the club, away from the dancers and the tables that circled them. Luckily, the building was old, with real windows that opened and shut, not those new, permanently sealed monstrosities that kept out any fresh air. She bent forward, her hands on the windowsill, enjoying the feel of the cool breeze against her face and shoulders, enjoying being alone for the first time that evening.

"Warm, isn't it?" said a silky smooth male voice.

She glanced up. A tall, muscular man with oversize, darkly tinted glasses and a long, thick mustache stood beside her, a little too close. He smiled at her. "Yes, very," she said, polite but cool, and again faced the window.

"This is my first time here," he said. His hair was slicked straight back and heavily pomaded.

She didn't reply.

"It's rather intimidating," he continued. "All these people. You never know if any of them will talk to you or not.

My friends told me to give it a try, though. They said . . . they said most people were pretty nice."

What was this guy doing, trying to pick her up or hold a session with Dr. Joyce Brothers? "And some want to be left alone," she said pointedly.

"That's very true. Do you come here often?" he asked.

He was dense or persistent or both. She folded her arms, still staring at the alley view of garbage cans and backs of buildings. "No."

"Oh? Why not?" he asked. He leaned his shoulder against the window frame and cocked his head, a casual pose, as if they were having a friendly chat. It was presumptuous. She wished he'd go away from *her* window.

She stiffened. "I haven't wanted to."

"Ah. Well, you're lucky. Yours is a much better reason than mine."

She'd had it. This boor was a walking cliché. "I know, you were too busy working, right? Something involving high finance, making lots of money, I suppose? Pardon me if I'm not impressed." She'd delivered the words with a sneering tone that should make any self-respecting male leave in a huff. It didn't.

"No, that's not it at all. But still, I don't blame you for not being impressed. There's nothing impressive about me, I'm afraid." She glanced his way. These were the first words he'd spoken that had any ring of truth. He shook his head, then bowed it, as if casting his gaze downward. Through his eyeglasses' dark tint, she couldn't tell for sure. "I've been alone too much," he added.

This guy had quite a line going. He'd almost taken her in, too. He was pretty good at this. "So you've come to a dance club to make up for it?"

He chuckled. "I can see you don't believe me. I don't blame you. My . . . my reason isn't very believable, I'm afraid."

"Now that I *do* believe," she said, not sure why she was still being civil. Well, sort of civil.

He adjusted his glasses. "Actually, it was pretty terrible—"

That did it. "Excuse me," she said, and turned to leave.

"Wait. I'm sorry. I'm making quite a mess of explaining." He quickly stepped in front of her. "My . . . my wife died some months ago."

"Sure." She tried to get around him.

"Here I thought you were a decent human being!" His lip curled in disgust, and he stepped back as if fearful of being tainted by her.

She stared at him in shock.

"I don't know the kind of people you normally associate with, lady," he said, "but I assure you, I wouldn't lie about my wife's death. You may be lovely, but no one is *that* beautiful." His voice broke, and he faced the window.

She felt guilty and very, very small over the way she'd spoken. When had she become so jaded? "Wait! I'm sorry." She touched his arm. "It was just after being hit on all evening, I was feeling, well . . . It was a callous thing to say."

He nodded, saying nothing, his back rigid as he stared through those dark, sightless glasses.

Uneasily she said, "It'll take time." She began backing away. "But you'll do all right, I'm sure."

"It's hard." He took a step toward her, then stopped. "Very hard." His voice was hushed, almost a whisper.

She forced herself to stop backing up even though he made her feel uncomfortable. Poor man. She had to remember that he was a new widower. He was facing the downside of marriage—from the ultimate togetherness, to a time alone. Suddenly, her heart ached for this man, for what he must have gone through. "I'm sorry," she said.

"What's your name?" he asked.

"Angie."

"Angie what?"

"Just Angie."

He gave a tentative smile. "Well, Just Angie, my name's Lee. I must confess," he continued, "I noticed you when you came in with that handsome blond fellow. Is he your steady?"

Perhaps their meeting by the open window hadn't been as much by chance as she'd assumed. This stranger—Lee—was far too inquisitive. "He's my fiancé," she said, remembering her earlier conversation with Stan. Also, being betrothed was a way to keep men such as Lee at arm's length.

"Ah. A lucky man," he said.

"Thank you."

One of the band's few slow dances began. "Since you're engaged," Lee said, "and the last thing I want is a woman who's available, would you do me the honor of this dance?"

"I'm afraid not. Thank you anyway."

"Oh. Well, I can't say that I blame you." An embarrassed blush rose on his cheeks. "I don't think I'd want to dance with me, either. I haven't been on a dance floor since who knows when. My wife was sick for a number of years before she died, you see. I just thought it'd be nice to see what it felt like again, in a safe situation. You're so lovely, though, I shouldn't have presumed. . . . I'm sorry. I didn't mean to offend you."

Again he bent his head and shook it slightly, as if berating himself for being foolish enough to ask her to dance.

"You didn't offend me."

"You mean you will dance with me?" His lips, his voice, smiled. But his eyes? "You're too kind." He held out his hand to her.

She hadn't meant that. She wanted to tell him he could easily find someone else to dance with. But his hand stayed outstretched, waiting. Well, what harm would one dance do?

She placed her hand in his, and his fingers quickly folded around it. They were firm and strong. His thumb lightly stroked her knuckles. "Soft," he said.

"What?"

"Your hand is very soft." He led her onto the dance floor, then faced her. "You're soft. I'd forgotten how soft a woman can be."

"Actually, I think I see my fiancé—"

"One dance." He took her in his arms. "We'll dance our way over to him."

She held herself back, feeling a sudden urge to run from him. Resting her hand lightly on his shoulder, she could feel his bulky muscles, much like a bodybuilder's. The strength he must possess scared her. But when he didn't try to draw her closer, she tried to convince herself she'd been overreacting. Paavo always accused her of doing that.

Still, up close, even in the dimness of the club, she could see that his mustache was strange—a fake?—and his teeth seemed too big for his mouth, almost as if they were an actor's prop. The pomade on his hair had a heavy, overly sweet smell.

She fixed her attention on a nearby couple, her mind clearly playing tricks on her where this man was concerned.

Hot, sweaty bodies packed the center of the dance floor. Elbows jabbed her. Someone stepped on her foot. Another person spun his partner into her back, knocking her flat against Lee as they danced. His body was surprisingly hard and muscular. "Excuse me," she murmured.

"It's all right." His lips grazed her ear as he whispered the words. A cold shudder trickled through her.

Frightened, she broke free. "I must find my fiancé," she said. "Good-bye."

He grabbed her arm and held it tight. Too tight. "Not good-bye, Angie. Until we meet again."

CHAPTER

$\infty\!\infty\!\infty$

TWELVE

"Who's been telling you these stories, Angie?" Marianne Perrault, a staff writer at *Haute Cuisine*, chased a piece of rubbery squid *sashimi* around her plate with her chopsticks. "Hugh and I have been married ten months, and we're forever going places and doing things together. Just last night we went out to dinner."

This was music to Angie's ears. Suddenly, her *sushi* lunch tasted much better. "That's so good to hear, Marianne," Angie said. "I remember last week we were talking about that new Afghanistani restaurant, and you said how much you wanted to go. Did Hugh take you?"

"No."

"Or that interesting Malaysian place you mentioned. Was that where you went?"

Marianne took a sip of warm *sake* from a small porcelain cup. "Actually, Hugh's a meat and potatoes kind of guy. He didn't want to try anything that might have ingredients he wasn't familiar with. Come to think of it, we were sort of rushed. I guess our dinner out wasn't such a great example."

"What do you mean? Where did you two end up?"

"Kentucky Fried Chicken."

CHAPTER

THIRTEEN

Stanfield Bonnette trudged up the Jones Street hill. The bus he rode after work left him off on Union Street, one block down from his apartment building. No bus tried to climb to the top of Russian Hill—it was too steep.

Someday, he might be able to afford a car, he thought bitterly. But even if he had one, parking was impossible in this city unless you had a garage—also prohibitively expensive. It was cheaper to bus and taxi everywhere. Especially when most of your money went to paying rent, as his did.

But he enjoyed his top floor apartment. It always impressed his dates, and he only went out with women he wanted to impress. It's just as easy to fall in love with a rich woman as a poor one, he told himself. Unfortunately, the only rich woman he'd met so far that aroused more than a passing interest cared far more about some homicide inspector than she did about him. Last night, she'd given him a start with her question about marriage. He should have known better than to react the way he did, tipping his hand that way. That she laughed made the bitter pill even harder to swallow.

And anyway, just what did that detective have that he didn't?

He stopped walking a moment to catch his breath. This hill was so steep that every so often some steps appeared, built right into the concrete sidewalk, supposedly to help high-heeled women walk downhill.

He'd made it to the top of the hill, the corner of Jones and Green streets, where his apartment building stood. He entered the lobby. A man wearing sunglasses, a San Jose Sharks cap, and carrying a bouquet of roses jumped back from the mailboxes. Startled by Stan's appearance, he bent his head downward, the brim of his cap hiding all but his chin from view.

"Sorry," the deliveryman mumbled. "There don't seem to be no doorman."

Stan didn't usually talk to strangers, not even ones carrying flowers. He'd lived in the city long enough to be paranoid about everyone and everything. "One is usually here," he said, keeping his distance. "He must have stepped away for a minute."

"I got some flowers for Angelina, the address is this building, but I don't know her apartment number."

"Angelina? You mean Angelina Amalfi?"

"Amalfi. Yeah, that's her."

More flowers for Angie, Stan thought. Probably from her hotshot detective. The guy probably heard he took her dancing last night, and now he wants to mend fences. Why didn't she just ditch the guy as he suggested? Well, the heck with him. If he couldn't get her address straight, that was too damn bad.

Then a wicked thought occurred to him. Why not hijack the flowers? Redirect them to his own apartment and never let Angie know Paavo had sent them. All's fair in love and war, he reminded himself, feeling good about how clever he was.

"She lives right here, in Apartment 12 ... 1202," he said.

"Twelve-oh-two," the man repeated, his head still downturned as if bowing to Stan. "Thanks. I'll take them up."

"I'm going up there," Stan said. "I live across the hall, so I don't mind saving you a trip. Anyway, she's never home in the afternoon."

"Oh . . . she's not? Okay, then. Thanks, pal." The man shoved the flowers at Stan and hurried away.

By the time the elevator let Stan off on the twelfth floor, he was feeling a little guilty about what he'd done. Just a little.

Paavo knocked on Angie's door. He had left work promptly at 4:30, almost unheard of for him, driven across town to shower and change, and made it to Angie's place before their six o'clock date. The last thing he wanted was to be late.

Last night, he'd phoned and phoned, not giving up until he reached her instead of her answering machine. She didn't tell him where she'd been, which wasn't like her at all. It made him feel strange. Suspicious. Where had she gone? With whom? But to show that he trusted her, he didn't ask.

Instead, he made a date with her for this evening, and he planned to keep it. Particularly if she was going to star in her own TV show. He wondered if he'd be able to compete with the type of men she'd meet. Or if she was already growing tired of him, and that's why she'd been out so much lately and not saying where.

That something about the two of them was troubling her was clear. Since she'd been so secretive recently, he couldn't help but suspect she'd met someone new or was, at minimum, having second thoughts about their relationship.

When he heard the doorknob turn, his pulse quickened. She opened the door.

She wore a lace-trimmed, ivory-colored silk top and matching wide-legged pajama pants. The outfit was soft, expensive, and feminine—just like Angie. She smiled, and in a moment he held her in his arms and kissed her. He gave the door a shove with his foot and listened for the click of the latch, not even wanting to turn away for the time it took to shut the door properly.

"I missed you," he said, all his earlier doubts foolishly vanishing in the glow of her smile. "But I don't want to wrinkle your pretty new outfit."

"Wrinkle it," she ordered.

His grin, he suspected, was too wide, too lopsided, and too out-and-out dopey, but that was how she made him feel. How easily she could get him to smile, even laugh, still surprised him. Before meeting her, he'd almost forgotten how.

"Where are we going to dinner?" he asked, still holding her.

"*Chez* Angelina."

"What?"

"We're eating right here."

"Here? I didn't want you to work. I wanted to take you out."

"You expect me to give up a chance to keep you all to myself? No way!"

His eyes crinkled into a mischievous glint as he took off his sport jacket and loosened his tie. "All right, Miss Amalfi," he said. "If you want me to yourself that much, then you've got me." He dropped his jacket on a chair and stepped toward her.

She placed her hands against his shoulders, backing up. "Wait! When did you last eat?"

He kept walking forward and she kept backing up until she backed into her Chippendale desk. He leaned forward and kissed her. "Who cares?" he murmured.

Who indeed, she thought, wrapping her arms around his shoulders. She was right, suggesting they stay here this evening. His kisses were dizzying, soon driving all thought from her mind. Her arms tightened around him, and she pressed her body against his as their kisses deepened. He even made her ears ring . . . and ring . . . and . . .

"Oh! The timer." She pulled away.

"What timer?" he asked.

Adjusting her clothes she headed toward the kitchen. "Dinner."

"Now?"

"This meal," she said, keeping her voice low and sultry, "will be a seduction in itself." Then she winked.

Big blue eyes widened with pleased curiosity.

She laughed. "Come on, big man. You can help."

He followed her into the kitchen and checked pots, pans, and bowls as she proudly announced a dinner of filets mignon, lobster tails, asparagus tips, saffron rice, Caesar salad, red and white wine, and sourdough bread. For dessert, one Italian rum tart for Paavo. She'd given up dessert for Lent, after all. The only thing left to do was to fire up the heavy skillet and put the two thick filets mignon in the bed of melted garlic butter.

A shave-and-a-haircut beat sounded at the door.

"Watch the filets," she said to Paavo, who was slicing the sourdough. "I'll take care of this."

She hurried across the living room and peeked through the peephole before opening the door. "I'm busy."

"And hello to you, too," Stan said cheerfully, slipping past her into the apartment. "Where were you all afternoon?"

"I don't have time to talk, Stan. Go home." She stayed at the door.

"But I brought some dessert for us." He tossed her a paper bag. "Also, I wanted to tell you about my day today. There was even a strange deliveryman." He crossed the living room and sank into her sofa.

"That sounds fascinating," she said drily. Leaving the door open she looked inside the bag. "One cookie?"

"But it's a Mrs. Fields. Very rich. We can split it. How about some coffee? Dinner smells great, by the way. I can tell you about the delivery while we eat."

"Angie, you'd better check these steaks," Paavo said, stepping into the dining area from the kitchen. He stopped short, his eyes narrowing as he gave Angie's neighbor a quick once-over. "Well, well, look who's here."

Stan jumped to his feet. "Oh, I didn't know you had

company, Angie. And here I thought you'd want some intellectual conversation. Oh, well, some other time." He snatched back the paper bag with the cookie. "By the way," he said, dropping his voice seductively, "thanks *a lot* for last night." He lifted an eyebrow at Paavo as he sauntered from the room. Angie shut the door behind him.

"You were with Bonnette last night?" Paavo asked, his eyes glacial.

"It was nothing." Angie tried to push him back into the kitchen.

"Bonnette seemed to find it special."

"Pay no attention to him."

"You haven't said where you two went."

"No." How could she tell him she'd gone with Stan to take a cold, calculated look at the singles scene. She found it wanting. Badly. "We went to the Sound Works."

"A dance club?"

She nodded.

"I see."

"No, I don't think you do. Stan said we should go out to celebrate my upcoming audition. I agreed."

His gaze was hard. "That's right. I was busy last night, wasn't I?"

"I waited, but—"

"It's okay, Angie," he said quietly. "I understand."

"Stop saying you understand! Stan's a friend."

"Right. And the Sound Works is the kind of place to go to with a friend. Lots of single people go there—to dance, meet each other. Why shouldn't you go as well?"

Could all that sarcasm be masking a twinge of jealousy? She wondered if he'd ever experienced such a thing before?

"I knew you'd understand," she said, hugging him. "Let's go eat."

The man looked positively baffled as he followed her to the table. Once the food was on, though, they quickly put aside Stan and his cheap innuendo.

"You're a genius," he said, dipping his last bite of lobster into the warm, clarified butter.

"I know." She took a piece of her lobster with her fingers, slathered it in butter, and lifted it to his lips.

He ate, then caught her hand and licked the butter from her fingertips one by one. She shut her eyes, reveling in the slow, lazy sensuousness of his tongue against her fingertips. When he finished with her pinky, she reached for another piece.

"Uh, uh," he murmured, taking her hand and drawing her from her chair to his lap. "You taste much better than lobster." He pretended to take a bite out of her chin, her jaw, her neck. His hand slid down her waist to her hips. Where he touched, she sizzled.

"I miss you so much when we're not together," she whispered. "The days seem so empty."

"And the nights," he murmured, carefully pulling her top free from the waistband of her slacks.

She loved him, but her head spun. She felt confused. A little scared. Never one to keep things inside, she had to tell him how she felt.

She drew back. "I have to talk to you, Paavo," she said seriously. "I know we agreed that our relationship needed time to grow, to mature, and to see how things might work out between us, but . . ."

His hands stilled. Eyes wide, he stared at her.

Could he be reading her mind? she wondered. Could he be looking so stricken just because she thought it might be time for them to discuss marriage?

Suddenly, the phone rang. They both nearly jumped out of their skins at the shrill sound.

It rang again. "You'd better answer it, Angie. It might be important."

"I'm sure it's not. Let the answering machine—"

He stood, lifting her out of his lap and helping her stand. "I told Homicide they could reach me here tonight, if anything came up."

"All right, all right. I'll get it." She kissed him. "You stay right there."

He started to follow her to the phone.

"Freeze, Inspector!"

He threw up his hands and, as she picked up the phone, he sat back down.

"Yes?" she said curtly.

"Hey, there, Angie. How ya doin'?"

She groaned inwardly. She knew that jubilant voice. Paavo's homicide partner.

"Actually, I'm kind of busy."

"Say, is the Big P.S. there?"

She winced. P.S.—an afterthought. That's what she'd be once Paavo took this phone call. "He's here," she said with a sigh. "Hold on."

She handed Paavo the phone. "It's your partner."

He put the phone to his ear. "Yosh, what's up?"

He listened for a couple of minutes, then frowned. "What was her name?"

Angie caught the "was." God, no, she thought. Another homicide. She prayed she was wrong.

"City Hall? Is that why the chief's worried?"

Was someone killed at City Hall? she wondered. She rubbed the chill from her arms.

"Got it," he said, then placed the phone back in its cradle. As he turned, the expression on his face told her Yosh's call was more than just informational.

"You don't have to leave, do you?" she asked.

"I'm on call this week."

"My God, Paavo, there *are* other homicide inspectors in this city! We were supposed to have this time together."

"I'm sorry, Angie. This isn't the way I wanted our evening to end."

She looked at the unhappy, yet determined look in his pale blue eyes. When he turned them on her that way, she couldn't argue with him. "I'm sorry, too, Paavo. I shouldn't have snapped at you. It's not your fault."

He put his hands on her waist, pulling her close. "Maybe it's for the best. Maybe that talk . . . about our relationship needing time . . . maybe we need more time before we have it."

He was right, she realized. They weren't ready to talk yet. She nodded, burying her face against his shoulder.

He held her a long while, his hands stroking her back, massaging it, as if he could rub away her troubling thoughts, the havoc Yosh's call had brought to their evening.

"If it's not too late," he said softly, "may I come back for dessert?"

She tilted her head back and looked at him, her hands on his shoulders. "Come back, Inspector, no matter what time it is. Dessert will be waiting."

He gave her a kiss that nearly broke her heart, and she didn't know why.

CHAPTER

∞∞∞

FOURTEEN

Paavo and Yosh arrived outside the homicide victim's Twin Peaks apartment building at just about the same time. This normally quiet neighborhood had a number of onlookers attracted by the appearance of a police car. A uniformed officer waited for them and led them through the spectators, into the building, and then upstairs to the third floor, where a group of tenants had gathered in the hallway.

Another officer stood outside the door of the deceased's apartment, guarding the crime scene.

"Looks like she's been dead a few days," Officer McPherson said, his complexion a decided gray as he described going into the apartment with the landlady and finding the woman. "According to the landlady, the victim's name is Tiffany Rogers. She was about twenty-three, single, and white."

A middle-aged woman wearing a floral blouse over turquoise slacks, her short, black hair streaked with gray, approached them. "I'm Harriet Donovan, the manager of this building."

Paavo and Yosh introduced themselves. "Are you the one who found the victim?" Paavo asked.

"Yes, I did." Her voice shook nervously. "I immediately called the police. I didn't touch anything, I don't think . . . "

"How did you get into the apartment?"

"I knocked, but the door was locked." She worried her bottom lip as if unsure about making the next statement. "I have a key. I . . . I think I'm within my rights to use it, I mean—"

"It's all right, Miss Donovan," Yosh said soothingly. "You certainly had to check on her."

"Yes." She raked her hair behind one ear. "That's what I thought, too."

"What caused you to look for her in there?" Paavo asked.

"I was asked by her sister, Connie. Apparently, yesterday Tiffany didn't show up at work at City Hall and didn't call in sick. When she didn't show up again today, and didn't answer her telephone, her boss became concerned and phoned the sister. The two of them aren't very close, I understand, but Connie called me to see if Tiffany was sick and had unplugged her phone or something."

"Does her sister live nearby?"

"Yes, over in the Sunset."

"Have you told her about this?"

"No." She put her hand to her throat and took a step backwards. "I'm sorry. I guess I should have, but . . . "

"That's all right, Miss Donovan," Yosh said. "We'll take care of it. You've been a big help to us already, we want you to know. And I suspect we're going to need your help a lot more before this is over, so you stay right nearby, okay?"

She nodded quickly, her eyes wide.

"I knew we could count on you," Yosh said.

He and Paavo stood before the victim's apartment door. Paavo gave a light push and the door swung open easily. Rogers's body lay in the center of the living room, the once-white carpet beneath her nearly black and thick with blood. Her face was almost white, her eyes and mouth open, the eyeballs clouded, and her lips dry and leathery.

The odor was stomach-churning—the iron scent of blood and the acrid, sour smell of body fluids bubbling out of her mouth.

They stepped closer, easing along the perimeter of the room, where it was least likely they might disturb any evidence. A robe covered the victim's arms and shoulders, but the front lay open. Long-stemmed red roses, wilted and dead, had been haphazardly tossed around her body, the blood beneath them looking as if it had flowed from their own death throes.

The stab wounds were deep and long. The sheer number and placement over the breasts and pubic area looked like the work of a sexual psychopath. Paavo turned away in disgust.

San Francisco had been spared one of those for some time—since the Zodiac murders in the late sixties and early seventies, and later, the Trailside killer. Both had chosen their victims at random. Both had preyed on young, single women.

He could only hope this wasn't another. They were the most difficult to catch—and the ones who, if not caught quickly, were the most likely to kill again.

His gaze met Yosh's. Each of them knew what was uppermost in the other's thoughts.

The photographer arrived, and soon after, the crime scene investigators. Taking one look at the blood, they dressed themselves in clear plastic booties, overalls, and gloves, then began the ritual of recording the scene. Paavo and Yosh stood back from the body, careful not to contaminate any evidence. They hadn't approached it, and wouldn't, until after the CSI unit finished its job.

Apparently, when the landlady phoned the police to report the murder, she had mentioned that the victim worked at City Hall. That had been enough for Hollins to take an immediate interest in the case. The City Hall involvement could go nowhere, or go straight to the mayor himself. Hollins wasn't taking any chances. Neither were Paavo or Yosh.

While the crime scene unit worked, the inspectors went through the apartment building, talking to Rogers's neighbors. Most of the tenants were single, living alone or with roommates, worked all day, and had busy evenings. Most hadn't seen Tiffany for days, and hadn't expected to since she wasn't a homebody at all. Everyone knew she had an "important" boyfriend whom she'd go off to meet somewhere two or three times a week. She never brought him to her place. They all figured he must be married.

The inspectors also asked if anyone had heard any strange sounds or noticed anything out of the ordinary around the apartment building over the last three or four days. No one had.

"Here's the sister's name and phone number," Miss Donovan said, handing Paavo a slip of paper. "She's waiting to hear from me."

The name Connie was written in a tight, precise hand.

Paavo went to the manager's apartment on the first floor and dialed the number.

As gently as possible, he broke the news. He asked her to come to the apartment building. Not only did he need to talk to her, but—after the body was removed—she could readily determine if anything had been taken or was drastically out of place in the apartment.

He doubted it, though. Looking at Tiffany's mutilated body, he knew robbery wasn't the motive here.

Hours and hours had gone by, and still he sat in the green Honda across the street from Angie's apartment building. His bladder was full, but that was all right. He was thinking, planning. He liked to figure out puzzles, and to him, Angie was a puzzle.

He had watched Smith leave after only a little more than an hour with the woman. Leaving so soon didn't make sense. He should have stayed longer, like all night. *He* would have.

Instead, Smith left. Alone.

He didn't get it. Was Smith involved with Angie? Was she really engaged to the blond fellow who took her to the Sound Works? They'd scarcely danced with each other. Maybe she'd lied to him when she told him the blond was her fiancé? Or maybe she was two-timing both men?

Women were such liars. Who could tell what they were up to? They all lied and cheated. Except Heather.

A vague memory tried to take shape, but he pushed it away. Heather was perfection, everything a woman should be.

Not like this Angelina Amalfi.

Damn! He pounded the dash. Was she the cop's slut or not? He had to find out.

He'd enjoy finding out, in fact. Getting to know her better. A lot better. Angelina Amalfi was a beautiful woman. Small. Delicate. Like Heather. He had liked the way she felt while they danced. The way she smelled. Her perfume had the scent of roses. Roses. How perfect.

He remembered the way she'd smiled at him. Flirted, even teased. She laughed at his jokes, his wit. By the time he was through charming her, she was wild for him. And hot. Wet and hot.

And when they danced, he saw her surprise at his body, his strength. She waggled her tail good then, rubbing against him, letting him know how much she wanted him. But her fiancé was there, so she had to hold back. Damn the man.

But later that night, when she and her so-called fiancé were off somewhere screwing, maybe she'd shut her eyes and think of him. Imagine it was *him* that she was touching, *him* deep inside her.

His breathing grew heavier. Thick and raspy. He lowered his hand *there*, even though it wasn't nice to touch himself. Not nice. He pressed hard, enjoying the discomfort. The throbbing.

This Angie was so much like Heather. His Heather. Heather had been hot for him, too.

It would be like Heather. All over again.

CHAPTER

———— ∞∞∞ ————

F I F T E E N

As Paavo and Yosh crossed the grand foyer under the dome of City Hall, their shoes made a loud clicking sound on the marble floor. The building was quiet and empty in the early morning hour, before the offices opened to the public.

Tiffany Rogers had been a secretarial assistant to one of the most influential members of the Board of Supervisors—longtime member Maxim Wainwright. Paavo and Yosh had an appointment with him and everyone who worked closely with the murdered woman.

"Come right in." A white-haired, navy blue–suited woman, reeking of efficiency, held the door open for the inspectors. "Supervisor Wainwright is expecting you."

She showed them into a small but smartly furnished office. The oak desk looked as if it must be worth several grand.

"I'm absolutely shocked by this!" Wainwright, a tall, gray-haired man, exclaimed as soon as the introductions were made. "So is everyone who knew her. She was a wonderful young woman. Vivacious and charming."

Paavo took in the wringing of the man's hands, his

strained, overly helpful, concerned manner. At the same time, he gave scant credence to the supervisor's words. All new murder victims were wonderful people—or, at least they were the first time a homicide inspector spoke with their friends and relatives. But that facade usually faded after another visit or two.

Paavo pulled his notebook from his breast pocket. As soon as Wainwright stopped enumerating Tiffany's virtues, Paavo and Yosh began their routine series of questions about Miss Rogers's job, her relationship with her boss, her coworkers, and if she'd ever complained about coworkers or anyone else stalking her, threatening her, or bothering her in any way. To each question asked, Wainwright replied that he saw no indication that there had ever been a problem. Tiffany had only worked for him for two months. She'd been a clerk in Accounting, and came highly recommended. Her current position had been as an assistant to Mrs. Brinks, the woman who had greeted them. In fact, Wainwright added, he had scarcely ever spoken with Miss Rogers. All his conversations had been with Mrs. Brinks.

When asked who had so highly recommended Miss Rogers, his reply was "everyone." He couldn't think of any single individual.

Letty Devon, an elderly woman, had been Tiffany's supervisor in Accounting. "She was precious. A lovely girl. She would have gone far as a civil servant." Letty wiped the tears from the corner of her eyes.

"How long did she work for you?" Paavo asked.

"Five months. She'd been in the typing pool before that for three months, I believe."

"You know, Mrs. Devon," Yosh said, "or Letty? May I call you Letty? It's a pretty name. Old-fashioned."

Mrs. Devon smiled and nodded. A red half-dollar-sized spot appeared on each withered cheek.

"I was thinking, Letty," Yosh continued, "didn't

Tiffany move up awfully fast? I mean, only three months in the typing pool, then only five here before she was promoted to working for a supervisor seems pretty remarkable."

"Yes. It was fast." She pursed her lips.

"I bet a lot of people spend their entire career in Accounting. A very good career, too."

"You're quite right." Her shoulders stiffened, and she held her head a little higher.

"Would *you* have moved her that fast?" Yosh asked. "Did you recommend her to Wainwright?"

"Well," she squirmed.

"You can tell me," Yosh nodded encouragingly.

"Actually"—she lowered her voice as if afraid someone was eavesdropping—"I recommended against it."

"Oh?"

"She wasn't ready. Not at all."

"Then how'd she get the job?"

"I don't know the specifics, but I know in general."

"Yes?" Yosh leaned closer.

Letty Devon cupped her hand over her mouth as she said one word. "Connections."

Wainwright had mentioned that Tiffany's closest friend at work had been an accounting clerk named Manuela Rodriguez. Paavo told Mrs. Devon he'd like to speak to Rodriguez. Devon offered her office to the inspectors for their interview. "Whatever I can do to help," she announced.

Manuela Rodriguez was in her mid-twenties with raven black hair and enormous, soulful eyes. Her plum suit was tasteful, yet tight enough and short enough to be alluring instead of businesslike. As she entered the office, she tightly gripped a large man-sized white handkerchief.

Her gaze was blank as she studied Yosh, but grew lively when she noticed Paavo. She met his clear blue eyes with frank interest before giving him a slow, suggestive smile.

Usually Yosh was Mr. Congeniality with potential witnesses, and Paavo was the one who sat back, noted reactions, and then asked the most biting questions—the bad cop to Yosh's good. But seeing Manuela's reaction to Paavo, the two inspectors switched roles without saying a word to each other.

At Paavo's first question—how long she'd known Tiffany—Manuela's already-red-rimmed eyes began to tear. "We met about a year ago. Tiffany was still in the typing pool. We used to like to go to parties and all kinds of stuff, you know, when neither one of us was dating anybody special. You know what I'm saying?" Paavo nodded, and Manuela crossed her legs, her already-short shirt riding even higher. "For the last couple months, though, she didn't go no place with me. She was, like, seeing somebody. But I don't know who. And she wouldn't say."

"Why not?" Paavo asked.

"Top secret, that's all. I figured, like, the guy was somebody here at work."

"Had she dated men from work before?"

"Yeah, sure. Didn't work out, though."

"Miss Rodriguez," Paavo said, "did Miss Rogers tell you about those other affairs?"

"Yeah, sure."

"Why didn't she this time?"

"He was, like, you know, some big shot. Or married. Probably both. She'd never dated a married man before. I didn't think she would now, but she—" She stopped there and folded her hands over one knee.

"Go on," Paavo urged.

"I shouldn't say." Manuela shook her head. "I'm just, like, guessing."

"That's all right, you were her friend," Paavo replied. "Anything you guess interests us."

"Well, she was, like, you know, ambitious. If some big shot took an interest in her, even if he was married, I think she'd go out with him."

"What do you mean by ambitious?" Yosh asked.

Manuela gave him a long look, then shrugged.

"Tell us," Yosh insisted. "Did she want to get ahead here at work? Was she looking for someone to set her up? What?"

"You name it," Manuela said.

"No, Miss Rodriguez," Yosh said. "You name it."

"It would be a big help to us," Paavo added.

Manuela studied her fingernails. "Tiffany liked nice things, you know. She always went out with men who'd give her presents. Expensive presents. But mainly, she wanted to get a job that made enough money that she could tell all men to go stuff it if she wanted to."

Paavo leaned back in his chair. Manuela's gaze slowly traveled from his shoes along his long, lean body up to his eyes. She gave him a sultry smile. "Before she got the job in Wainwright's office, had she been seeing anyone?" he asked.

"No. We was going to a lot of parties. Having a real good time. You know what I mean?"

"What about after?"

"After?"

"After she got her job with Wainwright."

"We didn't go no place together after. She was already seeing her mystery guy."

"Do you remember the last party the two of you went to together?"

"Sure. We were, like, invited to a party with a crowd from the Hall of Justice, mostly. A few from City Hall."

"Cops?" Yosh asked.

"No. No cops. I don't hang around with cops. Too much trouble, you know. These guys were big shots. Real big."

"Names?"

"I don't remember. But it was at Bimbo's 365 Club. Other people might remember. Not me."

Paavo nodded. "Okay, Miss Rodriguez. If you do remember anything, give me a call." He handed her his card.

She studied the card a minute, then faced him again. "You got really nice blue eyes, you know," she said, then smiled. "Maybe I got to, like, rethink my thing about cops."

Angie woke up late, groggy with a horrible headache.

Paavo hadn't returned for dessert last night. She berated herself for waiting up for him until almost three, when she had given up and gone to bed.

No use going back to sleep, she decided and stumbled into the kitchen. Grinding Graffeo coffee beans for some strong Italian roast, she had to admit that attempting to discuss marriage with Paavo was definitely one of her dumber moves. She wasn't ready yet.

As she sipped her coffee, the cloudy grogginess began to clear from her brain, and the world came into focus once more. After last night's meal, she didn't feel like eating breakfast. She probably shouldn't eat for a week if she didn't want all those calories to go straight to her hips. Her battle against becoming pear-shaped was constant and vigilant. She eyed some little round *biscotti* her mother had given her—hard, made with very little sugar if one discounted the smidgen of white icing on each. They were made for dunking into hot coffee.

No, she'd given up dessert for Lent. Maybe she should give up thinking about marriage as well? The more she thought about it and asked about it, the more confused she was becoming.

She couldn't sit here all day thinking about Paavo and marriage and cookies. There were more important things to think about, like how long she'd have to wait before auditioning for the television job, or a more immediate concern, what she'd write about for *Haute Cuisine* magazine.

She wanted the magazine article to be something special, if for no other reason than that her archrival, Nona Farraday, had recently written her way from freelancing for the magazine to a position as a staff writer. To Angie, Nona was Lex Luthor to her Superman, Siskel to her Ebert, Beavis to her Butt-head. No, scratch that.

Professor Moriarity to her Sherlock Holmes. Much better.

And just as Holmes and Superman rose above their rivals and defeated them, so must she come up with an article that would turn heads and gain her the attention and respect of the press, the public, and the culinary world.

She had to find something so unique, an experience so exceptional, that people would take note.

The Wings Of An Angel. Visions—angelic visions—of the strange little restaurant came floating back to her. Hosanna in the highest.

The flavor of the meatballs and sauce returned as sharply as if she had a plate of food before her. It was unique, wonderful. If the chef would use the sauce in a few other dishes, the restaurant would succeed easily.

But the men running it clearly needed help.

Her help.

She knew a fair amount about running a restaurant. She'd reviewed them for over a year, worked at LaTour's for a short while before it closed down—due to no fault of hers—and even spent a week setting up a menu for a New Age inn. She knew a number of restaurateurs in the Bay Area as well as in France.

Besides that, helping the owners would give her something to do while she waited for her TV audition. Magically, her headache vanished, her grogginess and ill temper lifted, and the perfect plan popped into her head.

She dressed with care, wanting to look chic but casual, and settled on a Hanae Mori white-and-black pants outfit. She'd get Wings's chef's attention yet.

She rode the elevator to the basement garage, got in the Ferrari, and drove down Union Street to Columbus Avenue. She stopped off at a grocery store, bought some food, and then continued on to the restaurant.

When she arrived, she was pleased to see a young couple sitting in the window eating heaping platters of spaghetti and meatballs. "Hi," she said cheerfully to the same waiter she'd had the last time she was here—a cross between Joe Pesci and Fred Flintstone.

She had slipped the shopping bag with her few groceries onto her arm, holding it like a purse. She didn't want the waiter to pay it any special attention.

The waiter stopped in his tracks and stared as if he couldn't believe what he saw. "It's you."

"I couldn't stay away. The food's delicious and the service truly memorable."

"Yeah?"

"May I sit?"

"Go ahead."

Since he wasn't about to seat her, Angie found herself a table. "I'm glad to see you're getting more customers."

"Yeah, well we tol' Vinnie we didn't have no choice."

"No choice? You make it sound as if he didn't want anyone here."

The waiter frowned. "It's a long story."

"I see," Angie said, although she didn't. She took the menu from him. "What's your name, by the way?" she asked.

He pronounced it carefully. "Oil."

"Oil? That's an odd name."

"Yeah. My ma was real fond of royalty, I t'ink."

"Royalty?" What royalty was associated with oil? "You mean like a sheik?"

"Yeah. Chic. Dat's me."

"My name's Angie."

"Oh. Yeah, well, I gotta help dem udder people." The waiter went off to take care of the couple. Angie had the distinct feeling she'd missed something. She opened the menu. It still said "Columbus Avenue Café."

"Oh, Oil!" Angie called, as the waiter headed toward the kitchen. He stopped and faced her. "Excuse me, but is there any reason for me to look at this menu? I mean, is the cook serving anything besides spaghetti and meatballs today?"

"No."

She handed back the menu. "I'll have spaghetti and meatballs."

"What do you wanna drink? And we don't have no caffe latte no more."

"I see. How about Perrier?"

"Perry. . . ?"

"You know, water."

"Water. No problem."

A short while later, the waiter brought her a plate of spaghetti—just as delicious as she remembered—and a glass of water, no ice, straight from the tap. This restaurant needed even more help than she thought it did.

"Oil," Angie called once more when she saw him stick his head through the swinging doors to see how his three customers were doing.

He walked over to her table. "Whatsa matter now?"

"Would you tell your cook that I think he's marvelous. Also, I'd like to help him put more choices on the menu."

"Why? He got da spaghetti right."

She braced herself. Now, she'd see if her plan would work or not. "I work for the government," she said, trying to sound bureaucratic. "I give cooking assistance to new restaurants."

The waiter stepped back. "You're from da government?" His eyes narrowed. "You don't look like you work for da Man."

"It's a new program to help the small businessman," she said hurriedly. "There's been so much criticism that government doesn't help small businesses, that this administration came up with our little way to change all that."

He frowned. "What parta da government you from? You gotta badge?"

"You never heard of us, I'm sure. A small bureau—and no badges."

"So what's it called?

Good question. "Alcohol, Tobacco, and Cookware."

"Oh. Dat sounds kinda familiar. Jus' a minute." He ran into the kitchen.

Earl skidded to a halt in front of the stove. "'Ey, Butch! We got a retoin customer."

"Somebody came back for more?" Butch stopped stirring the spaghetti sauce and wiped his palms against his formerly white apron.

"Da broad. An' now she says she's from da government, and she wants to help you cook better."

"Why does everybody think there's somethin' wrong with my cookin'?" Butch grumbled.

"Maybe sometime you gotta feed somebody somet'in' besides spaghetti an' meatballs."

"Vinnie says we ain't supposed to feed nobody nothin'—except we can't throw the customers outta here. That ain't kosher."

"But she's from da government. If we don't let her help, she might shut us down. Or call da FBI."

"Or worse," Butch muttered. "Our parole officers."

"And dey might look in da basement."

"We're stuck," Butch announced glumly. He felt for his long-gone shoulder holster.

"You t'ink we oughta tell Vinnie?" Earl asked.

"And put him in a worst mood? No way. We gotta keep this quiet. Tell him she was snoopin' around, so we put her to work in the kitchen. That way, she'll keep busy and won't find nothin'." He frowned. "Anyway, a woman's place is in the kitchen."

"What if she hears noise from da basement?"

"We'll tell her it's rats. Women hate 'em. She won't have nothin' to do with the basement."

"I don't know," Earl said. "My ex-wife usta say da only kinda rat she hated was da two-legged kind."

"She oughta know."

"Dat's right—she run off wit' No-Nose Nolan—an' he's a rat."

"Yeah, yeah. Look, we gotta stall. Tell her to come back in two days."

"I'll try, but I t'ink she's kinda stubborn. Like Vinnie."

"Naw. She ain't big enough."

Earl went to the swinging doors and tried to push them open. They wouldn't budge. He tried harder. They gave only a little. If anything it seemed they wanted to open inward, toward him. It was all he could do to stop them from smacking him in the face. He wasn't amused.

Carefully, he let go of the doors and stepped back. When they didn't open in on him, he curled his arms against his stomach and, leading with his left shoulder like Lawrence Taylor going in for a tackle, he leaped, both feet leaving the air, and hurled himself against the doors.

Angie decided the swinging doors must be broken. They wouldn't open into the kitchen, no matter how hard she pushed against them. With her shopping bag on her arm, she grabbed hold of a door handle and, stepping to the side, yanked the door open.

The waiter named Oil flew past her like a cannonball and headed straight toward the other customers. Angie had noticed that they'd been sitting waiting for their check. It was about time Oil began taking his job seriously.

She stepped into the kitchen, undistracted by the sound of breaking dishes behind her.

"Whadda you want?" In front of the stove, a small, wiry man wearing a disgustingly dirty apron bounded around on the balls of his feet. Angie figured he must have just burned himself on a pot.

"My name's Angelina Amalfi." She placed the shopping bag on the large butcher block. "You must be the cook here."

He scowled at her and her bag. "You the Fed?"

"Let's not think about that." Angie looked around the kitchen in amazement. It was fully stocked with restaurant equipment and everything looked quite clean—probably well scrubbed by the owner so that he could rent it out. "I'm here to help get you started. I've got lots of experience in restaurants. I even once worked at LaTour's, which was quite famous before it unfortunately shut down."

"I don't know no LaTours, El Tours, or LaTrines, and I don't want no government agent in my kitchen. I don't even vote."

"As I said, just forget about that. I'm afraid I don't know your name."

"Butch Pagozzi."

"Italian, just like me. I should have known that when I tasted your meatballs. *Parl'italiano?*"

"Huh?"

So much for consanguinity. "I want to compliment you on your spaghetti and meatballs. They're quite unique." She began going through the shelves of food. There was little there except a twenty-pound box of spaghetti, cans of tomato paste, and a few containers of Italian seasoning. Hamburger meat was in the refrigerator, plus French bread—exposed to air and getting hard—and big cans of a variety of stews, chili, and strange processed foods no self-respecting restaurant would be caught dead serving.

"Where's the rest of your food?" she asked.

"I didn't wanna spend much money 'til we got some customers," Butch said.

"You're not going to get customers unless you spend money to buy the food to bring them in."

"Yeah, but we don't have no money to spend. So the customers get the spaghetti, or they take a hike. It's a tough world, lady."

These boys were in trouble. "You really do need to have more on your menu than one thing." She began going through the spice shelves. They had a good supply of all kinds of spices, but nothing to spice up. She looked with frustration at the shelf. There wasn't a single spice that could give Butch's sauce and meatballs their special flavor.

"It'll be easy for you to build an interesting menu on

the base of the spaghetti and meatballs that you already have, you know."

Butch swaggered. "Sure. I know that."

"Good," she said, trying to hide her disbelief before going back to opening jars of spices and smelling them to see what was fresh and what had turned old and sour or flavorless. "What's your recipe for meatballs?" she asked nonchalantly.

"Nothin' special."

Damn. She hoped he'd just blurt it out. "You use ground beef, right?"

"Extra lean."

Extra lean? Angie didn't let her skepticism show. "And I suppose you put in salt, pepper, oregano, chopped onion, garlic, bread crumbs, and an egg to bind it?"

"I know how to make meatballs. I don't need no Fed—"

"But your meatballs are different. What else do you put in?"

He folded his arms. "Nothin'." His look dared her to contradict him.

"I'm not being critical. I'm interested. There's got to be something more. The taste—"

"Basil. Yeah, basil."

"Basil?"

"I put in a little basil. Always have, always will," he said with a pugnacious, smug smile.

Basil wouldn't do it. Basil would give a lightly scented herbiness to the meatballs, not the pungent, salty tanginess that had her so baffled. "And?"

"Nothin'." He fidgeted. "This is a real third degree, lady."

She'd just have to watch and find out.

"To show you how serious I am about helping out," she said, "I'll show you right now how you can double your menu with almost no additional work or expense on your part."

"I don't believe it."

"You don't?"

"No way."

Using the cheese and French rolls she'd bought at the grocery, she quickly made the sandwich she had in mind. She spooned Butch's spaghetti sauce on the inside halves of a split roll and then halved three meatballs and placed them on the bottom portion of the roll. She sprinkled coarsely grated mozzarella on top of the meatballs, then spooned on more sauce to melt the cheese. Angie put the sandwich together and sliced it in two with a triumphant flourish.

"Hey," he said. "It looks good enough to eat!"

"That's the idea."

One of the swinging doors opened all the way and hit the wall with a loud thud. Earl stood in the doorway. He held his hand to his forehead and blinked rapidly, as if he couldn't quite focus.

"Oil!" Angie cried. "What's wrong?"

"You better sit down," Butch said, taking his arm. "What happened?"

"I'm stronger'en I t'ought. After I knocked open da doors, I ran so fast, I hit da post out dere and musta knocked myself out. When I woke up, da customers was gone—wit'out paying for da food. Dey stiffed us, da lousy crooks!"

CHAPTER

SIXTEEN

"You've got to keep City Hall out of this case. As far as the press knows, she was a typist. Nothing more. Mumble when you say where she worked." Lieutenant Hollins got up from behind his desk, walked around to the front of it, and leaned against the edge. Paavo and Yosh sat facing him. They'd just completed briefing him on the Tiffany Rogers investigation. Hollins made it a point not to get involved in his men's investigations unless political heat was turned on. In this case, the heat was on high.

"Her friends and coworkers are at City Hall, and there's a good chance the guy she's been seeing is there as well," Paavo said.

"It's our only lead, Chief," Yosh added. "So far, the CSI unit can't even find a suspicious fingerprint to lift. The crime scene is clean as a whistle. She always met her boyfriend away from her apartment. We aren't sure where yet. We've got a few leads we're still checking."

"So you've got nothing except for a dead woman lying in her own blood on the floor of her own living room!" Hollins added.

"We have to follow wherever the leads take us," Paavo said.

"I'm not saying not to, all I'm saying is keep the press away." Hollins paced back and forth in front of his desk. "The mayor and the Board of Supervisors want this murderer caught right now. This isn't the kind of publicity they want for themselves or the city. I mean, if someone who works for them isn't safe, who is?"

"Aw heck, Paavo." Yosh turned to his partner. "The supervisors said they want us to catch this murderer fast. Here I'd planned to take my sweet time with this case."

Paavo couldn't help but grin.

"Cut the comedy, Yoshiwara." Hollins stuck an unlit cigar in his mouth and chewed. "This case is number one for you both, got it?"

"We are not dropping the Nathan Ellis case," Paavo said with an edge to his voice.

"Calderon and Benson can baby-sit it for you for a few days—until you catch Rogers's killer."

"Nobody has to baby-sit our case. We've spent days on it."

"With City Hall involved, I don't want any hint that the Rogers case doesn't have your full, undivided attention."

"What about Debbie Ellis? She thinks her husband's case has our attention." Paavo's eyes were narrowed, his only sign of anger.

"Calderon will handle her all right."

Paavo and Yosh kept silent.

Hollins said, "Get out there and find Tiffany Rogers's killer before City Hall comes down on all of us."

On her way to City College, Angie gave herself some extra time so that she could drive by Paavo's house to see if he was home. He'd been so busy with his latest murder case, she hadn't seen him for a few days. His car wasn't in front of the house—his small cottage didn't have a garage—and his cat, Hercules, was sitting on the fence in the sunshine.

Angie was quite sure Hercules spent his days heckling any dogs who went by on a leash.

When Paavo was home, Hercules was usually inside asleep after scarfing down a full can of 9-Lives. Once Angie brought him some fresh crabmeat, shelled. He refused to eat 9-Lives for three days thereafter. Paavo made Angie promise she'd never do anything like that again.

She tried the door, but after receiving no answer, she continued on her way to City College, where she taught a noncredit adult education course on the history of San Francisco. The class, as much as it was an asset to her students, was also to help her with her historical study of the city—the book she'd been working on for several months.

Writing the book might not have been interesting, but her class was a different story. In it, she didn't want to just look at the politics of the city—which had been fascinating, decadent, and corrupt—much like any other American city's, but to view it from the point of view of the kinds of people who lived here long ago. She wanted to talk about the San Francisco of longshoremen and teamsters, of gamblers, gold diggers, and the Barbary Coast, of the only city to successfully call a general strike, the Left Coast home of the Wobblies.

As the class studied about each new ethnic group that moved into the city, she cooked up a small dish or two when the lesson began, and as each topic ended, she took the class to a restaurant that specialized in the cuisine of that particular nationality. If you can't walk in their shoes, you can at least eat in their kitchen, was her motto. What better way to learn?

She brought her charges to Yuen's Gardens for *dim sum*, L'Etoile for bouillabaisse, Italian Seasons for manicotti, Speckmann's for sauerbraten, and Tommy's Joynt for a pint of the Guinness. It was expensive, but her class attendance skyrocketed, and she didn't have a single dropout— an achievement unheard of in adult education classes.

Pulling the Ferrari into the faculty parking area, she cut

the motor and gathered up her books and lecture notes. As she got out of the car, she noticed a man walking her way. There was something strangely familiar about him. He wore a N.Y. Yankees baseball cap and sunglasses, jeans and a blue parka. When he saw her watching him, he stopped walking, gave a half smile, and leaned casually against a black Beemer. It somehow didn't look like it was his car. In fact, he didn't look like a member of the faculty. Something about him made her uneasy.

No, she was being silly. Ever since she'd danced with that creepy guy at the Sound Works, she'd been seeing monsters in every corner. There was no reason for such paranoia. Heck, the poor guy was probably a new student here to check out the faculty—especially the female faculty. A schoolboy stunt. Nothing more.

She held her books tighter and hurried toward the school building, trying not to look his way.

CHAPTER

SEVENTEEN

"So tell me, Kirsten," Angie said on the telephone to the old friend she used to see quite a bit before Kirsten's marriage, "you and Al have been married for almost two years now. How's it going? What do you think of it?"

"What do I think? What do you mean?"

"You know. Do you recommend it? Any problems I should know about?"

"Problems? What makes you think there are any problems?"

"I'm sorry. I didn't mean there were problems. I was just—"

"You heard about Alan with that woman, didn't you? They work together, that's all."

"No. I never—"

"I know what you're thinking! I didn't realize it had become common knowledge already. But I'm glad you told me. You've always been my friend, haven't you, Angie?"

"No. I mean, yes, I'm your friend, but about Alan and that woman—"

"My God! Everyone knows, don't they? They must

be going everywhere together! Making a laughingstock out of me! Alan swears they're just working, but if so, how would you know about it? How would all my friends know? Work, *hah*! Thanks for telling me!" The phone went dead.

"Telling you? Kirsten, wait. Kirsten? Hello? Hello?"

CHAPTER

EIGHTEEN

He parked a block away from the house. It wasn't safe to park any closer. The judge had apparently noticed him sitting in his car a few times, and had begun to peer a little too closely, to grow a little too suspicious.

This was the morning. He had it all planned. Anticipation made his pulse race. He sat and waited for his breathing to return to normal, his pulse to slow a bit.

The first thing was to make sure no one noticed him. No one at all. He didn't want to throw up red flags before his entire plan—all of it—had succeeded.

His fingers tightened on the steering wheel. It was time to leave the car, to walk to the lush grounds along the Palace of Fine Arts, to stand behind the fir tree with the thick trunk and low, heavy branches, just as he had the past three days. There, he'd wait until the judge left the house to go on his morning walk along the Marina Green's waterfront path to Fort Mason for a cup of herb tea, and then walk home again. It seemed to be a health routine. It wasn't going to be very healthy for his wife, though.

He got out of the Honda and pulled the driver's seat forward so that he could reach into the backseat for his bouquet of roses. An SFPD black-and-white appeared at the intersection and stopped at the stop sign.

He kept his head down. He could all but feel the policemen taking him in, probably calling in the license plate on his car to the DMV. What'd they think they'd discover? That the car had been stolen? Maybe they would check the registration. Did they really think he'd be so stupid as to register it in his own name?

Not that it mattered. He knew all about the DMV, their computer system, and the cops. He knew it'd take a long time before the cops put two and two together. He'd be finished here by that time.

In the rearview mirror, he watched the police car turn onto his street and slow down as it neared him. He waited, not moving, until he heard the sound of the engine as the car drove past. He glanced up, perspiration dripping from his forehead, and watched the car turn the corner.

They might have seen him. They should have. They must have. He breathed harder. What if they remembered something about him? Or his car? He had to be careful. His heart felt ready to burst from his chest. Patience, that's what he needed. It was necessary to be patient now.

It was a straight shot from here to Richardson Street and the Doyle Drive approach to the Golden Gate Bridge. By the time the cops went around the block, he'd be long gone. He jumped into the driver's seat, started the car, and sped away.

Today, the old woman was lucky. But her luck wouldn't last.

Paavo sat in an overstuffed easy chair in Tiffany Rogers's living room. The morning sunlight streamed in from the window, bright and cheerful, in stark contrast to the ugly dark stain before him. The body and most of the evidence had been long removed, indexed, categorized, sliced, and diced to be studied, analyzed, and preserved.

Fingerprints, hair follicles, blood types, DNA, anything

that could potentially be matched with a suspect, once one was identified, had been collected. The estimated time of death put it the evening before the first day she missed work—about forty-eight hours before the police were called. A six-inch military-style combat knife appeared to be the murder weapon. The roses strewn around her body and the single rose on her bed were from florists because the thorns had been trimmed and the stem cut at some fancy angle. Checking on florist shops, he'd learned there were more of them in San Francisco than he'd ever dreamed, including a flower market that was also open to anyone who wanted to get up early enough. He'd tried gathering information about customers who'd bought a dozen long-stemmed roses three or four days earlier, but after checking with just a few florists, he quickly abandoned hope of tracking down the killer through that means. The numbers were far too high, and a number of purchases had been cash transactions by men—as if they very suddenly found they needed to give someone a dozen roses. Paavo could understand that.

No vase had been found filled with water for the flowers. Nor was there a florist's box anywhere in the apartment. He couldn't imagine any woman leaving a dozen long-stemmed roses lying about to wither and die. Whoever killed her must have brought the roses with him.

A gesture of a lover? Of someone wanting to court her? If, even after receiving the roses, Tiffany spurned the man's advances, could that have driven him to murder? She hadn't been raped, so it wasn't a sexual assault.

The kind of killer who could have committed such a grisly murder and then stopped to pick up a florist's box and its wrappings wasn't anyone who had just committed a crime of passion. Someone had planned to murder this woman.

He walked around, looking out windows and in closets, trying to get a feel for the place and what had gone on here.

The apartment Tiffany lived in was supposedly secure.

There was a locked, steel front door, requiring the occupant to buzz the person into the building. Yet, time and again it happened with this type of security that after someone had legitimately buzzed in a friend, a trespasser would stop the door from relatching. He would hold it open about a half inch, and, once the legitimate caller was out of sight, the trespasser would enter.

The night Tiffany was killed, however, none of the other residents remembered having had a visitor or having let anyone in for any reason. A couple of people came in late that evening. They insisted they had been careful not to let anyone sneak in after them, but it might have happened.

Even if the murderer sneaked past the front door, Tiffany would have had to open her door to him. Why would she? A single woman would worry about how some stranger had gotten into the building and up to her apartment?

None of this made sense unless the man had been someone she knew. Someone bringing her flowers. She let him in, and then he killed her.

Neighbors up and down the block were questioned, but no one had seen a man carrying a box that could have held roses.

The police tried lifting prints off the buzzer to Tiffany's apartment, the front door handle, even the underside of her toilet seat, but found nothing, which meant the killer wore gloves or wiped off the prints. Again, the sign of premeditation.

In the meantime, a picture was emerging of Tiffany as a vivacious, ambitious young woman who had suddenly turned quiet. Everyone was convinced she'd been seeing someone who had warned her not to say anything about their relationship. Paavo asked why, but no one could say.

It also became clear that neither age, looks, nor interests mattered to Tiffany in the men she dated. If they had money or power, preferably both, they were date bait to her. In the last two months she had found someone to date who was so special—for whatever reason—that she hadn't even told her best friend or her sister who he was, although it had become obvious that she and her sister weren't very close.

Paavo had searched through her desk and papers, trying to find some clue as to who the mystery man was. Maybe Tiffany no longer wanted to keep his identity a secret, and maybe he didn't like that. Whatever had happened between them, Paavo needed to find the man and question him.

There were few papers in the desk, no books, and Tiffany's reading material consisted of the *National Enquirer, Star,* and a single edition of the *Chronicle* dated nearly a week before she died.

The day after her sister, Connie, had ID'd the body, he had accompanied her back to the apartment to go through Tiffany's jewelry and clothes. They found gold and diamond jewelry from Moulin et Cie, Sans Souci Jewelers, and her namesake, Tiffany's. She even kept the boxes, as if to prove the jewels weren't paste.

Connie told him that the diamond tennis bracelet from Sans Souci Jewelers was new. It might have been from the new lover.

Sans Souci was where the Fabergé egg thief had killed Nathan Ellis. Could there be a connection between this death and Ellis's? It seemed too big a leap—but then Paavo had never believed in coincidence. He'd check it out.

He walked into the bedroom and looked at Tiffany's clothes hanging in the closet. Since meeting Angie he'd come to appreciate the simple lines and small details that separated quality clothing from that which was simply expensive. Tiffany spent more than the average working girl on clothes, that was obvious, but she hadn't learned quality yet. The outfits were full of the kind of frills and ruffles Angie wouldn't be caught dead in.

Paavo took the jewelry box with the tennis bracelet from the drawer and put it in his pocket.

He left Rogers's apartment and went straight to Sans

Souci Jewelers. The owner, Philip Justin Pierpont, was in the store working the counter with one of his clerks. He hadn't yet hired a replacement for Ellis.

"Hello, Inspector," Pierpont said. "Any news on the killer?"

"We're still working on it. I've got something here I'd like you to check out for me." Paavo opened the Sans Souci box to disclose the bracelet. "Does this look familiar?"

"Quite. We ran a special on those for Valentine's Day."

"Is there any way you can check to find out who you sold this one to?"

"Of course. We didn't sell many of those. They weren't the best-quality diamonds. Usually, if someone is looking for a diamond bracelet, they're willing to spend a little more money to get top quality stones even if the size is smaller than they originally wanted."

Paavo gave the box to the jeweler.

"We keep a record of all our merchandise." He put on his jeweler's magnifying glass and carefully inspected the diamonds. "Yes, it appears to have been one of ours." Next, he led Paavo into his office, where he looked up the bracelet on the computer.

"Ah. Here we go. We sold five. Two to women in the city. One to a couple from Los Angeles, one to a man in the city, and . . ." He stopped talking as he studied the computer. "This is strange. I almost never see a transaction like this." He glanced up at Paavo.

"What is it?"

"We keep records of credit cards and checks. That's the way almost all of our customers pay us. Not in this case, though. The bracelet was paid for in cash. There was no need to get any customer information, not even a signature."

"If the transaction was that rare, there's a chance the clerk might remember it, right?"

"Absolutely. Except in this case."

Paavo suspected he knew the reason before he even asked his question. "Why?"

"The clerk was Nathan Ellis."

* * *

As Paavo took off his jacket and hung it on the back of his chair, he looked at the flurry of notes and messages left on the desk in his absence. He added to them the names of the people who'd used checks or credit cards to buy diamond bracelets at Sans Souci, as well as the name of the clerk who had worked with Ellis the day the diamond bracelet cash purchase had been made. Except for early morning, Pierpont always had two employees in the store at the same time.

The clerk, Meredith Park, was off work that day. Paavo tried reaching her at home, but there was no answer. Next, he quickly disposed of the other buyers—all were able to give solid information as to what happened to the bracelet they'd bought.

He was about to try Park's home again when the phone buzzed.

"Smith here," he said.

"This is O'Rourke in Robbery. We just got a call I think you might want to check out."

"What's it about?"

"A jeweler. Said a small guy with a fake beard came in, held him up at gunpoint, and stole just one thing. When my lieutenant heard what it was, he said I should call you."

Paavo could think of one object only that could cause the Robbery detail to think of him. "An imitation Fabergé egg?"

"You win the big banana."

Paavo stood. Hollins had given Nathan Ellis's case to the team of Calderon and Benson. But they were out working on another case at the moment. The possibility of a tie-in with Tiffany Rogers's murder existed, but also he remembered his interview with Debbie Ellis, how she begged him to find whoever killed her husband.

"I'll be right there," he said.

CHAPTER

NINETEEN

Angie sat in the family room of her parents' Hillsborough mansion with her father. He had a hockey game on the TV, a basketball game on the radio, and the TV remote control in his hand. Periodically, he'd flip through the channels to be sure he wasn't missing anything else. Salvatore Amalfi wasn't a sports fanatic by any means, but since his bypass surgery, the doctors told him he had to back away from his retail shoe business. He was too naturally competitive and needed to find a way to relax and not worry about how each of his many stores was doing.

Looking at him scowl and complain about the Sharks' play on the TV and the Warriors on the radio, Angie thought he didn't seem to be following orders about being noncompetitive at all.

She sighed and kept watching, glassy-eyed, while talk of power plays, hat tricks, and slap shots swirled around her. She couldn't have given the score if her life depended on it. The more she thought about it, she wasn't even sure why she was here. All she knew was that she hadn't felt like spending a Friday night home alone hoping Paavo would show up.

Her single girlfriends, those few there were left, would be out on dates, and she didn't want to disturb the married ones.

Everyone seemed to have someone to belong to but her, she thought, indulging in a heavy dose of self-pity. So, she came to the place she did belong—home to her parents. She was always welcome here.

Although, considering that her mother had gone off to bed with a book, and her father was engrossed in TV and radio, they, too, didn't seem terribly overjoyed at her unannounced arrival. She heaved a heavy, rueful sigh.

"*Che c'è*, Angelina? I haven't heard so many sighs since I took your mother to see her first Marcello Mastroianni movie."

"It's not funny, Papà. I'm trying to figure out my future."

"Your future? That's no reason for such a long face. You're young, healthy, with a good education. You can do whatever you want. So, what is it you want?"

"Well, maybe I want to get married."

"Married? You mean to that fellow with the strange name? *That's* what you want for your future?"

"I'm not talking specifics here, Papà. In general. Marriage? Career? Both?"

"You haven't settled on a career yet. I think you should. How can you think of giving up what you've never had?"

"It's not for lack of trying." She heaved another sigh.

"*Il poliziotto*—he's your problem. You *do* want to marry him, don't you?"

"I'm not sure. I mean, what is marriage?"

"It's a life sentence, and you're too young for it." Suddenly, he jumped to his feet, staring at the TV. "No! The Sharks just scored. I've been watching for two hours, the score one to nothing. Detroit's favor. The Sharks tie, and I miss it!"

So much for her future. "Sorry, Papà. I'm going to bed," she said, standing.

He put down the remote, his dark eyes studying her for a long time. He was still a handsome man, tall and distinguished despite the shadows his illness had brought to the area under his eyes and the sallow color to his skin. "Don't be sad, *bambina*. There's so much in life for you to see and do and experience. Take your time. Life's a wonderful thing, Angelina. Now get out of here. They're going to show a replay."

She walked to his side, rested her hand on his shoulder, and kissed his cheek. "Good-night."

He touched her fingers lightly, and she left the room.

Before going into her bedroom, she stopped to say good-night to her mother.

She knocked on the bedroom door. "Mamma?"

"Come in, Angelina," Serefina said. The bedroom was large, with an adjoining sitting room that overlooked a small creek, and a bathroom that was larger than the living room of Angie's apartment. The room was furnished with Italian antiques, the pieces lavishly carved and ornately finished in an off-white color with pink-cast faux marble, and trimmed in gold paint. It would have been gaudy except that it was so inherently Italian, it made Angie feel comfortable and secure.

Her parents' bed was king-size, and the mattresses sat high off the ground. Serefina was sitting on the bed, propped up with pillows, and had tears streaming down her eyes.

Angie's heart nearly stopped. She could feel the blood drain from her face as she stared at her mother. "Mamma, what's wrong?" she cried. She ran to the side of the bed, her mind swirling. Was it her father's illness? One of her sisters? Serefina? Not Serefina—her mother couldn't be sick!

Serefina dabbed her eyes with a lace handkerchief. "It's this book. It's so sad. *Che terribile*. It's called *The Bridges of Madison County*. It's about a poor husband who goes away from home to help his family, and his back is no sooner turned than his wife has an affair with some drifter photographer! She doesn't even know the man!"

Angie took a deep breath to calm herself. "Mamma, I don't think that's the point."

"Not only that, Angelina—*Dio! Che disonore!*—this terrible wife . . . she's Italian!" Serefina tossed the book to the foot of the bed.

"It'll be all right, Mamma. Most people won't remember that about her. She didn't act very Italian."

Serefina dried her eyes. "Maybe you're right. That story—that's not what marriage is all about."

"It's not?" Angie sat on the edge of the bed.

"It's two people building a life together. It's the union between the two that makes them strong and let's them survive whatever life throws at them."

"You really believe that, Mamma?"

"*Veramente*." She took Angie's hand. "When me and your father were first married, he worked two jobs. Almost eighteen hours he was gone, six days a week. It didn't matter, though, to how we felt about each other. If anything, it made our love stronger because we saw how much we hated being apart. We worked hard so that we could make this time to be together."

"I know you did, I remember."

"And you know what's strange, Angelina, as much as I adored your father when I was a young wife, I love him even more now. When young, our love was the flame of a match— sharp and hot and bright. Now, it's like the fire of coals—dry and warm and solid—and will last until we are but ashes."

Angie nodded. "It's good to hear that."

Serefina looked surprised. "You didn't know?"

"I should have, shouldn't I?" She stood up. "I think I'll go back home tonight after all."

"You are home."

"I mean, to *my* home. I love you, Mamma."

"*T'amo*, Angelina. But before you go, will you hand me my book again. I tossed it way down there by my feet."

Angie arrived home before midnight, and about a half hour later came the knock on the door she'd been hoping to hear for the last few nights. She ran to the peephole and looked out.

"Paavo." She opened the door.

He came in, closed the door behind him, then took her in his arms and held her tightly. "I missed you," he murmured, his voice heavy with weariness and longing.

"I missed you, too," she said, running her hands over his hair, damp from the night fog. She gazed up at him. "Can you stay awhile? Shall I put on coffee? Have you eaten?"

"No, to everything." He gripped her shoulders and held her back so that he could see her better. "Don't bother. I wanted to see you, to be sure you're all right."

"You could have called me." The words blurted out, seeming to come from nowhere, even though she'd meant to be supportive, nonaccusatory. She'd have to backpedal rapidly.

"I tried a couple times, but there wasn't any answer."

That was his excuse? "I have an answering machine. You could have left a message. You could have said, 'Angie, this is Paavo. I'm at work, but I wanted you to know I was thinking about you.'" Great, she thought, now I sound even more like a shrew. She walked away, toward her petit point sofa. He followed.

"I do think about you, whether I talk to machines about it or not."

She bit her lip. It was serious turn-over-a-new-leaf time for her with this man. "I know," she whispered, then, louder. "I understand."

"You do?"

He seemed shocked that she could be understanding. "Of course! You don't like answering machines, and you're busy with your job. It's important to you. I can accept that."

His eyes narrowed. "Have you bought more ballet tickets?"

This suspicion of his about her motives was pretty darn insulting. "I meant what I said! I understand."

"Well, all right, but . . . "

"But what?" She tensed.

"Nothing."

She studied him carefully. The words of her parents, her friends, spilled over one another, adding to her confusion. Her voice was hushed. "I'm important to you, too, aren't I?"

He took her hand and sat down on the sofa, then pulled her down after him. Wrapping her in his arms he said, "If you weren't important to me, I wouldn't be here. I'd be off somewhere, like Yosh, taking a quick nap."

"I went to my parents' house tonight," she said softly. "I was going to stay there, wondering if you'd even know or care. Then I felt silly for playing such games and came home."

"Never play games with me, Angie."

Her breath caught. "I won't," she whispered. "I love you, Paavo. Like a match."

"A what?"

She wrapped her arms around his neck, and no further explanations were needed.

CHAPTER

∞∞∞

TWENTY

The morning air was damp and thick with fog. A good day to die.

He waited until the judge left the house for his morning walk, then tinkered with a radar encoder until his universal remote unit signals meshed with those of the main controller of the garage door opener. Next, he put on a double pair of latex gloves.

Checking carefully that no one was near, no one could see him, he aimed the remote at the garage door and clicked. The door unlocked. He sprang toward it, stopping it before it lifted more than a couple of feet off the ground. Then he dropped to the ground and rolled under it into the garage.

Quickly hitting the release, he pulled the door to a closed position again, then lay still and waited for sounds of neighbors or passersby who might have seen or heard him.

He listened, too, for sounds from the living quarters overhead, trying to hear them over the sound of his own heavy breathing.

All was quiet. He started to stand.

"Luke?"

He froze, his heart hammering at the sound of a woman's voice. "Luke, is that you?"

Sharp-eared old bat. There were stairs in the back of the garage leading up to a door to the house—probably to the kitchen. He darted to the bottom of the stairs and crouched down, expecting the wife to open the inside door to investigate further. But there was no sound of footsteps. No sound at all from upstairs.

She must have decided she was mistaken.

He crept up the stairs slowly, ready with each step for a loud creak to give him away.

The stairs were solid. Quiet.

At the door that led to the house proper, he twisted the knob, praying the door wasn't locked. His prayer was answered.

Slowly, he pushed the door open. The kitchen was large, yellow, with two walls of cabinetry and, over the sink, a window box filled with tiny plants in four-inch pots. The room was empty.

Where had the woman gone?

He shut the door behind him, holding the knob until the last moment. The latch made a tiny click. He pushed in the button in the center. If the old man came back that way, he'd find the door locked.

Not that it would matter. He'd be too late to save his wife, anyway.

She was in the house somewhere. From the kitchen door, he could see a hallway. The way these San Francisco houses were built, he knew it led to a living room and dining room in the front of the house and to the bedrooms in the back. Quietly, he moved toward the door, half-expecting her to appear in the doorway with each step he took.

A loud whistle sounded. He snapped his head toward the stove. A teakettle.

Hurling himself behind the kitchen door, his heart racing, he waited. But despite the noise the kettle made, he didn't hear the woman hurrying down the hall to turn it off.

She would come eventually, though. He could wait right here for her.

The loud kettle jangled his nerves. Perspiration formed on his forehead. He tried to remain there, without moving, to wait for her. It'd be so much easier that way. He covered his ears, needing to cut off the kettle's shrill scream. No! That wouldn't be safe. He had to listen for her.

Where was she? Could she be hard of hearing? She had heard noises in the garage, though, had called out her husband's name. What in the hell could she be doing that was more important than turning off her goddamn teakettle?

Control. He needed control. He flexed his hands, his fingers. But the noise grew louder, shriller. Steam shot from the spout. It squeezed the air, choking him. He clawed at his throat. If he shut the flame under the kettle, would she notice? Would it alert her?

Where the hell was the bitch?

He'd have to find her, kill her, then turn it off himself. That was the only way to stop the noise that was making his head split, making it hard for him to think.

His hand against the frame of the kitchen door, he darted his head out into the long hallway. She wasn't there.

Keeping his back against the wall, he sidled along the hallway toward the living room. The room was empty, as was the dining area between it and the kitchen.

That meant she had to be in the back of the house, in one of the bedrooms.

Suddenly, he didn't mind the loud whistling of the teakettle. It masked his footsteps as he eased his way, once more, down the hall.

He reached the bedroom without her seeing him and peered inside.

She stood beside the bed, her back to him, wearing only a slip, hose, and brown, low-heeled shoes. Her clothes had been neatly laid out before her on the bed. She picked up a pink blouse and put it on. He watched, mesmerized, as she proceeded to fasten the many buttons that lined the front of it. Next, she reached for a brown skirt and stepped into it, hiking it up to her waist, then spending a considerable amount of time smoothing the blouse and slip once more. Such a pity, he thought, so much trouble for no reason.

She buttoned the skirt. As she worked the side zipper, looking down, giving it her full attention, she began to turn in his direction.

He pounced. She opened her mouth to scream, but his hand covered it, muffling her cries and forcing her back on the bed. He lay atop her, crushing her with his weight. She fought, kicked, tried to get away, to scream, but she was no match for him.

His blood pounded. His temples throbbed and a fiery redness built against his eyes. The incessant whistle in the background, the squirming of her body beneath him on the bed, heated him. He backed off a bit, closing his eyes as he let her struggle, enjoying the feel of her, remembering what it was like to have a woman writhe beneath him. Helpless. Captive. He opened his eyes.

But instead of young, beautiful Heather or Angelina, beneath him was this old hag. Disgust raged at her. Filthy slut, tempting him that way, making his body do things he didn't want it to do with someone ugly like her. He pulled the combat knife from his back pocket. She'd never tempt him again.

He took the rose from the back pocket of his jeans and placed it on her pillow. It was smashed and dark, and most of the petals had fallen off, but he didn't think the police would care. They'd get the message.

He wiped off the knife on the blood-soaked bedspread, then took off his shoes. He didn't want to track bloody shoe prints onto the carpet—that'd give the police too clear a picture. But he'd never heard of tracking sock prints before. Especially heavy woolen socks.

In the kitchen, he shut the gas off under the shrieking teapot, then went to the hall closet and took out the judge's trench coat and felt hat. Putting on his shoes once more, he walked out the front door, down the stairs, and up the street to his car.

Paavo sat in the living room with Judge St. Clair. The judge was hunched in the center of the sofa, his hands covering his face. His trembling had stopped, but the slump of his shoulders, his bowed head, created about him an immutable sense of defeat and pain.

"Tell me exactly what you did after you found her," Paavo said gently.

The judge lowered his hands. His eyes were red-rimmed, his cheeks blotched from earlier tears. His mouth worked awhile before he could get the words past a tightened throat. "I didn't even have to touch her. I knew. I knew she was . . . But I did touch her. Her hand, her face. They were already cold, and her eyes . . ." He swallowed and waited a moment or two. His hands shook. "I took a bath towel from the linen closet and covered her with it. I know I shouldn't have, but the way he'd left her . . . She was always such a proper lady. I couldn't let her be found that way. I just couldn't. I'm sorry!"

Paavo put his hand on St. Clair's shoulder. "It's all right. Anyone of us would have done the same."

The judge nodded, and tried to hold back his tears.

Paavo left him and went back into the bedroom. Homicide Inspectors Rebecca Mayfield and her partner, Bill Sutter, were the on-call team this week. But one look at the crime scene and Rebecca contacted Paavo. It looked frighteningly similar to the way he and Yosh had described Tiffany Rogers's murder.

"Did the judge know anything that might help?" Rebecca asked.

"It's hard to tell. He's in a bad way," Paavo answered.

"You're pretty sure it's the same guy, though?"

"It's got to be. The way he's stabbed them, the rose on the pillow. Just one difference. This one was even more brutal."

CHAPTER

TWENTY-ONE

Angie's third sister, Maria, looked up from the catalogues and files spread out on the floor and scowled. They'd never been close, and that look reminded Angie why.

Maria was the serious, religious one in the family. Everyone thought she'd become a nun. The family was shocked when she eloped with a saxophone player from Pier 17, a jazz nightclub on the Embarcadero. No one knew Maria even liked jazz.

Now, she acted as publicist for her husband—and had turned the name Dominic Klee into a household word for jazz buffs. They now owned the Jazz Workshop, where Klee's Quintet played when they weren't touring. Maria straightened the catalogues into a stack and then turned her full attention on Angie.

"Did Papà send you here?" she asked, her eyes narrow. "He can't believe we're not starving."

"I didn't even tell him I was coming," Angie said.

Maria flicked her waist-length, straight black hair off her shoulders to fall smoothly down her back. With no makeup, rows of silver bracelets, and heavy, dangling silver earrings, she grew more exotic every day.

"So, what's this about, Angie?"

"I'm trying to learn about marriage," she said. She knew Dominic had to leave Maria and their son at home while he toured, and, in a sense, Paavo was gone a lot, too, because of the long hours he worked. Angie found his schedule, or lack of one, hard to deal with. "I was just wondering if Dominic's being gone so much bothered you?"

Maria shrugged. "What can I say? It's his job. His life. It's what he loves, and I love him."

"But he's working in nightclubs. There's drinking, drugs, women throwing themselves at him. I mean, he's very . . . um . . ." Angie wasn't sure of the word to use around her religious sister.

"Sexy?" Maria offered.

"Well, yes."

"Don't I know it." Maria's face broke into a smile as she thought about her husband—a smile that Angie realized had nothing religious about it.

Her sister grew serious. "I trust him, Angie. I have to. For our marriage, it doesn't matter if he's home or away. I've found the perfect way to deal with it."

"Oh, good." Angie was desperate for answers. "How do you do it?"

"I pray a lot."

CHAPTER

TWENTY-TWO

Angie sat at her tiny kitchen table and absentmindedly stirred her morning coffee. The other night, before he left, Paavo had told her he had been working on the well-publicized case of the young typist from City Hall. That was why he and Yosh were putting in such long hours. It was also clear that he was irritated that Nathan Ellis's murder had been put on the back burner, so to speak.

She read the *Chronicle*'s account of Tiffany Rogers's murder and the investigation. She also reread earlier accounts of the jewelry store killing.

Tiffany was just a year younger than Angie. She had been born and raised in the city, and had attended parochial schools here. For all Angie knew, their paths had probably crossed. Paavo had mentioned that Tiffany had a sister named Connie. Connie Rogers ... that sounded familiar for some reason. But Connie was four years older than Tiffany—three older than Angie. Angie probably didn't know her, but maybe one of her sisters did.

No one seemed to have any idea why Tiffany had been killed. What if it had something to do with her family? Something that anyone who knew Connie might figure out? She could easily make a few phone calls. What harm could it do? It might help. And Paavo was so tired lately, working this case, as well as the jewelry store murder.

She picked up the phone and dialed her sister Frannie's number. Connie and Frannie were just about the same age.

"Never heard of her," Fran said.

Undaunted, Angie tried her middle sister, Maria. Maria was irritated at such a dumb question. Angie should have known Maria wouldn't bother to remember anyone who hadn't gone to morning mass each day before class. Caterina and Bianca were probably too old.

That left her cousins. She started with Loretta, the one who owned Herobics and kept in contact with lots of people, doing all she could to make them feel guilty about not getting enough exercise. But Loretta didn't know Connie.

Then she tried her cousin Gloria, who was married and sang in a church choir. She didn't know Connie either.

What about her male cousins? Connie and Tiffany were good-looking women. She knew exactly which cousin to call.

"Buddy, how ya doing?" she said. Buddy Amalfi lived in South City, the natives' name for South San Francisco. Years would go by without her seeing or talking to Buddy, but when they made contact again, it was as if they'd talked only yesterday.

"Hey, Angelina, long time no see."

"I've been busy. Listen, I've got a favor to ask."

"Ask away."

"I'm trying to find a woman named Connie Rogers. She's about your age, went to school here in the city."

"Connie . . . Connie . . . Connie. Sure, I remember her. Come to think of it, I went out with her a couple of times in high school."

"I'm trying to find her. Do you know where she is?"

"God, I haven't seen her in nine, ten years."

"It's important, Buddy."

"Well, let me work on it. I still keep in touch with a lot of the old gang."

"Tell them her sister was just killed, that should get them thinking harder."

"Her kid sister? Killed? What do you mean killed?"

"Tiffany was stabbed to death. She was a typist. It's been all over the papers."

"Holy! I'd heard some woman was stabbed. Good Christ! I didn't pay any attention to the name. Poor Connie. Okay, I'll get right on it."

Angie hung up and looked at the phone with a self-satisfied air. When she took an interest in something, she didn't fool around.

"I t'ought we'd be outta here by now," Earl said as he chipped at the cement wall with a hammer and chisel.

"We would be if you two bozos didn' waste all your time talkin' to the lowlife that comes in here." Vinnie sat on an upside-down wastebasket and puffed on his cigar as Earl worked. Butch stood at the top of the stairs listening for customers and keeping an eye on his kitchen.

"I didn't ask to talk to 'em," Earl protested. "I don't even like being a waitpoison."

"What's he talkin' about, wait poison?" Vinnie looked up at Butch.

"One of the customers told him waiter and waitress were sexist," Butch said. "Now he thinks he's s'posed to be politically correct."

Vinnie looked at the ceiling. "Still payin' me back, ain't ya, God? Stuck me with these two. I hope you're havin' a good laugh."

He noticed Earl had stopped working to look at him. "So dig, already," he ordered.

"I t'ink we need a jackhammer," Earl said.

"God, he's dumb!" Butch muttered. "How we gonna find a jackhammer?"

"We could steal one," Earl reasoned.

Butch came down the stairs. "Sure. We'll go down to

the corner store and swipe some cigs, a bottle of whiskey, a jackhammer—"

"Shut up, both of you," Vinnie said. "I'm thinkin'."

"That's a revelation," Butch grumbled.

"Shut up I said!" Vinnie bellowed. "I got it. We're gonna get a big drill and use it at night when no one else is around."

"Except maybe some cops drivin' by," Butch sneered.

"I t'ink we should take toins standin' watch," Earl added. "Den, if we see a cop car, we can holler down to toin off da drill."

"Holler? Over the sound of a drill?" Vinnie glared at Earl, then turned to Butch. "What's he got for brains?"

Butch just shook his head. "I think I hear a customer."

"You're sure?" Paavo asked. He stood in the office of Sans Souci Jewelers and faced the clerk who had been working with Nathan Ellis the day someone paid cash for the tennis bracelet.

"Yes, sir. That's all I can tell you." Meredith Park's steady gaze met Paavo's. "Tall, distinguished, Caucasian, and between fifty and fifty-five, I'd say. Prematurely gray. Sort of okay, I guess."

"What do you mean, sort of okay?"

"Let's say, he wasn't my type. Too slick—like a politician, maybe. In fact . . . no. I don't know." Meredith shrugged.

"Would you recognize this man if you saw him again?" Paavo asked.

"That's hard to say. There was something vaguely familiar about him, but I'm just not sure."

Paavo nodded. Distinguished, gray-haired, middle-aged. Given all he'd learned about Tiffany, the description sounded perfect for one of her boyfriends. The question was, who was he? What was his name? "If you think of anything more, let me know."

"I will."

Paavo turned to leave.

"Oh, Inspector. One other thing."

"Yes?"

Meredith Park turned shrewd, intelligent eyes on him. "It's probably nothing, but a couple days before Nathan was killed something peculiar happened. It's been on my mind. I didn't want to bother you because I doubt it means anything, but since you're here . . . "

"It's fine, Mrs. Park. Tell me."

"A woman came into the store asking about the Fabergé eggs. She was probably in her late thirties, early forties, five-foot-three or -four, with long brown hair, dull and lopped off at the ends as if she'd cut it herself. Anyway, it was only a day or so after we'd put the eggs out for our Easter display."

"Yes?"

"So, out of the blue she asked if they were from the original Fabergé artisans in Europe. I said as far as I knew there was some connection to the famous studios—that's how they were allowed to use the name. Then she asked if the quality was at all the same. I said of course not, that original eggs were found only in museums."

"Go on."

"She asked if that were true of all Fabergé pieces. And I told her the real eggs were priceless, and even the small Fabergé pieces, these days, would be valued in the hundreds of thousands of dollars, if not more."

"So I've been told," Paavo said, not seeing why that mattered.

"Well," Meredith Park leaned closer, "when I told the woman that, she turned so pale I thought she was going to faint."

Paavo nodded thoughtfully. "If you see this woman again, I'd like you to call me right away."

"Will do, Inspector."

CHAPTER

∞∞∞

TWENTY-THREE

Angie walked into her classroom to find a cellophane-wrapped bouquet of long-stemmed red roses in the center of her desk. Could they be from Paavo? she wondered, although he wasn't exactly the flowers-giving type. Maybe he'd sent them because he'd been too busy to see her lately?

She searched the flowers for a card.

She hadn't heard from Paavo in a couple of days. The city was astir in the wake of the murder of a retired judge's wife, and Paavo was in charge of the investigation. This was another one of those cases where she saw more of him on the local TV newscasts than she did in person.

The press speculated that the same crazed murderer who had killed the typist had also killed the judge's wife. They made much of the fact that Tiffany worked for a supervisor—the city government connection, they called it—which led them to dub the case the Municipal Murders.

The mayor and Board of Supervisors were furious at the gory attention given to their administration, as if bad government had led to the murders. No matter how much political pressure they exerted on the press to stop its coverage of the murder investigation, the interest continued. Finally, they realized there would be only one way to end the examination—for Homicide to catch the killer. Paavo was in the middle of a firestorm.

No card. That was strange. Who would send her such beautiful roses and not give his name? It had to be Paavo.

She quickly shuffled through the stack of papers the school's administration office had left in her mailbox. Information about some fund-raising events, a faculty meeting for the regular staff, a meeting to introduce the new third assistant vice administrator, a list of some supplies that wouldn't be bought because there was no money, another list of books that wouldn't be bought for the same reason, and a card telling her about a late enrollee into her class, W.C. Lake. She flipped it over to see if it was a joke. She'd spent enough vacations in England to know their meaning of WC, and tied with "lake" made her wonder. She put the card aside. Probably just some unfortunate American name.

"Does anyone know who brought me the flowers?" she asked the few students, retirees mostly, who'd arrived early for her class.

"A sweet young man. Rather shy," Lynette answered. "He said he was signing up for your class, but he couldn't stay today, and hoped you'd forgive him."

Something was strange about this. She'd had students sorry they'd missed class before, but none had been sorry enough to bring her a gift. Not even a posy of pansies, let alone roses. Especially since this was just an adult ed class. No grades and no credit.

"Did he give his name?" she asked Lynette.

"I don't think so."

"He said you'd know him when the two of you finally met," Herman said, looking up from his notebook.

"He did?" Angie was more confused than ever.

"He seemed to be quite a fan of yours," Joan, another student, added, then smiled. "I thought he was a bit smitten myself."

Angie tried to put aside thoughts of her mysterious,

smitten student while she gave her lecture, but it was difficult. Particularly as the strong scent of the flowers permeated the front of the classroom.

The lecture dealt with President Warren G. Harding's visit to San Francisco. He checked in at the St. Francis Hotel and promptly checked out—permanently. The public was told he'd died of influenza and exhaustion due to a tour through the western U.S. and Alaska, but rumor had it that he'd been poisoned.

No one has ever found out, to this day, what the real story is.

When the class ended, Angie began to gather up her lecture notes. She, Lynette, and Joan were going out for coffee after class. Usually, Angie had some decadent chocolate dessert—but not during Lent.

"Roses, Angie?"

She knew that voice. Paavo stood in the doorway scowling at the flowers.

"They're from one of my students," she said, smiling broadly.

"They look a little wilted," he said as he approached her desk.

Spoilsport. But then, maybe he was jealous that he hadn't thought of giving her flowers himself? "It's the thought that counts," she said.

"Sorry. I didn't mean to pick on your student." He glanced at the two older women standing nearby, gawking at him and taking in every word he and Angie said. "I guess you're busy. I should get going."

"No, not at all. These ladies are Lynette and Joan, two of my students. They used to work for the government."

"Oh?" Try as he might, he couldn't make himself sound the least bit interested.

"We're retired now," Lynette said, a big, friendly smile on her face. "We were going out to have some coffee. Want to join us?"

"No, thanks. I don't think so. I guess I'll catch you later, Angie." He backed up a step.

"We'll make it another time," Joan said. "You two young people don't need us. Right, Lynette?"

Lynette kept looking from Paavo to Angie and back. Joan jabbed her with her elbow. "Oh. Right!" she said, and they left.

"Sorry about that," Paavo said. Alone with her now, he walked to her side and tucked back a curl that had fallen too near her eye, then bent forward and kissed her quickly.

"It's okay," she said. "You've been pretty busy yourself, Inspector."

His gaze caught the flowers. "It's been no bed of roses."

She put her hands on his arms. "It sounds like you're getting a lot of pressure from City Hall," she said, concern in her voice.

He held her waist. "You could say that."

He wasn't the type to admit to more, no matter how ugly it could get. And she knew local politics could get very ugly indeed. "Where's Yosh?"

"He's gone home for a change of clothes and some home cooking. He also wants to make sure his wife and kids don't forget what he looks like."

"Did he drop you off?"

Paavo nodded. "I saw your car in the lot. I've wondered what you've been up to."

"Me?" She felt her cheeks burn as she thought about her conversations on marriage with friends and family. She dropped her hands from his arms and turned away. "A little of this, a little of that. Nothing special." She stuffed papers into her briefcase.

He paused. "Nothing special? What about your roses? They seem pretty special."

"They're from a student."

"You've been pretty busy charming him, I guess."

"What's that supposed to mean?" She snapped the briefcase shut. He took hold of the handle before she did.

"How about I take you out for that cup of coffee?" he asked.

She took a deep breath. "Shouldn't you eat and freshen up like Yosh? I suppose you have to go back to work?"

"In a couple of hours."

"Tell you what, let's go to your place so you can relax, change, shower, and feed Hercules. I'll make something for you to eat." .

"You don't have to do all that."

"I know. And I know you don't expect me to. That's why I don't mind doing it."

He wasn't sure what to say. He wanted her with him, wanted to be together, but she had been acting so strange lately he didn't know what was going on. Just what did "a little of this and a little of that" mean, anyway?

She picked up the roses. He wished she'd left them. He wished he'd thought of bringing her flowers. He wished . . . a lot of things. He eyed the roses. From a student . . . sure they were. As they walked down the corridor, the smell of the flowers brought back to him the scent of death and blood.

She carried *his* roses, he thought, carried them against her breast. His smile vanished, though, when he saw the detective behind her. He'd almost forgotten about Smith. How could he forget? He was letting her distract him from his mission. Letting thoughts of her as a woman . . . as *his* woman . . . get in the way. He couldn't allow that.

He adjusted his glasses and leaned forward. He liked how gently she carried the roses. One of them touched the hollow of her throat. He could almost see it pulse with the warmth of her blood. Red blood, like his roses. Sacrificial blood.

How would it be to offer her blood instead of an old woman's or a young whore's on the altar of revenge? She was more innocent. Innocent like Heather. Hers would be the blood debt paid—no, not paid—there was no redemption to be had. On Easter his work as avenger, not redeemer, would be complete.

He followed the white Ferrari. She drove straight to Smith's house. It was becoming pretty clear that despite her blond fiancé, she cared about Smith, and that the feeling was mutual. That was all he needed to know.

Despite himself, though, disappointment filled him. Too bad he had to kill her.

Paavo's kitchen was always a challenge. She picked up a box of Kraft Macaroni and Cheese. Why would anyone waste money buying something packaged that was so easy to make? A little pasta, fresh grated cheddar, or even better, fontina, add some onion powder, salt, cracked red pepper, milk, and butter—and of course, a little garlic never hurt anything—and it was ready.

Hercules let out a howl at the back door. It had to be intuition, Angie thought as she let him in, that told him when she was in the kitchen. The sight of the big, tough tom making little mewls and rubbing against her ankles made her laugh.

She scooped a teaspoon of mayonnaise onto a saucer. "That'll have to do until I get back," she said. As soon as she heard the shower running, she hurried to her car and drove to a good market not too far away.

She knew Paavo had been living on Dunkin' Donuts and wanted to make him something substantial.

Using the key he'd given her to let herself back into his house, she hurried into the kitchen, gave Hercules a small salmon fillet, and then put Paavo's French lamb chops into a marinade of red wine, vinegar, olive oil, bay leaves, and peppercorns. She sautéed fresh garlic and red pepper flakes in olive oil, and added chicken stock. When it came to a boil, penne pasta went into the pan. Once the liquid boiled again, she put broccoli florets atop the mixture, covered it, and let it cook until the pasta was done. As it cooked, she broiled the lamp chops and made a small green salad.

It was funny, she reflected, as she prepared the meal, but she had always thought she'd end up with an epicure—

someone who enjoyed and knew good food and wine the way she did. Paavo wouldn't know a truffle from a mushroom, beluga caviar from trout eggs. Where had she gone wrong? Not only that, she didn't even care.

But then, the staff writer at *Haute Cuisine*, Marianne Perrault, dined with her husband at Kentucky Fried Chicken. At least Paavo appreciated good food when he had the time to eat it.

"Angie, what's this? I didn't want you to go to all this trouble."

His face was shiny from his shave and shower, his hair slightly damp, and he smelled like Old Spice after-shave. She turned back to the pots and pans, forcing her thoughts back to cooking instead of other things he made her think of. He had to eat and go back to work even if she didn't. "It's no trouble," she said. "I enjoy it."

He wrapped his arms around her shoulders and nuzzled her neck. "I enjoy you."

"Go sit down," she said. "You'll make me burn the food."

"If I wasn't half-starved, I'd try." He lifted the pot lid to look at the pasta, and then checked on the broiling lamb chops. "Where did you get all this?"

"Ve haf our vays."

When the pasta was al dente and the broccoli crisp but tender, she drained the mixture, leaving a little as a sauce. She put pasta, broccoli, lamb chops, and thin-sliced hot cherry peppers on plates and served them.

"How are your cases going?" she asked as she sat to eat. "Any luck yet?"

"Not yet." He tasted the penne pasta. "This is delicious."

"I thought you might like it. You seem to enjoy good food."

"Sure. You're a wonderful cook."

That wasn't exactly what she meant. "The newspapers are saying the same person killed both the judge's wife and the City Hall typist."

"So I've heard." Each bite of the small, thick lamb chops tasted better than the last. He could get used to coming home to Angie's cooking very easily. It was all he could do to stop himself from shutting his eyes in ecstasy.

"What do you think of renting movies for entertainment?"

He glanced up at her. "What *kind* of movie?"

"I don't know . . . I was going to ask you that."

"What's this about?"

"Nothing. Just curious."

He thought a moment. "Well, Yosh was singing the praises of *Kung-fu Killer* the other day."

"Oh, dear."

He chuckled at her stricken expression and quietly enjoyed the rest of the meal.

As they cleared the table, Angie said, "You know, Paavo, the press wants to link the Rogers and St. Clair murders, but Tiffany worked at City Hall and superior court is at the Hall of Justice, right?"

"True."

"I guess it's possible," Angie said, "even though the judge worked in one place and Tiffany in another, that they came into contact with the same people—the same madman."

"We're checking on it, over and over again." Paavo put the pot and cooking utensils in the sink. "The most logical thing is that the two women knew someone in common. So far, though, we haven't found anyone at all. Not even a hint of a mutual friend."

"If there was a connection," Angie said, putting the spices she'd used back in the cupboard, "between the judge and Tiffany, why kill the judge's wife? Wouldn't the judge have been the most likely victim?"

"Exactly. The press hasn't bothered to ask that question. I guess they haven't figured it out yet. We're checking out Wainwright, Rogers's boss, and everything connected with the office, but so far it's another zero."

"The City Hall connection might be pure coincidence.

A lot of people are involved with city government these days."

"I'll look at coincidence last."

Angie couldn't let Paavo's case go. "Tiffany was single, right?" she asked, filling a dishpan with soapy water. Paavo didn't own a dishwasher. "What about her boyfriend? Who was he?"

"She was seeing someone, but she wouldn't tell anyone who he was." Paavo wrapped the garbage in old newspaper and took it to the can in the side yard. "No one's volunteered any info," he shouted.

"That's suspicious," she called out to him. "Why wouldn't she say?"

Back inside, he grabbed a dish towel. "Her friends think he was someone important in city government. Probably married."

"No woman who's got an exciting, powerful new boyfriend isn't going to give at least a hint about him to someone. It's just not possible."

Paavo thought a moment about Angie's words, wiping the dishes until they squealed. He took every job seriously. "That's what's strange. If anything, she was a person to flaunt her successes, not hide them."

"See? Who was she close to?"

"A woman at work."

"That's all?"

"Far as we know."

"You've got to be missing something."

There was a pause, and Angie was about to rush in with an apology about her runaway mouth. He stared intently at her. "Yes. I know."

He put down the dish towel. "As soon as I put out some food for Hercules, how about a lift down to the Hall? Yosh is probably there already."

She wiped off the rim of the sink and countertop. The kitchen was spotless. "I fed him already. Let me get my jacket." She headed for the living room for her jacket and purse.

He grabbed her hand as she rushed by. "Did I thank you for the dinner, Miss Amalfi?"

"Not properly, Inspector Smith."

"Then let me do so now, even if you do get flowers from strange men."

"I never—"

He stopped her protests.

CHAPTER

TWENTY-FOUR

Three days later, Angie stood on the steps of Ss. Peter and Paul's Church, where she'd gone to light a candle in memory of her grandfather on his birthday. This was one of those special, sunny spring days when the sky was a cloudless, brilliant blue. Against the colorful buildings of North Beach, clusters of easygoing people shopped or dined or played in the park and gave the area the busy, friendly Mediterranean flavor it was famous for.

Angie crossed Filbert to Washington Square and sat on a park bench. For a few minutes, at least, it was an afternoon to enjoy.

"I have a lot of experience with marriage."

Angie turned at the sound of the loud, gravelly voice. Behind her was a tall bush, and on the other side of it was another bench. She couldn't see who sat on it.

"I didn't know you'd been married," a slurred, younger-sounding voice replied.

"Can't even remember how many experiences with wedded bliss I've endured, son. I'm a marrying man, I am."

"You like it, do you?"

Angie pressed herself hard against the back of the bench to hear better what the marrying man had to say.

"I do. Hey! See what I mean? The words 'I do' just roll from my tongue like butter on a hot cob of corn. The little ladies I was married to, though, they were a problem. Women have these hang-ups, you know."

"I didn't know that."

Anxious not to miss a word, Angie knelt on the bench and leaned into the bush.

"Yeah. About stuff like having a job. Staying sober. Taking a ridiculous number of baths. They forget the ecstasy."

"I see."

"I had one wife, every time I'd hop into bed, she'd hop out. Now, of course, she just might not have felt worthy of the marital gift I was about to bestow. But for some reason, she used to say odd things, like I was overwhelming. I never understood what she meant, unless it was my charm. That was one of my shorter marriages."

"I can understand that."

"You know, son, the carnal seems to be another hang-up with women. I got a theory. Men and women are different, and I don't just mean in the obvious way. I'm talking sex drive. I figure from the time a fellow knows it's possible, he's raring to go. But the little lady's sex drive peaks later. Probably posthumously."

Angie listened to the two guffaw over this a long time. Then the younger-sounding one said, "At least you understand them."

"I hate to disillusion you, but despite my vast experience, they're still a mystery to me. So much so—I'm not ashamed to admit—I'd just as soon pay for it. But you know something, even the pros feel unworthy of me. It's amazing. I've got to be one hell of a guy."

That did it. She *had* to see this wondrous marrying man. She grabbed hold of some branches and spread them apart, but still couldn't see through the thick bush. Leaning farther over the back of the bench, she grabbed more branches and was trying to separate them enough to see through when she lost her balance and toppled headfirst over the bench. Holding on to the bush, she belly flopped on top of it, causing the branches to sway under her weight and carry her up to the back of the opposite bench. She looked right into the bloodshot eyes of two scruffy men. They jumped to their feet.

The older one, a seedy but still faintly debonair character in his shiny too-tight striped suit and bowler hat worn at a jaunty angle, proudly puffed out his chest as he smiled down at her.

"There, son. See what I mean? They're always falling for me."

Earl ran out of the kitchen and came to a screeching halt when he saw who stood near the entrance waiting for a table. "You back?"

Angie looked around to see if he could be addressing anyone else. No, she was the only one here. "Yes."

"Which table?"

"How about the same one as last time?"

He led her to the table and even held the chair out for her. She pulled a twig she'd missed earlier off the leg of her slacks and sat. He handed her a menu—the same Columbus Avenue Café menu with the name lined out.

She gave it back. "What's on the menu today?" she asked.

"T'ree t'ings."

"T'ree? I mean, three?" she said with surprise. The cook must have taken her advice and expanded the menu. "How wonderful! What are they?"

He squeezed his eyes shut, counted with his fingers, then opened them and looked at her. "Spaghetti wit' meatballs, spaghetti wit'out meatballs, an' a meatball sangwich."

She clasped her hands to her forehead. "I think I need to pay the cook another visit."

"He's busy."

Angie looked around the empty restaurant. "Give me a break!"

Just then another customer came in. A rather plain man, he had short, spiky brown hair—not spiked like a punk, but spiky like someone whose hair had been cut a little too short and who hadn't ever learned to control his cowlicks, and thick, black-rimmed glasses that rode too high on the left and too low on the right, making him look like his head was perpetually cocked.

He was also tall and surprisingly muscular-looking. There was something familiar about him, but she couldn't remember having met him before.

He smiled shyly in her direction. She smiled back. Did he know her?

"See?" Earl looked at her smugly. "What did I tell you?" He walked over to the new customer. "You wanna eat?"

"Um, yes. I believe so."

"Okay. Follow me." Earl led him to a table near Angie. "Here's da menu. I'd recommend da spaghetti an' meatballs."

Angie turned around to watch. The customer looked from her, to Earl, to the menu, then folded it shut and handed it back. "Sounds good to me," he said.

Earl went back to Angie's table. "You decided yet?"

"How about a new waiter?"

"It ain't on da menu. How 'bout spaghetti an' meatballs?"

She held her head. "Not today. I think I'll pass, in fact." She stood, picking up her purse. "Tell the cook I suggest he look into polenta. There isn't a restaurant around that does it really well. The trick is to mix diced roasted green chilies—mild ones—in with it. If he wants to try it, I'll help."

She was ready to leave, but noticed that the customer had been listening to her conversation with the waiter. She didn't want him to get the wrong impression.

"Let me assure you," she said, "the spaghetti and meat-balls are truly delicious. I'm just tired of them."

"Thanks. I'm glad to hear it. This is the first time I've eaten here. I'm new to the city."

"Well, welcome." She couldn't help staring.

"Is anything wrong?" he asked.

"I'm sorry. You look a bit familiar."

He looked at her as if she were mad, then grinned. "I remind you of Mel Gibson, maybe?"

Even his smile and attempt at humor didn't lesson the sudden uneasiness she felt. "Hunger must be causing my eyesight to do strange things. Sorry. Enjoy your lunch."

"It was nice talking to you." He gave her a friendly, almost–puppy-dog smile. Placing his elbows on the table, he steepled his hands, and leaned forward, toward her. "Hurry back," he said.

CHAPTER

$\approx$

TWENTY-FIVE

District Attorney Lloyd Fletcher slowly leafed through the reports from the Crime Scene Investigations unit, the photographs and laboratory tests, as well as Paavo's and Yosh's notes on interviews with Tiffany Rogers's coworkers, neighbors, and family. When he finished, he did the same with the folder on Velma St. Clair.

"Frankly, I expected much better from you, Smith," he said.

Paavo wasn't surprised to hear a remark like that from Fletcher. Still, it stung. "The guy the judge used to see hanging around each morning hasn't shown up since the murder. We've got an idea of what he looks like. Also, a kid who lives across the street from Tiffany Rogers's apartment described a man with the same build carrying a long, white box—sounded like a florist's box—the night Rogers was killed. It's got to be him."

Fletcher ran his hand over his thick white hair as if to smooth it, except that every strand was already in place. "A tall, muscular white guy who wears a baseball cap and aviator sunglasses. Let's see, that probably describes ten thousand or so men in San Francisco alone. Maybe twenty to thirty thousand if we take in the whole Bay Area. I'm not impressed."

"We're still working on finding Rogers's boyfriend. She has to have left some clue, somewhere, as to who he might be."

"You're wasting your time. Everyone said she'd gone out with the man for two months or less. And why would her lover have killed the old woman? No, you're barking up the wrong tree there."

"But with City Hall—or at least, city government—involved in both murders, plus the missing boyfriend, there are too many questions whose answers all point in the same direction. The key has to be right here—someone close."

Fletcher shot out of his chair, placed his hands on his desk, and leaned forward. "Or you might be wrong. You might be ready to ruin a man's career because of an indiscretion with some bimbo who had the bad taste to get herself killed."

Paavo stared, taken aback by the vehemence of Fletcher's outburst. The man had a reputation for being pristine. If not, Paavo would wonder about his remarks. Despite his reputation, in fact, Paavo still wondered.

Fletcher straightened and tugged at his shirt cuffs as he paced in front of this window. "How much clearer can I make myself, Smith? You are not to involve City Hall, the Board of Supervisors, or anyone connected with city government in this case. These women were murdered by some psycho, and I'm not going to have you disturb any political types in this city more than you already have. Do you understand me?"

Paavo tried to tamp down his simmering anger. "City government is our one constant."

"Keep away from the Board of Supervisors. That's an order."

"Hi," Angie said as she walked into Everyone's Fancy, a small gift shop on West Portal Avenue. "Are you Connie?"

"Yes," the clerk, a pleasant-looking woman with shoulder-length, light brown hair, looked wary.

"I came to give my condolences. My boyfriend is the homicide inspector working on your sister's investigation, Inspector Paavo Smith."

Connie's eyes teared, and she went back to rearranging some glass swans. "Do you always visit the families of your boyfriend's cases?" The expression on her face showed how macabre a pastime she considered that to be.

"My goodness, no. But it turns out that you went to high school with one of my cousins. We were talking about this and that, and I mentioned how scary it was that two women were killed with the same MO—that's modus operandi—and my cousin said he knew you, but that he hadn't seen you since high school."

"Really?" Connie's expression told Angie she wasn't inclined to believe her. "What's his name?"

"Dan Amalfi. Everyone calls him Buddy."

For the first time, Angie saw Connie's caution lift and a pretty smile brighten her plain face. "Buddy! You're Buddy's cousin? He was *so* handsome."

"He still is."

"I can imagine." A splash of color appeared on her cheeks. "What's he doing now? Married? Kids?"

"No kids. Divorced. Not even after twelve years of parochial school could he keep his marriage together. A mistake from the start."

"I know the feeling." Connie put the last swan in place. "I had twenty-six months of sheer hell."

It was on the tip of Angie's tongue to ask *why*. Why would a marriage turn so sour so quickly? Didn't she know the man she married well, or had she ignored the faults that were there, until it was too late? But she wasn't here to learn about marriage, she was here to help Paavo. "Buddy's marriage lasted only eight months."

Angie knew why that marriage failed—the two kids married right out of high school—young, horny, and both dumb in the way only teenagers in love could be about the real world and the mundane problems of making a home in it.

"Buddy remembered me when he read about Tiffany?" Connie asked.

"Your poor sister," Angie said gently. She wasn't here to discuss Buddy.

Connie rubbed her arms as if chilled. "My God, it's still such a shock."

"I'm surprised her boyfriend never showed himself." Not subtle, but to the point.

"How'd you know that?"

Angie sensed Connie's wariness taking over again. "It was in the papers, remember?"

"Oh. Well, she did her darnedest to keep his name a secret, so I guess even after she's dead he'll keep his name out of it."

"It sounds mighty suspicious if you ask me," Angie said. "When Buddy and I were talking about it, we couldn't imagine a woman being happy about some guy and not ever saying anything about him."

"It's true, though," Connie insisted. "Tell Buddy she was really close-mouthed about the guy."

"It has to be she was ashamed of him, then. Don't you think? I mean, I talk about Paavo all the time. I talk about what he says, what he does, even what he thinks—at least, when he tells me. And this is despite my family being completely opposed to me going out with a cop—at least, everyone is except my mother, who likes Paavo—but the rest of them, well, you know how families can be."

"Do I ever. Mine is the same way. You should have heard everyone when me and Keith got divorced. You'd think it was all my fault. What about Buddy?" Connie asked suddenly. "Was the family angry when he got his divorce?"

"More disappointed than angry. But, you know Buddy. He could charm the scales off a toad. Everyone got over it fast enough."

"That's Buddy. Say hello to him for me, won't you?"

"Of course."

"In fact, bring him by. We've got great gift ideas here. Tell him, he doesn't even have to buy anything. I'd like to say hello."

"I'll tell him."

"He sure was handsome. We dated a couple of times—once to the movies, and another time to Charlie Markowitz's party," Connie mused, leaning on the counter.

"Buddy mentioned it," Angie said.

"He remembered?"

"Yes. Anyway, I was just thinking about Tiffany—"

"Poor Tiffany." Connie straightened. "Every time someone mentions her, it's like an electric shock all over again."

"Did she ever talk about what it was that attracted her to the man she was dating, or what they did together—I mean, where he took her on their dates?"

"It was clear he had money. That kind of thing was important to Tiffany. She never named the places he took her to. Instead, she'd say something like 'He took me to a big fancy restaurant in Marin where he wouldn't be recognized.'"

"Interesting. His picture must have been in the newspapers or on TV for him to have worried about being recognized."

Connie shrugged. "You never know. San Francisco is small in many ways. Look how you found me."

"That's true. I'd suspect, since he felt okay about going to Marin, he worried that *old* San Francisco, not tourists and commuters, might recognize him. That means he's just a local big fish."

"That's how it sounded."

"How did she refer to him?"

"As her friend. That's all."

"Hmm, I wonder . . ." Angie was going to have to ponder this awhile. She looked around the gift shop. "Oh, my!

Look at these." She went to a case with a display of Russian eggs.

"Aren't they beautiful? They're made by modern Fabergé artisans. The Easter gift for the person who has everything."

"I guess so. They aren't cheap, are they?"

"No, but there's so much significance in eggs and Easter, we actually do sell a few of them each year."

"They're wonderful. I've seen a couple of them on display in a little jewelry shop next door to an interesting little restaurant, The Wings Of An Angel on Columbus Avenue. Do you know the place?"

Connie shook her head.

"Their spaghetti and meatballs are great."

Connie nodded absently, still staring at the eggs. "Tiffany loved those eggs." Her eyes welled up, and suddenly she was in tears. She reached into her pocket for a wadded-up tissue and wiped her eyes. "I'm sorry. I just remembered that one of the last things she said to me was that she'd ask El to buy her one, and now—"

"El?"

"El, yes. *El amigo*. That's what she and her pal Manuela called him—her friend, the friend. Sometimes just El for short."

"You don't think El is the letter of his name?"

"I guess I never thought about it. Tiffany said she called him El because of Manuela."

"Did you mention this to Paavo?"

"I doubt it. I hadn't even thought about it."

"El," Angie murmured, still eyeing the eggs. "These are so special. I wonder if anyone would be interested in an article on them?"

"An article?" Connie paled. "Are you a journalist?"

"Don't worry. Not the way you mean it. I write reviews of restaurants, and sometimes I do other articles about food or cooking. I'm trying to get a television show started. I should be called to an audition any day now."

"Television! Wow, that is so exciting! God, I'd die if I

had to go on TV. I'd stand there with my mouth open and make a complete fool of myself. You're very poised, though. You'd be great."

Angie gave a brave smile. "Thank you. I hope so."

"What will the show be called?"

Her smile vanished. "They're thinking of calling it . . . *Angelina in the Cucina*."

Connie's eyes widened, and then she started to laugh.

CHAPTER

$$\infty\infty\infty$$

TWENTY-SIX

The Coventry Hotel was in an old, unprepossessing building with a brass nameplate so small it could have been a mail slot. As such, one was unprepared for the elegance behind the wood and glass front door, the lush sofa in red-and-gold brocade, and matching striped chairs set on Persian carpets under a massive crystal chandelier. Mahogany and faux marble antiques finished the Old World ambience of the lobby. The rooms promised to be every bit as elegant.

Paavo faced the manager, a slight, balding man, every bit as haughty and sophisticated as the furnishings. "We found your matchbook in the victim's apartment. We're wondering if she was ever a guest."

James Sneed studied the photo Paavo handed him, then gestured for the desk clerk to join them. "Tiffany Rogers, you say?"

"That's right."

"She doesn't look familiar to me at all. If I may be so bold, she doesn't strike me as the sort who would be one of our regular clientele. We run a highly respected hotel."

"I'm sure you do."

The desk clerk reached their side. "Inspector Smith, this is Arthur Mills. Do you recognize her, Arthur?"

"Not at all."

The manager handed back the photo. "Sorry, Inspector."

Paavo tucked it in his breast pocket. "Do either of you work nights?"

"Our guests are rarely here *only* at night," Sneed said.

Paavo repeated his question.

"No."

"What time does your night shift report? And also, I'd like to take a look at your guest register for, let's say, the past eight weeks."

Paavo went through the guest register carefully, but saw nothing at all that jumped out at him as odd. Not even any repeat names. He gave the material back to the manager. "Everyone who stayed in this hotel is listed here, is that correct?" he asked.

"Well . . . not exactly," Sneed said.

"What do you mean?"

"The city rents a suite here at all times. They keep it for special guests because it's nearly impossible to find superior accommodations in this city on short notice. In summer, the suite is filled constantly. That's not the case this time of year. Several of the, er, dignitaries of the city have access to the suite—keys, in other words. They come and go as they please."

"They don't have to check in and out at the front desk?"

"We ask them to. But we know they don't all do so."

"Do you have a list of people with keys?"

"We only issued one—to the mayor's office. But I know more have been given out because the maids have told me they've seen different people entering or leaving on occasion. Of course, the height of propriety is always observed."

"Of course," Paavo said. "Thanks for the information."

* * *

Angie telephoned Paavo that evening. "I'd like to go with you to Mrs. St. Clair's funeral tomorrow afternoon," she said.

There was a long pause. "You know how much I enjoy having you with me, Angie," he began, "but—"

"My father knows Judge St. Clair. I'll represent the family. He shouldn't go anyway, his heart, you know. It's not good for him to be around murder victims."

"I'm not going there as a social gesture."

"I know. You do your thing, and I'll have enough etiquette for both of us."

"What's the real reason you want to go?"

"No real reason, other than I want to be with you. By the way, I met Connie Rogers."

"You *what*?"

"She's an old girlfriend of my cousin Buddy. In fact, she's still interested in him, if I'm any judge."

"Where did this cousin suddenly appear from?"

"What's that supposed to mean? I've got a lot of cousins you haven't met yet."

"It means that it's pretty convenient that your cousin's love life involves the family of my murder victim."

"You are *so* suspicious, Inspector. Look, Tiffany's older sister and a number of my relatives are near the same age, and all went to Catholic high schools in the city. It's natural at least one of them would know her. How many Catholic highs do you think we have here?"

"Obviously not enough to keep you out of my cases."

"Before you complain, let me tell you about 'El.'"

Angie told him about her conversation with Connie Rogers the previous day. After leaving Connie's, Angie had driven straight to City Hall. She found her voting district's supervisor and made a pest of herself until she received an in-house telephone directory that gave the names of each department head in city government, their deputies, and their mid-level managers.

She concentrated on the department heads. Tiffany liked men with money and power. She wouldn't have bothered with a mid-level manager, and the deputies were also iffy. Angie found four top level people whose names started with L. The chief of Police and a member of the Board of Supervisors were both named Lawrence, the district attorney was named Lloyd, and Llewellan was the chief of the Department of Sanitation. Besides them, the mayor's executive officer was named Luis.

Now, she needed to see how these men looked and acted—to see if any of them might seem the sort of man Tiffany could have been interested in. Since it was likely that they knew the judge, they might be at the funeral. It was a good place to check them out.

"Hold everything, Angie. First of all, how do you know El is the first name? Why not the last?"

"I admit it's a guess. But all the women I know refer to their boyfriends by their first names. Maybe it's a Catholic school thing, but last names are usually used as a joke."

"Before you go rushing off with this, let me talk to Manuela. If she's the one who came up with *El Amigo*, it's just a blind alley."

"I knew you'd help!" Angie said.

He seemed to make a strange guttural sound before hanging up the phone.

The next day Paavo picked Angie up at her apartment, and they rode in his old Austin Healey to the mortuary.

"I talked to Manuela," he said as he drove.

"What did she say?"

"That she knows nothing about 'el' and never used the term '*el amigo*.'"

"All *right!*"

A large crowd stood outside the building talking in hushed tones, and an even larger crowd was inside.

Paavo circled the outside group, then did the same indoors, to get a sense of who was here. Angie followed, trying to get a glimpse of those on her list of L names.

"Tell me, Paavo," she whispered, holding his arm, "which one is your boss, Lawrence?"

Paavo put his arm around her waist, speaking quietly into her ear as he looked over the crowd. "It wouldn't matter if the chief of police had ten *L*'s in his name, he didn't date Tiffany Rogers."

"How do you know?"

"His wife would kill him."

"Some men can be pretty sneaky."

"Not from their wives—or not for long," Paavo said. "That's him. Blue suit, gray hair. That's his wife in the green suit. I've known him for ten years, Angie."

"Hmm." Angie nearly bored a hole through him trying to figure out if he looked like someone Tiffany might have dated. "His eyes are shifty," she announced.

Paavo turned her to face in another direction. "Forget him," he said, but even as he said it, he thought of the Sans Souci clerk's description of the man who bought the bracelet for Tiffany. No. Impossible.

"Do you see any of the others?" Angie asked. "I know what Supervisor Coglin—Larry Coglin—looks like, but I haven't seen him here. Isn't it suspicious that he wouldn't come?"

Paavo frowned. "Could be. Lloyd Fletcher, the DA, is the tall, white-haired fellow near the judge." Fletcher was another one who met the clerk's description. Paavo thought about his strange conversation with Fletcher. How the man had insisted that he not pursue finding Rogers's boyfriend. That it could ruin a man's reputation and not lead to the killer, anyway. Could Angie actually be on the right track here?

"I've seen him before. He wants to be mayor, I hear."

"So they say."

"And the others?"

"I don't know the chief of sanitation—you're on your own there. And I don't see the mayor's XO."

"X—, oh, the executive officer. All you government types talk in letters. Say, I wonder if the *L* isn't an initial for a name at all, but a job? An *L*? What job could that be?"

"No government job just has one letter. Bureaucrats are always too long-winded. You know that."

"Considering his fling with Tiffany, how about Ladies' Man?"

"That'd be LM."

"You're so precise, Inspector. Let's find the—what did you call him? The XO."

Paavo noticed a deliveryman hovering nearby holding a bouquet of roses up in front of his face. If he never saw a rose again, it'd be too soon. All the flowers should have been up by the casket already, though. Why would a deliveryman—

"Oh, look, Paavo!" Angie leaned close against him. "There's someone new at the door. Good-looking, too. Hispanic, I think. Could he be Luis the XO?"

Paavo faced the doorway. "That's him."

"Let's go over there. I want a better look at him."

"Wait."

"What?"

He turned back to check on the deliveryman. Paavo let go of Angie and slowly starting walking toward the casket. Near the side exit, he saw a bouquet of roses lying on the ground.

He scanned the room quickly, then hurried out the exit. It led to a side alleyway. He ran down the alley to the street, to find another crowd milling about, getting into and out of cars and talking. He saw far too many of them wearing gray slacks similar to the deliveryman's.

The man's upper body seemed to be clothed in beige— a sweater, most likely. But his face . . .

All Paavo could remember was the sight of the roses.

CHAPTER

TWENTY-SEVEN

Paavo picked up the crime lab report, read it once quickly, then threw it down on his desk. "No good news, I take it," Yosh said.

Paavo handed it to him. "They couldn't lift any prints off the rose display, not even off the vase they were placed in. It had to have been him, standing right there, listening to me, laughing. Damn! I looked right at him."

"Hey, you weren't the only one. I missed him, too. I mean, you expect to see flowers being delivered to a funeral."

"What if that was the way he got into Tiffany's apartment? What if he wasn't someone she knew at all, but just some guy delivering flowers? She might have opened the door for him."

"Could be," Yosh agreed. "She wouldn't want the flowers to die. Instead, she did."

"A deliveryman goes along with what the kid saw," Paavo said. He felt a sudden chill as he remembered the roses one of Angie's students had delivered to her.

"What's wrong?" Yosh asked.

He shook away the feeling. "Nothing. By the way, who would you say is the biggest gossip in Homicide?"

"Benson wins hands down. Why?"

"I'm curious about our friend the DA."

"Careful, Paav."

"I know."

Yosh picked up the DMV report Paavo had been reading and scanned it quickly. "I thought we had him when those patrolmen wrote down the green Honda's license number. Now I see the car's registered to a dead man."

"I asked for a bulletin to go out on it anyway. I'd like to talk with this ghost driver."

"A hundred bucks and you can buy any kind of ID you want on the street," Yosh said. "They make things tougher for us all the time."

"Ain't it the truth," Calderon muttered as he walked into Homicide, scowling harder than usual.

"Hey, buddy," Yosh said. "How's it going?"

Calderon winced. "Another robbery."

Paavo and Yosh jumped up and crossed to his desk. "Another fake egg?"

"Who would have thought this city would be so lousy with phony Russian eggs? That was the fourth robbery. Some weird little guy with a fake beard and black wig. Not hard to spot, I'd say. Maybe I should transfer and help solve their cases? Those guys need lots of help if they can't nab someone going around looking like a bearded Charlie Chaplin."

"In other words, no new leads on Nathan Ellis's murder?"

"I followed up on what the clerk at Sans Souci told you—the one who said some woman was asking a lot of questions. Seems a woman who looked like her was at this gift shop the day before the attack."

"Good work," Yosh said. "It sounds like the thief is a woman."

"Not so fast," Calderon cautioned. "Me and the guys in Robbery thought of that already. So, to check it out, I went into a jeweler's that wasn't robbed, gave the same descrip-

tion, and asked if a similar woman had been in the store
the day before, asking questions. They, too, said yes.
About five of them. In other words, women ask about
Fabergé eggs. What else is new?"

"Great," Yosh said. "So much for that theory."

"Don't rule it out completely," Paavo cautioned. "Not
yet, anyway. The reaction of the woman the San Souci
clerk spoke to wasn't normal, no matter how often women
ask about such things."

"I guess we could track all the women who show interest in the eggs if we didn't want to do anything else for a
few weeks."

"We've got until Easter," Paavo said. "Then the eggs
disappear, and so does our murderer. A little over three
weeks."

"We'll get him," Calderon said, showing more energy
than usual.

"Let's mark the city map with the stores that were
robbed," Paavo said. "Look for a pattern."

"With little Easter bunny stickers," Yosh said.

"The only pattern is that the robberies happen on
Tuesday—so far. It's nothing I'd count on, though. Easter,
good God! Who'd have thought Easter would bring out the
wackos? I thought people weren't religious anymore?"

Just then Bo Benson walked in. "Excuse me," Paavo
said, "but I've got some gossip to catch up on."

"You've got to do it, Connie," Angie said. She faced
Connie across the counter of Everyone's Fancy.

"I don't feel right about it." Connie wiped dust and fingerprints from the carousel horses and tried to shut out
Angie's arguments.

"Don't you want to know who was dating your sister?
The guy didn't identify himself to the police, didn't even
go to her funeral. But there's a chance he knows something
about whoever killed her. And there's always the chance
he killed her himself."

"And the judge's wife?" Connie said, dusting faster.

"So the killer's a psychopathic government big shot. Wouldn't be the first time."

Connie wielded her Windex bottle. "It was random, Angie. It had to have been. Some serial killer. It'd be just like my sister to take up with a Ted Bundy type."

"Paavo doesn't think it was random. He thinks there's a reason those women were chosen—we just don't know what the reason is yet."

"I don't know, Angie. I hate to do anything that might mess up the investigation. Besides, I think my sister really fell for this guy. It wasn't like her not to brag about whoever she was seeing, but she kept quiet about him. Could be beeause she loved him."

"All the more reason to find out who he is. The investigation is stalled. His own boss is trying to stop Paavo from talking to City Hall." She paused to chew her lower lip. "Gee, I wonder what Lieutenant Hollins's first name is? I'll have to ask Paavo—if I can manage without him bellowing at me about it."

"Paavo bellows?"

"I seem to bring out the best in him. Anyway, I know my idea won't mess up anything. You can close the store for a couple of hours, then come back here."

"I don't know. It's close to Easter and Passover. I'm selling a lot of little gifts."

"Speaking of gifts," Angie said, "you should get rid of those Fabergé eggs. Someone's been going around the city stealing them."

"You're kidding. Who'd want to steal such a thing?"

"Nobody knows, but Paavo was involved because one of the clerks was killed by the robber."

"Oh no!"

"Oh, yes. Homicide calls it the Easter Egg Murder. Let's carry them in the back, then get out of here. Okay?"

"I give up. Let me move the money to the safe first. Could you lock the door, Angie?" Connie waited by the cash register.

Just as Angie was swinging the door shut, a strange-looking little man, dressed in black clothes, wearing what looked like a wig and fake beard, appeared before her. "Sorry, you'll have to come back later," Angie announced, then shut the door in his face and flipped the sign to CLOSED.

The two women drove in Angie's Ferrari to Tiffany's apartment, where they spent some time going through her closets. Most of the belongings would be given to charity or sold off. Finally, they found the perfect thing.

An hour later, they went to Tiffany's hairdresser, who was only too happy to oblige despite a salon of customers. A big tip helped.

"Actually," Connie said, "it looks pretty good, doesn't it?"

"Very good," Angie said with a critical eye. The light blond color and short, stylish hairdo were a definite improvement over Connie's mousy brown side part and fringe. Next, she meticulously applied makeup, a pair of Tiffany's long, dangling earrings, and exchanged Connie's low, comfortable shoes for a pair of spike heels.

"Let's go," Angie said with a burst of excitement. The other woman looked uncertainly at her, but nodded.

They started out at City Hall. Up on the second floor, they went to the mayor's office. The reception area was large and elegant, decorated in an eighteenth century style reminiscent of the White House.

A receptionist smiled pleasantly as Angie approached.

"I need to see the mayor," Angie announced.

The gray-haired woman reached for her appointment book. "Do you have an appointment?"

"No, but it's very important."

She gazed up at Angie. "What is it regarding?"

"East and West Pakistan."

"Pakistan?" She blinked rapidly several times behind her bifocals. "I don't believe there are East and West Pakistans any longer."

"I know, and that's the problem. I'm part of the Coalition to Resurrect All Pakistans. The acronym is unfortunate, but it does not reflect on our cause! Our group believes the city of San Francisco needs to be involved in this! We are the city that knows how! We're in the forefront of *all* important movements, and this, I assure you, is a most important movement."

The receptionist stood. "I'm sorry, miss, the mayor is out."

Angie squared her shoulders and smoothed the front panel of her red Ellen Tracy suit—the kind businesswomen called a power suit. "I'm not leaving until I speak to someone in authority. This means a lot to the people of this city."

The woman frowned, but the suit obviously did its job. "Let me get the mayor's executive officer." She disappeared into the side room.

Yes! Angie thought. The XO himself.

Luis Hernandez came out of his office. He was the epitome of charm as he smiled broadly, extending his hand in greeting, his gold Rolex and diamond pinkie ring flashing, his thousand-dollar Ralph Lauren suit fitted to emphasize each bulging biceps, triceps, and deltoid. "Mr. Hernandez," she shouted as they shook hands, "how nice of you to see me."

He halted, surprised at her outburst, and looked around. At just that moment, Connie appeared in the hallway at the entry to the mayor's suite of offices. She turned her back to the door and looked over her shoulder, as if someone had called her, then she continued on, wobbling slightly.

Angie saw Hernandez eye Connie, saw his gaze do a rapid up-down as if admiring her good looks, and then turn back to Angie. He seemed calm and unflustered.

"What can I do for you, Miss, er—?"

"On second thought, maybe Pakistan is better off as two countries. I mean, maybe it's not even a San Francisco issue, although that's hard to imagine. Thanks for your time, Mr. Hernandez."

As he gaped speechlessly at her, Angie ducked out of

the reception area, grabbed Connie's arm, and the two of them hurried away from the mayor's office.

"Nothing," Angie said.

"These heels are killing me," Connie said unhappily, as she tottered beside Angie.

They found Lawrence Coglin's office down the hall in the Board of Supervisors suite. Angie stepped into the office, leaving the door open wide behind her. Connie remained, again, in the hallway.

"Is Supervisor Coglin in?" Angie asked.

The secretary, a young woman with hair that had been teased and moussed to incredible heights and eye shadow applied with a trowel, gave her a withering look. "Yes, but he's busy at the moment."

"I just want to see him one second to give him this petition." She held up a large manila envelope stuffed with papers.

"I'll see that he gets it." The secretary took hold of the edge of the envelope.

A small tug-of-war ensued until Angie pulled it back and clutched it to her chest. "I've got to give it to him personally. I represent two thousand constituents—two thousand voters—and it'll just take a minute."

"What is it regarding?"

"PG & E."

"Utilities?"

"Does the supervisor want to irritate two thousand voters?"

"All right, one moment."

In a minute Lawrence Coglin himself, all smiles, came out of his office. He was tall, with thinning brown hair, bushy eyebrows, wearing horn-rimmed glasses. In all other respects he was nondescript—the sort of man no one would ever notice if he didn't have a title before his name. "Hello, there, I'm Larry Coglin." He swooped down on her and gripped her hand in one of those knuckle-crunching handshakes that politicians seem to think makes them appear sincere rather than boorish.

"I represent the people of the Marina district," Angie said.

"Marina?" He glanced at his secretary, then back to Angie. "My area is the Sunset."

"It is?"

From the side, she saw Connie go into the same routine of slowly walking by, turning her head away from the supervisor as she looked over her shoulder, then continuing on. Coglin noticed her, but didn't bat an eyelash.

"I thought you were our supervisor. My mistake. I'm so sorry to have bothered you."

He smiled. "Well, if you ever move, keep me in mind."

"Sure thing!" Angie said, as she backed out of the office, then turned and hurried to Connie's side. "These people are either completely cold-blooded and insensitive, or innocent."

"Well, they *are* politicians," Connie said. "Are you sure we want to continue with this?"

"We can't stop now," Angie said, hurrying away from the Board of Supervisors suite. "We can forget the chief of sanitation. He's on a month-long junket to Paris to observe French public toilets. Believe me."

Connie followed as best she could in Tiffany's spike heels. The two ran down the long staircase and out the door to the Civic Center parking lot, jumped into the Ferrari, and rode the few blocks to the Hall of Justice.

"This is going to be harder," Angie said as she ushered Connie past the metal detectors and into the building.

"Maybe we should just forget it," Connie said. "These guys aren't fooled."

"Don't worry," Angie said encouragingly. "Anyway, I think it's a terrific idea. Your lipstick needs a touch-up."

"But it's your idea." Connie obediently took a peek in her compact.

"That's what I mean. Let's go."

They rode to the DA's offices on the third floor. Angie went up to the receptionist. "Is Mr. Lloyd Fletcher in?" she asked.

"I'm sorry, he's observing a case in court this afternoon," the lanky black man said politely.

"Court? Which courtroom?"

He checked his calendar. "Courtroom C."

"Which floor is that on?"

"This one. On the opposite side of the building."

Angie and Connie had to walk past the elevators to reach the courtroom. "I don't like this one bit!" Connie whispered fiercely. "I'm sorry, Angie, but I'm leaving." She turned into the elevator bank and hit the down button.

"You can't leave." An elevator bell bonged and the up arrow lit. "The elevator is going up. You don't want it anyway." She took hold of Connie's arm and tried to steer her away.

"I'll wait." Connie dug in her heels and tried to pull her arm free. "I'm not going to the courtrooms!"

"You've got to," Angie insisted.

The elevator doors opened as the two battled.

Angie suddenly dropped her arm. There, in the elevator, his mouth open and his eyes bulging, stood Lloyd Fletcher.

Angie gasped.

Connie turned around and stared straight at Fletcher.

The DA stared back. The color leeched from his face. As if taking on a will of their own, his eyes slowly went from the stylish short haircut—cut and dyed exactly as Tiffany's had been, to the makeup exactly as Tiffany had worn it, to the form-hugging pink dress that was Tiffany's, to the pink suede pumps, then his eyes jerked back to Connie's face. For a moment, the two women thought he was going to pass out. He mumbled an apology, and hurried off the elevator.

Angie and Connie jumped onto it. As soon as the doors closed Angie whispered, "That was *him*! Did you see the expression on his face."

"Oh, my God." Connie leaned back against the elevator wall, her hand against her heart. "He looked at me as if he'd seen a ghost."

"He looked like a ghost himself! He's the one. He's got to be. My idea worked!" Angie cried. They looked at each other, shrieked, held hands together, and hopped about in a little victory dance. On six, the elevator doors opened. A group of lawyers peered in at the dancing women and decided to wait for the next one.

Angie pushed the button for four. "We're going to go see Paavo," she said. "Right now."

Both Paavo and Yosh were staring as if they couldn't believe their eyes. Seconds before they had been in the midst of the tiresome task of going over, once again, the interviews with Judge St. Clair's neighbors when a commotion erupted in the Homicide office. Angie flew in, her face aglow with excitement, made a beeline for Paavo, and grabbed his hands. He barely had time to register how beautiful she looked when his attention was caught by the woman tottering behind her on a pair of pink shoes with heels higher than the San Francisco Yellow Pages. Behind her came the secretary, trying to grab the wavering woman, whether to support her or hold her back, he wasn't sure. Angie let go of him and, for some reason, got involved with the other two.

He stared at the blonde and quickly realized two things. First, that the three women were all talking at once. Second, what Angie had done.

He stood and held his hand up. Miraculously, the talking stopped. The secretary let go of the blonde, Angie stopped trying to free the blonde from the secretary, and the blonde kicked off her high-heeled shoes.

"Hello, Miss Rogers," he said.

The secretary looked baffled.

"It's okay, Elizabeth," he told her. She scurried back to the relative sanity of her desk.

"We did it, Paavo!" Angie grabbed his hands again. "I can't believe it, but we did it! We found out—"

"Angie," he interrupted, placing his hand against her

back and steering her toward an interview room. "Let's not disturb everyone."

She looked around to see that the four inspectors in the room had stopped work and were staring at her. She smiled hesitantly.

Yosh hurried over to join them.

"Hey there, Angie," he said. "How ya doin'?"

"Top of the world, Yosh."

He carefully took in the other woman. "Connie Rogers, right?" he said. "New hair color. New style, too. Very nice."

Connie's cheeks flamed. "Thank you."

The four entered a small, soundproof interview room and shut the door. Paavo and Yosh sat on one side of the metal table, Angie and Connie on the other. Angie had the distinct impression she and Connie were on the wrong side of the table here.

"Lloyd Fletcher," she announced proudly. "He took one look at Connie dressed up this way, and I thought he was going to pass out. He's got to have been Tiffany's boyfriend."

"Do you know what's going on, Paavo?" Yosh asked.

Paavo folded his arms. He had to do it—the urge to dole out corporal punishment for such a childish stunt was over-whelming. "I'm afraid I've got a good idea. You two didn't parade Connie in front of every man whose name began with an L, did you?"

"Why not?" Angie asked. "Anyway, we only had to check out three of them since you insisted the chief of police couldn't have been involved and the sanitation boss is out of town."

There was a short silence, then, carefully pronouncing each word, Paavo said, "What do you mean by 'check out'? You can't just go waltzing up to those men and say you want to see them."

"Maybe some people can't," Connie said, then cocked her head toward Angie.

He fought a strong desire to unfold his arms. "Don't explain. I don't want to have to arrest her."

"It was all perfectly legal," Angie assured him. "These men are politicians, after all. Anyway, no one batted an eye but Fletcher. He's our man."

"He's been involved in the Rogers and St. Clair murders because of City Hall. He's seen photos of Tiffany. You might only have seen him reacting to the fact of the resemblance."

"No. You and Yosh reacted to the fact of the resemblance. His reaction was much stronger. More . . . more visceral."

"It's true," Connie said, nodding vigorously. "You wouldn't believe the expression on his face, the way he stared at me. It was creepy."

"They might be onto something," Yosh said. "You can't say Fletcher's been cooperative, and Benson told me everyone says he's been acting peculiar lately."

"There you go!" Angie cried. "Now, I've just got to—"

"The man's the district attorney, Angie," Paavo said firmly. "You've got to do nothing, and *especially* do nothing that might cause him to realize you two set him up."

"I know, I know. It's police business."

"That's right. I'll talk to him."

"Talk? There's got to be a better way," Angie said. "I mean, what could you say? Seen any dead girlfriends lately?"

Connie winced.

Angie was horror-struck. "Oh, Connie, I'm so sorry! I didn't mean to be disrespectful."

"It's okay, Angie. At least *you're* trying to be helpful."

Angie saw Paavo's and Yosh's irritation at Connie's slap at the police. At times, even *she* recognized when she'd gone too far. "Let's go, Connie." She grabbed Connie's arm and hustled her out of there. "See you around, fellas."

CHAPTER

$\infty\infty\infty$

T W E N T Y - E I G H T

He ducked behind the Volvo wagon parked on the Jones Street hill as a car drove by, its headlights sweeping the area before it. The nearest parking he could find for his Honda, now with a new coat of black paint, was two blocks away.

He didn't want anyone to see him there, outside the garage to the apartment building where Angelina Amalfi lived. The garage door was locked, but all he needed was for one person to come home. Just one. That person would use a remote control, open the door, and park—and he'd slip in before the garage door shut again.

He'd tried to rig up his remote to open the door, as he had done at the judge's house, but this security system was much more sophisticated. It'd be a chore to break, and why take the time when this way was so easy. Tenants were careless. A good reason to take advantage of them.

He'd already waited there two hours, ever since midnight, for someone to drive into the garage. The fog had come in and the air was damp, but he wasn't cold. His body felt neither warmth nor cold—he was beyond such mundane things.

If no one came home tonight, he'd be back tomorrow. What did a day or two matter?

He ducked again as another car turned onto Jones Street and started up the hill. This one slowed. When it reached the garage, it turned onto the driveway. He scrunched down farther behind the Volvo, waiting. He heard the garage door squeal open. To his surprise, the area became flooded with light as the garage's interior lights came on—a safety precaution. In a moment, he heard the revving of the car's engine as it moved slowly into the garage.

He hurled himself forward, against the outside wall of the building, hoping the shadows would keep him hidden. Crouching as low as he could, he darted through the opening, flattened himself against the inside wall, then scrambled quietly for a dark corner.

He waited. The garage door stayed open for what seemed like an eternity when, finally, he heard it rumble and emit a high-pitched squeak until it shut with a thud. The people who'd driven into the garage, a man and a woman, got out of the car and walked to the elevator. He watched the man insert a key into the elevator, then the two of them got on.

The elevator, too, was secure. No problem. He didn't want to take the elevator anyway—he'd had enough of being trapped in a cage to last a lifetime. He'd take the stairs. She lived on twelve, but he could make it up that high easily. He'd worked out in prison, knowing the day would come when he'd have to rely on his strength, his body, to get him what he wanted. He went in the ultimate nerd—brainy, skinny, and a wimp. He came out buffed-up, handsome, and even more brilliant than before. A laugh bubbled up inside him. He loved irony.

When all was quiet, he took out his key chain flashlight and went to the car that had just driven in, used a jimmy to unlock the door, and lifted the remote control opener off the visor.

That was to make it easier if he ever had to come back. It was cold out there on the street.

Then he searched for the door to the stairs. He found it, just a little ahead. Someone had even stenciled the word "S-T-I-A-R-S" on it. Thoughtful, if illiterate.

Gripping the doorknob, he turned it. It didn't open. He tried again. The door was locked.

He looked around, flashing his small light at the walls, floor, ceiling. These people thought they were so clever, making the garage secure. But that meant all those in the building who used the garage always had to remember their elevator key, or the key to the stairwell. If they didn't, there was a phone so they could get the doorman from upstairs to come down and let them in. How many people, though, would want to call and make themselves feel foolish?

He spotted a tall cigarette tray in front of the elevator, a metal cylinder with a bowl of sand on the top. The elevator was probably a no smoking zone. Now, if some clever resident, knowing that not everyone remembered all their keys all the time . . .

He tipped the ashtray and flashed his light on the ground underneath it. He didn't see anything at first and was ready to give up, when the glint of metal against the gray concrete floor caught his eye. He bent lower, and, sure enough, there was the key.

He snatched it up. He had his doubts about using the elevator, though. If someone else got on, he couldn't explain his presence, and would have to kill the person. But how many people would be riding the elevator at 2:00 A.M.?

His heart pounding, he got on and pushed the button for twelve. As the door clanged shut, his body broke out in a sudden, cold sweat. He kept his finger on the Close Door button, in hopes that would trigger the mechanism to keep the doors shut and travel nonstop to twelve. The elevator lurched, then started climbing.

He reached under his jacket, and his hand closed around the handle of the combat knife as the elevator neared the lobby. This would be the most likely spot for someone else to get on.

He kept his eyes, unblinking, on the floor indicator. The lobby light was lit . . . would it stop? . . . then the 2 light came on. He breathed easier.

3 . . . 4 . . . 5 . . .

No one would be going between floors this time of night. He was home free.

6 . . . 7 . . . 8 . . .

The elevator lurched to a stop. He stared at the floor indicator: 9. What was going on?

The doors opened and a small child, wearing pajamas with little cowboys on ponies, stared up at him.

What the hell? His teeth gritted and his fingers tightened on the knife.

"Tommy!" A woman's voice shrieked. "Tommy, baby, what are you doing out of bed? Don't you dare get on there!"

He tried to make himself small, pressing his shoulder hard against the side, where the woman couldn't see him. His heart raced. If the kid got on and then his mother, he'd do what he had to. He couldn't have witnesses. But then he'd have to be fast with the Amalfi woman, which was too bad. He had planned to take his time with her, to enjoy her first. He scowled as hard as he could at the boy and in a deep, hushed whisper, said "Boo!"

Tommy's eyes widened, and he turned and ran to his mother.

He punched the Close Door button over and over until the doors finally shut. He leaned back against the wall, trying to breathe and get his heart back in his chest.

On twelve, the doors opened.

The hallway was well lit. There were only two doors on the floor—1201 and 1202. He turned toward 1202.

This would be the hardest part of the whole thing. If Angelina had a normal apartment door lock, he'd be able to get inside in about a minute with his MasterCard. If not, he'd have to try to get the door pick to work. He'd had it explained to him time and again in prison, and had practiced a lot, but it took a calm, cool hand. He would have done fine, except for that damn kid. Now his nerves were shot to hell.

He took out his MasterCard and slid it between the door and the jamb. Holding it almost sideways, he shoved it in farther, so that it bent around the door, then angled it downward until it touched the latch. Carefully, he worked the card until the latch caught, then farther until the card slipped from his fingers—and the door opened.

The apartment was pitch-black. He stood by the door, listening for any noise over the sound of his heartbeat and his own heavy breathing.

He thought again of the woman he'd held in his arms on the dance floor. The inspector's woman.

He'd make her his own, tonight. Before he killed her. He remembered lying atop the old woman as she'd struggled. How he'd reacted to the friction of her body against his. Just the thought of what he'd almost done with her had made him throw up later that day.

With Angelina, though, it'd all be different. She had wanted him. She'd smiled at him—even at the restaurant, she'd smiled and been friendly. He'd saved himself for her, just as he'd once saved himself for Heather.

As his eyes adjusted to the darkness, he could see a few shadows in front of him. He eased forward, expecting to find a chair or table blocking his path. Since the apartment remained quiet, he took out his flashlight and flicked it on, and gave the room a quick perusal.

The sight of his bouquet of roses on her coffee table brought a smile to his lips. He picked one up, gently lifted it to his nose, then, smiling, ripped the petals from the stem.

He tossed the rose aside when he spotted the telephone. Taking hold of the cord, he sliced it in two with his knife.

The kitchen was to the left of the living room, and just beyond it had to be her bedroom. He shut off the flashlight and headed for the room.

The air in Angelina's apartment didn't smell the way

he'd expected. There was a staleness, a masculinity to it. That had to mean she spent even more time than he thought entertaining men.

Now it was his turn to be entertained.

He stood in the bedroom, trying to make out her figure in the darkness. He inched toward the bed. What if she had her fiancé with her?

He hadn't thought of that before. That would change all his plans.

He could see the form of one person only on the bed. He smiled.

As he watched, thinking about her, he felt himself grow hard and reveled in the power it gave him. He knew exactly what he was going to do.

Still holding his knife, he groped around the top of her nightstand and found the telephone he was sure would be there. With a quick flick of the blade, he sliced that cord in two as well.

Feeling for the edge of the covers, he slowly eased them back. She lay on her side, facing away from him. Stretching his hand out, he let just one finger lightly touch her shoulder. He'd expected the feel of a nightgown, some lacy, fancy thing. Instead he felt bare skin. It shocked, yet thrilled him, and he snatched his hand back.

He lowered his zipper slowly, the metal teeth sounding as loud as machine gun fire in the quiet apartment. She didn't stir. Then, clutching the knife tight, he placed one knee on the bed, leaned over her, and then pressed his hand to her face, concentrating in the darkness on finding her mouth, stopping her screams. "Don't move," he whispered.

But her face was too big . . . too scratchy . . . bristly . . .

He yanked back his hand.

"What the—?" a masculine voice cried.

He slammed the knife down into the man.

The man screeched, arms and legs flailing in a tangle of bedsheets. He stabbed again, and the man gasped, then fell silent.

CHAPTER

TWENTY-NINE

The first thing Paavo saw as he stepped off the elevator was the pool of blood on the plush carpet between Angie's and Stan's apartments. Angie had phoned him and told him someone had broken into Stan's apartment and stabbed him. Stan had managed to crawl across the hall and knock until she opened the door. Paramedics were with him, and the police were on their way.

Both apartment doors stood open. Paavo's heart contracted painfully at how close such horror had come to Angie's quiet, elegant home. He glanced quickly into Stan's apartment. A patrolman had secured it until the crime scene investigators and the Crimes Against Persons detail arrived. He looked over the apartment, at the trail of blood from the bedroom to the front door and into the hall. Then his gaze fixed on a rose petal lying on the ground, and to the bouquet on Stan's coffee table. Roses. Another knife attack and roses.

He glanced over the room quickly once more. Robbery didn't seem to be the motive here. His eyes returned to the roses. Could it be coincidence? Lots of people had roses, after all. No, this was no coincidence.

He hurried into Angie's apartment. She was speaking quietly with a patrolman. Her hands, arms, and face were bloodied. Although he knew she hadn't been hurt, that the blood had to be Stan's, seeing her that way made him weak. She turned, and their gazes met.

In a moment, she was in his arms and he held her tight against his chest. He saw no tears, but her face wore a scared, hollow look that tore at him.

The patrolman walked up to Paavo, ready to question him, when he pulled out his badge. "Smith, Homicide."

"Gribbs, Central." The policeman sent a questioning glance from Paavo to Angie, and stepped back.

"Are you okay?" Paavo asked Angie, even as he ran his hands over her to assure himself that she was.

She nodded, then took a deep breath. "I was asleep when I heard a banging on my door." She shivered, and Paavo helped her to the sofa. He kept his arms around her. "I looked out the peephole, but couldn't see anything, then I heard someone moan. It was Stan, Paavo." Her voice broke. "It was awful." She put her face in her shaking hands. Paavo hugged her closer.

He looked at Gribbs. "Did you see the wounds?"

Gribbs nodded. "The cuts looked pretty deep. High, on his shoulders, front, and back."

"I've got to go to the hospital," Angie said, then glanced down at her bloodstained bathrobe. "I've got to dress."

Paavo helped her walk toward the bedroom. Her legs were wobbly as her adrenaline diminished, and the shock of finding her friend that way began to settle in. "I'll drive you there when you're ready," he said.

"Paavo, do you think that patrolman will let you into Stan's apartment to get his address book from his desk? I'd better telephone his parents. They live somewhere in Nebraska."

"I'll see what I can do."

"Why, Paavo?" she looked up at him.

"Why?"

"Why would anyone want to hurt Stan?"

The question hung between them, unanswered, as Paavo drove across the city to San Francisco General. When they arrived, Stan was already in surgery, and they were directed to the waiting area. Earlier, while Angie dressed, Paavo had phoned Yosh and asked him to get over to Stan's apartment. It wasn't a homicide, yet, but it was connected to the two they already had. He'd stake his life on it.

When he'd gone to get Stan's address book, he'd told the robbery inspector that Yoshiwara would be on his way to take over the investigation.

Now, as they sat and waited for the doctor to let them know how Stan came out of the surgery, Angie gradually calmed down and Paavo asked the question he'd been wondering about since his quick look around Stan's apartment.

"Did Stan tell you who gave him the roses?" Paavo asked.

"Roses? I didn't know he had any."

"Okay."

"Is it important?"

"It's nothing." He kissed her forehead as she rested her head on his shoulder. She was exhausted by the whole experience, physically as well as emotionally. He'd ask her more about the roses later, when she was more focused.

It was 7:00 A.M. before they got word that Stan was out of surgery and in intensive care. He'd lost a lot of blood, but nothing vital had been hit. With any luck, the prognosis was excellent. Paavo would try to question him, but he'd be surprised to find Stan coherent in much less than twenty-four to thirty-six hours.

Paavo took Angie back to his house. Something was going on that was very, very wrong, and much too close to Angie to suit him. He worried about her being alone. There was no logical reason, though, why he should worry about her.

Was there?

CHAPTER

T H I R T Y

Angie sat at a table in The Wings Of An Angel, drinking a cup of coffee and trying to pull herself together after the horrible night she'd had. Paavo had left for work before she woke up, so she took a cab back to her apartment. But thoughts of Stan plagued her, and she decided to go out for an hour or two.

She vaguely recalled Paavo's question at the hospital about roses, but everything had been in such a muddle she wasn't sure. Still, even today, she didn't remember Stan mentioning roses. He had said something about a strange deliveryman, though, hadn't he? What was it? *When* was it?

A customer walked in—the man with the lopsided glasses and the puppy-dog eyes she'd met a couple of days earlier. Earl showed him to a nearby table.

"You're crying." Puppy-dog eyes stopped as he passed her, his voice soft. "Is there anything I can do? Anything I can get you? Some water, perhaps?"

She shook her head. "I'll be fine. Thanks."

Earl pulled out a chair and waited impatiently until the customer sat. But he immediately turned in his chair and faced her again. "Would you like to talk about it?"

She wiped her eyes with her handkerchief and shook her head.

"I'm sorry." He folded his hands. "I didn't mean to pry."

"You didn't really," she said. "A friend of mine was. . . was hurt last night. He's in the hospital."

"How terrible! I'm so sorry. Will he be all right?"

"The doctors say so."

"Was it an accident?"

She sat up straight in the chair. The man was probably simply trying to be nice, but there was something about him she didn't care for. "No. He was attacked by someone. Some monster of a human being."

His eyes showed surprise. "Maybe it was a mistake."

"I don't care what it was. Whoever did it was evil, horrible!"

He reached for his water glass.

"Miss Angie." Earl stepped up to her with some coffee and a piece of pound cake. "Me an' Butch was hopin' dis might make you feel a little better. I tol' him how your friend was hurt an' dat you went up to da church dis mornin'. He said you was a good woman."

"I don't know about that, but thank you both. You're very thoughtful."

"You must be a regular here," the customer said, interrupting again. "Miss . . . Angie, is it?"

Earl stepped between the two tables. "Miss Angie don't wanna be distoibed. Is dere somet'in' you wanna eat or not?"

"Uh, yes. I do."

Earl handed him a menu. "I'd recommend da spaghetti an' meatballs."

He handed the menu back. "Fine."

Once Earl was back in the kitchen, the customer smiled at her. "My name's Carter, by the way."

She nodded and went back to reading the newspaper she'd brought in with her. The *North Beach Shopper* was new, a local advertiser that was given away door to door and left on sidewalk racks. She'd had a food column in an advertiser once. Didn't work out too well, though.

"I see you reading a neighborhood paper. I live near here myself," Carter added. "It's sure nice to have an inexpensive restaurant nearby."

"Yes, it is." She tasted the pound cake. As she suspected—straight from a grocery store shelf to her plate. Well, at least Butch and Earl had tried. She'd come here for nothing more than to spend a moment pulling herself together before calling Paavo and telling him that she was doing fine and was going back to her apartment. The attack on Stan had affected her deeply, but she understood that Paavo needed to concentrate on his cases and couldn't do it if he felt he'd have to hurry home to play nursemaid to her. The attack wasn't on *her*, after all. She had to get over the shock of Stan's being attacked. It was just that there were people in this world you never expect anything bad to happen to. Stan was one of them.

"Do you live nearby, Angie?" Carter interrupted again. "You seem to come here a lot."

"Not far."

"Maybe we're neighbors?" He gave her another of his puppy-dog smiles, yet his eyes had a hardness to them, a knowing glint at odds with the affable slackness of his mouth and jowls.

Something about the shape of his lips, the tone of his voice as he said her name was disarmingly familiar. Why? Where could she have met him previously?

They'd talked here once before. That must be what she was remembering. She tried to shake off the uneasiness she felt.

"I know all my neighbors," she said, making it clear the subject was closed.

"Oh, but—" He glanced past her, then turned around, suddenly finding the need to study his cutlery.

Peering over her shoulder, she followed his gaze to see Earl frowning fiercely at Carter. Earl walked over to her. "Miss Angie, I t'ink Butch could use a little help"—he cocked his head toward Carter— "if you'd like to come back into da kitchen."

"I'd love to."

"Just in time," Butch said as she entered. He stood over a large kettle with a wooden spoon. "I'm tryin' some polenta like you suggested."

Angie looked at the huge pot of golden polenta. He'd made enough to feed half of Italy. "Good. We'll use just a small batch of it to start. Did you roast any peppers?"

"They're in the oven right now."

Angie opened the oven door and found six large Fresno chilies. They'd softened nicely. She took them out and easily peeled off the hard, outer skin.

"You don't hafta let dat guy bug you none," Earl said, dishing out some spaghetti and meatballs.

"I don't want to be rude to your customers, Oil."

"What oil?" Butch asked.

"Him." Angie pointed.

"Earl?" Butch asked.

"Earl?" Angie repeated.

"Yeah, Oil. You was pronouncin' it jus' right, Miss Angie," Earl said.

She nodded. "Ah. I see. Anyway, I can handle that guy Carter."

"He's a bad egg, Miss Angie." Earl stated. "You keep away from him when I ain't around to look after you, okay?"

Butch hurled himself at the back door. "'Ey, Vinnie, get up here quick," he yelled. "You gotta come hear this!"

"Who's Vinnie?" Angie asked, stirring the polenta. "And why is he in the basement?"

"Yeah, Butch," Earl said. "You're so smart, tell da lady what's he doin' in da basement."

"It, uh"—Butch looked at the door to the basement then back at Angie—"it ain't a basement. It's an apartment. We stay down there to save money on rent."

"Oh? How clever. Restaurants are expensive to start up, that's for sure."

"What's all the yellin'?" Vinnie stepped into the kitchen.

"This is the Fed we was tellin' you about," Butch said. "Angelina Amalfi, meet Vinnie Freiman."

Vinnie frowned as they shook hands. "You called me to meet a Fed? Thanks, Butch. Just what I always wanted to do."

"Yeah, well, wait 'til you hear Earl. He's protectin' her from the other customers."

"Yeah?" Vinnie looked from Earl to Angie. "But if she's a Fed, maybe the other customers need protection from her?"

"I just don't like da looksa dat guy," Earl protested.

Angie mixed the pepper and polenta in a bowl. "You think he's some kind of crook?"

"Takes one to know one," Butch muttered, whereupon Vinnie stomped on his foot. Butch yelped.

Earl poured a glass of red wine and put it on the tray he was preparing.

"So," Vinnie said to Angie, "you teachin' Butch here how to cook?"

"I know how!" Butch grumbled.

"He's not bad," Angie said. She put some of her polenta and pepper on a plate, heaped grated Romano cheese on top, then spooned some of Butch's special spaghetti sauce over it and handed the plate to Vinnie. "Try it."

He took a spoonful. "Hey, this is good."

"What a screwball! Didn't I tell you dat guy's no good?" Earl came back into the kitchen, the tray still full of food. "Here I do all dis woik an' he takes off wit'out eatin'. He shoulda tol' me he was tireda waitin'.'"

Paavo walked into Homicide and tossed his notebook on his desk. Frustration was evident in every step he took.

"I guess it didn't go so well," Yosh said.

"No. St. Clair couldn't pick out anyone in the mug shots who resembled the guy he'd seen outside his place.

We doubted he could. Sometimes I don't like being right."

"I'm not having any luck either," Yosh said. "The car registration was filled out a couple of weeks ago in San Francisco. We tried to lift prints off the form, but it's been through too many hands. A handwriting analyst is looking over the writing, for whatever that's supposed to be worth."

"It'll give the chief something to say at the next briefing—police bring in handwriting expert to help solve vicious murders. Why does the public think some quack can do it better than us?"

"Because superstition is easier than hard work."

"Good point."

Paavo picked up the drawing the police artist had done based on St. Clair's description. There were no distinctive features shown—only a baseball cap shading the eyes, aviator sunglasses to cover the cheekbones, a straight nose, full lips, and a heavy jaw. The guy was apparently around six feet, muscular arms and shoulders, but slim waist and hips. Sounded like someone who worked out.

He could stop by a few gyms, Nautilus, whatever, and pass around the artist's sketch. A long shot, but maybe worth a try. There were a lot of those places, though. And would someone with such a clunker of a car have money for expensive gyms?

He could concentrate on inexpensive ones. Start with the Y, maybe? Where else? Heck, the cheapest places he knew of with workout equipment were prisons.

Prisons. An ex-con? Hanging around a judge? Possible. Very possible, in fact.

What if Angie was right about the DA? Fletcher and Tiffany's boss, Supervisor Wainwright, were friends— Paavo saw them at the Court House together. And Tiffany got the job through "connections." A judge and a DA. Interesting. Could there have been some trial, some case, they were both involved in?

But it wasn't the DA or the judge who were killed. It

was their women. Was that the connection? Or, was it a coincidence?

Damn. Much as he hated to think it, he had to believe that a criminal case, a trial, was the connection. He didn't have anything else to go on. And he never did like coincidence.

He tried reaching Angie again. She wasn't at her place or his. Where could she have gone—and would she tell him this time where she'd gone, or would she give him more of her mysterious nonanswers?

He tried the hospital. Stan hadn't awakened yet.

Paavo put down the phone in frustration. It was going to be another one of those days.

Myron Liu had worked in the computer center at the Hall of Justice for nineteen years, starting as a clerk and working his way up to the prime programmer in the department. He should have been made supervisor last month. Instead, he was passed over, again. This time for a woman brought in from San Francisco State University who didn't even know the police administration's computer system. He was sick and tired of it.

He watched Homicide Inspector Smith walk into their shop. He rose from his desk to help, when Ms. Smart-stuff stood up and gave him a look that told him to sit the hell back down and get to work.

He'd been helping Homicide for fifteen years. No one was better at filling their requests than him. Now, she was going to cut him out of this part of his job as well. What was up? Did they want to fire him?

He kept his head down as Smart-stuff came up to him a couple of minutes later.

"Here's a request from Homicide that I want you to get right on." She slapped a form on his desk. "I want a computer printout of every case that Judge Lucas St. Clair and attorney Lloyd Fletcher were involved in together."

"When Lloyd Fletcher was DA or even before that?" Liu asked.

"I said *all* of them, didn't I?"

He nodded. "You want complete SF records?"

"I want it as complete as you can make it!"

He lowered his gaze once more. "Really? As complete as that?"

"You *do* understand English, don't you?"

His cheeks burned. "I'll start the search immediately."

"Good."

Clenching his teeth to stop himself from telling his boss exactly what he thought of her, he began the development of a search program that accessed court databases throughout California, from tiny Yolo County, to the city and county of Los Angeles.

He looked over what he'd done. On second thought, she'd said she wanted it as complete as he could make it. He changed "California" to "US." Yes, Ms. Smart-stuff, he thought, I *do* understand English. I can make this search very complete indeed. He just hoped Inspector Smith wasn't in too much of a hurry.

CHAPTER

THIRTY-ONE

"I'm sorry, Mandy," Angie said. "I didn't think you'd be so busy at seven-thirty at night."

Mandy Dunleavy, one of Angie's best friends in high school, dropped into the rocking chair. "If I don't get the kids down early, I don't have any time to myself."

"Time for you and Collin, right?"

"Yeah, right."

"Do you expect him home soon?"

"Like I'm supposed to know? I'm just his wife. Why would he tell me? I cook, clean, keep the house. Does Collin care? Does he help?"

Angie tried not to show her surprise. Mandy and Collin were inseparable in high school and married shortly afterward. Angie and had always thought of them as the perfect couple.

"I'm sorry." Mandy sat wearily. "I don't know what got into me. What was it you wanted me to help you with?"

"Well . . ." Angie cleared her throat, suddenly having her doubts as to whether this was the right time to ask her questions.

"Yes?"

"You and Collin were always so much alike. You had so much in common. It made me wonder if that's a key to a happy marriage?"

Mandy gave a hollow laugh. "Me and Collin?"

"Yes."

"We were alike, weren't we? We shared everything once."

"Exactly. Isn't that important?"

"I don't know, Angie. For the last few years, we've seemed to grow more and more apart. Without shared interests, there isn't much else between us."

"I'm sorry. I didn't realize."

"Oh well, we might work it out. Who knows? There are times that marriage is really good—even mine and Collin's." She glanced at the clock on the mantel, ticking the minutes by. "But there are other times, Angie, when the kids are in bed, and the house is quiet, and you watch the clock and wonder where your husband is, and who he might be with . . ."

Mandy's gaze grew flat, haunted. "Times like that, marriage is the loneliest experience you've ever had in your whole life."

CHAPTER

THIRTY-TWO

Angie sat at a table by the window of The Wings Of An Angel, reading her script for the TV show she would audition for the next day. Thank goodness they'd finally called her. After all, she might have had other irons in the fire if they'd waited much longer—something a whole lot better than a show on a predominantly Farsi station, too. On the other hand, considering the butterflies in her stomach with this audition, if it were any bigger, they'd have to carry her out to the TV cameras on a stretcher.

"I was hoping I'd find you here again."

A shadow fell across her script, and she looked up to see Carter standing in front of her. "Oh, it's you," she said. Earl's warning rang in her ear.

"It's good to see you again, Angie." He slid his hands in his back pockets. "You make this restaurant special."

Earl ran up to Carter. "You back? You gonna stick around dis time and eat?"

"I intend to."

"We don't like guys who order food den skip out on us. Dat's a warnin', bud. You can sit over dere."

"Oh . . . well . . ." He looked expectantly from Angie to

the empty chair at her table and back, but when no invitation was forthcoming, he went with Earl to the next table.

Two other tables had customers—two women at one and a man at the other. Angie was glad to see that a few other people had begun to discover the restaurant. She had brought in some lace curtains she no longer used and helped Earl hang them this morning. They added a nice touch. She also gave him a brochure from a restaurant supply house for some white tablecloths and napkins, and suggested old-fashioned wooden chairs to replace the aluminum ones. The fifties decor just didn't do it for her.

Earl took Carter's order, then stopped at Angie's table on his way to the kitchen. "I forgot to ask, how's your friend doin', Miss Angie? Da one who got stabbed."

"Much better. Thanks, Earl."

"He know who stabbed him?"

"I don't think he ever saw the man."

"Yeah? Dat's too bad. You call da police about it?"

"Of course!"

"Yeah, I shoulda figgered dat. Dey know anyt'in' about it?"

"Not yet. Actually, my boyfriend's got the case. He's a homicide inspector. We went to see Stan in the hospital last night, but he wasn't able to answer any of Paavo's questions yet."

"I didn't know your boyfriend was a cop. A cop and a Fed. Man, you two must have to follow laws about kissin'."

"Not quite," Angie said with a laugh.

"So, what's Homicide doin' wit' a stabbin'?"

"It's similar to a couple of other big cases he's got."

"Busy guy, huh? Guess you don't see him much."

"Not only that, he's got a third case, too. One where someone's been going around the city stealing fake Fabergé eggs. In one robbery, a clerk was killed. You better warn the jeweler next door. He's got one of those eggs in his window."

"Man, someone got killed 'cause of some kinda egg?

What's dis world comin' to? I gotta tell Butch. He's got a dozen of them."

"Wait," she called him back. "It's an art piece shaped like an egg. Some of them open up and there are delicate porcelain figures or jewels inside."

"Yeah? People buy dose t'ings?"

"They certainly do. A friend of mine works in a shop that sells them. I was thinking that she and I should make a prominent display of a bunch of them, then hide in the back room, and when someone tried to steal them, we'd call Paavo to make the arrest."

"Sounds kinda dangerous, Miss Angie, for a coupla gals."

"Not if you join us, Earl," she said, teasing him. His expression, though, remained serious.

"I don't t'ink so. But I'll ask Vinnie. He's got da brains in da gang—I mean, group."

A pager went off. The man sitting alone took it off his belt, looked at it, then stood to pay his bill and leave.

"I was joking, Earl," Angie said as she watched the man with the pager. "But actually, that's what we need—a silent pager. We need to put bugs inside a bunch of those eggs. Then, when the thief strikes, we could get it to beep silently and follow him to his hiding place. We'd catch him."

"Dat's a good idea. Maybe you oughta be a crook."

"Only problem is where to get such a device."

"Excuse me," Carter called, sliding his chair a bit closer to Angie. "I couldn't help but hear a bit of your conversation. I'm a licensed electrician, and I know some people who've been developing a prototype of a device very similar to what you're talking about."

Angie didn't like eavesdroppers, even if they might be helpful ones. It seemed a little too convenient, and this guy a little too pushy, to suit her. "That's all right. We're just doing a little speculating here."

"It's a very sound idea, you know."

Sound? What was he? A punster?

"I can see your skepticism," he said hurriedly. "But I really do know what I'm talking about, and I can access a lot of items not generally available. Take this." He reached into his shirt pocket, pulled out a small plastic case, and opened it. Inside was a tiny metal chip that looked like a wristwatch battery. "It doesn't look like much, but with it, I can break into very sophisticated voice mail and fax systems—and can make copies of every message or fax being sent to the number I'm tapped into."

"You can?" Angie studied the chip, unsure if she ought to believe him or not. But why would he lie about such a thing?

"Internet accounts, e-mails, home answering machines—they're easiest, in fact."

"Dere's always guys wit' big ideas, Miss Angie. You can't trust 'em."

Carter ignored Earl and kept right on talking. "There's another device that works like a reverse paging system. I install them in luxury cars all the time. They can also be used in dogs, cats . . . kids, although we don't do any of that yet. Suppose your car is stolen, or your child is kidnapped. You follow the beep, which is silent since you don't want to alert the thief or kidnapper, and it'll lead you to it."

Angie thought she might have heard about something like he was describing. "That's impressive," she said.

"My friends are working on a microchip that does the same thing. The chips should go for about a hundred dollars a pop."

"That's all?"

"The biggest part of the cost with cars is the installation—you don't want anything a thief can see and remove. Also, the ones for cars are a lot more powerful than the one I'm talking about for you. They're good for hundreds of miles. These microchips, on the other hand, have a radius of about ten miles. From the place where stolen to a fence who'll pay cash for them inside the city."

"Interesting."

"Yeah, until da car t'iefs and dose udders figger out howta break da signal."

"But in the meantime, Earl," Angie said, her mind racing with possibilities, "I wouldn't mind learning a little more about them."

"By the way, waiter," Carter said, moving to Angie's table, "I'd like another glass of wine."

"Dat guy's gotta go," Earl muttered, pouring some house wine into a glass.

"What guy's that?" Butch asked, checking on the Italian sausage he was now offering with omelets, polenta, or in a sandwich.

"Da one always hangin' around Angie. He's back."

"I think *you* wanna be the only one hangin' around her," Butch said. "She even has you puttin' up curtains like some little househusband. You two was really cute this mornin'." He snorted with laughter.

"Where's Vinnie? He downstairs?"

"Naw. Now she's got him buyin' chairs an' tablecloths. He's afraid she'll get suspicious if he don't. He don't want no suspicious Feds now that we're so close."

"We're close, huh?" Earl asked, turning a hangdog gaze on Butch.

"Yeah." Butch kept his head bowed, not wanting to look at his partner. He checked on his sausages. Angie had taught him to fry them in water instead of oil to make them less greasy. They were browning nicely. "It'll be nice to not have so much work to do alla time. Just sit around and count our money."

"Yeah. I'm really lookin' forward to it." Earl pushed the swinging door open a little way and eyed Angie talking with Carter. "You, too, Butch?"

"Sure. Me, too. Why not? You don't think I care about this place, do you?"

"Heck no, Butch. Me neither."

*   *   *

"I don't think this is something you should get involved in, Angie." Connie Rogers's worried frown annoyed Angie. Her plan was perfectly safe.

"I'm not getting involved. It's a test, that's all." She moved the miniature glass swan to the back of the display counter and the turtle to the front. Swans were out this season. "He's an electrician. He knows about such things. Tomorrow, I'm meeting him at the restaurant and buying one from him."

"But what if it doesn't work?"

"Then I'm out a hundred dollars and feeling duped. It won't be the first time," she answered. "Anyway, I bought the egg. It's mine to do with as I wish, right? And I wish to leave it in your shop. As soon as I get the device, I'll put it in my egg. Then, you take it to your apartment when you leave the shop at night, and I'll try to track it from my place. Since I don't know where you live, it'll be a great test. Then, if it works, I'll tell Paavo. The police can bug about five or ten eggs in the city, take all the others out of the stores, and when the thief strikes, they'll follow the beeper and catch him. It's so simple a child could do it!"

"If it's so easy, why don't the police use this pager-thing already?"

"Paavo says local police forces never have state-of-the-art equipment."

Connie looked dubious. "I don't like it."

"Look at it this way. If Paavo doesn't have to think about this case, he'll spend more time trying to find Tiffany's killer."

"But I thought Tiffany's case already had his full attention."

"It has, but you know him. He's got all the Easter Egg Murder information stored in his head. Whenever he hears anything about the case, he gets involved all over again. What will it hurt to try? My last idea turned out well, didn't it? Have confidence!"

"Why? You've got enough for both of us," Connie said, and then gave a sigh of resignation.

CHAPTER

$\infty\infty\infty$

THIRTY-THREE

"Quiet on the set! Take *eleven*? I mean, take eleven!"
SNAP!

Angie took a deep breath. Looking straight at the camera
she tried her best, under sweltering lights that hung within
inches of her face, to smile instead of cry. What she wanted
more than anything was to wipe away the perspiration dripping from her forehead. But that would smear her quarter-
inch-thick TV makeup. Considering that the makeup
artist's idea of female beauty was a face that resembled a
Barbie doll, that might not have been a bad idea.

The director, cameraman, and assistant—the only ones
there besides her—were hidden in the darkness, while she
stood in a two-by-four-foot area with a sink, range, and
butcher block counter, wearing a once-gorgeous Oscar de
la Renta blue dress with the sort of understated simplicity
she'd thought would look elegant on TV.

It did, before she began to drip with perspiration and
flour. Behind her, cardboard had been painted to look like
kitchen cabinets and a window overlooking a giant sun-
flower-filled garden, reminiscent of the road to Oz. Maybe
that's where she was, come to think of it.

"I've put two cups of flour and two cups of mashed potatoes into this bowl," she said, smiling broadly as she tilted the bowl toward the camera. Her head bobbed up and down so that she could look at the camera and not drop the bowl—as she had back in the fifth take.

"Now it's a matter of mixing the two together so that they form a sticky pasta dough for your *gnocchi*. Remember, even though it's spelled to look like 'ga-no-chee,' it's pronounced 'nyohk-key'." She smiled again.

"Watch those smiles! Television is serious business," growled the director, who clearly fancied himself the Ingmar Bergman of cooking shows. He'd already interrupted her during take four to explain that this was a cooking lesson, not a lecture on Italian pronunciation or an advertisement for cosmetic dentistry. Takes one, two, and three hadn't made it to the insults stage. But after that, things had gone from bad to worse.

Stiffening her shoulders, she put the bowl with three cups of flour, one large potato, mashed, and one and a half cups of water under the mixer, hit the On button for the heavy tongs to whir, and jumped back out of the way. At take six the director had upset her so much that she failed to add the water, so when she turned on the mixer dry flour shot all over the studio, burying her and the set in a cloud of white powder. She still had some in her hair. So much for her $175 styling job. Instead of sexy blond highlights, she had aging white globules.

The next take had ended because they hadn't gotten all the flour off the camera—or the cameraman—and it looked like she was cooking in the middle of a snowstorm. A sneeze ended take eight. The film ran out on take nine. And an attack of giggles from the director's assistant ruined take ten.

But now the mixer whirred nicely. When the dough looked to be the right consistency, she stopped the blades, grabbed a dollop of the mixture, pulled and tugged at it, and then broke off a tiny piece and tasted it.

"Fine. Now we're ready—"

"*WHAT do you think you're doing?*"

"Testing it."

"You're not supposed to play with the product with your fingers!" The director stormed into the lights to face her, waving his hands in the air. "And we certainly don't advocate eating raw dough on our program. *Tell* the people what it's supposed to look like, Miss Amalfi, so that they can see for themselves if it's ready."

"But . . . you can't tell by just looking."

He got down on one knee. "Pretend, Miss Amalfi. This is television, after all."

She wasn't in the least amused by this man's histrionics. "Fine," she said.

He got up and went back to his chair. "Let's start from this spot."

In the dark, someone snickered.

"Three, two, one. Take twelve." *SNAP!*

"See how the flour and potato have combined to form a dough. Once that's done, it's time for you to make the gnocchi. Here's a simple way to do it. Take about a half cup of dough." She grabbed a small handful of it. "Then roll it into a long tube, about a half inch around. After that's done, lay the tube down on a cutting board and cut it into two-inch-long pieces. See these cute little tubes? That's the way you need to make them. Then, you take that lovely cut glass bowl that's been sitting in your dining room, probably doing nothing but gathering dust, and you carefully turn it upside down—"

"*Stop! Right there! Hold everything!*"

The director marched over and planted himself in front of her, his arms crossed over his chest.

She gave him a cold stare. "Yes?"

"You think this is some kind of joke, don't you?"

"Not at all."

"You think that because you don't like the name *Angelina in the Cucina* that you can come here and make a laughingstock out of this show!"

"What did I do?"

"If you tell people to take that damn bowl and put it on their heads, you're out of here, lady. Do you understand?"

"All I'm doing," she explained calmly, "is trying to show my audience the best way to make the gnocchi." She turned the bowl upside down. "You take one little tube of rolled dough," she said, demonstrating as she spoke, "and put three fingers along the tube, then press down in the center and r-o-l-l it along the cut glass. This way, you get a hole in the center of the tube, and indentations from the cut glass make a pretty pattern. You can also roll it along a cheese grater, but that's tacky for television."

"I'm not going to have you stand here and tell people to poke their fingers into pasta and roll it on the outside of bowls! Television is art, Miss Amalfi. Not play school!"

"But if you don't form the *gnocchi* properly, the center will be doughy and heavy and taste horrible!"

"Do it some other way!" he bellowed.

Angie got down off the phony kitchen platform. "I'll do it right, or not at all. After all, I know what I'm doing, which is more than I can say for you!"

"How dare you! You . . . you *ptomaine pusher!*"

"I'll bet Yan Can Cook never had this kind of trouble." She picked up her bowl, gave a harrumph, and marched out of the studio.

He sat on a stool in the basement telephone closet just off the garage of Angelina's apartment building and studied the phone lines and cabling. If only I could show you, Angelina—my Angelina—how truly brilliant I am, you'd be even more impressed with me, he thought. The lines were marked to the different apartments, but to be certain, he used the cellular phone he'd lifted from an unlocked Lincoln Town Car in the garage. The phone book showed an A. Amalfi. He dialed the number.

"Hi. This is Angie. I can't answer your call . . . "

Smiling, he attached her phone wire to a large metal box and turned up the volume control to listen to the rest of her message. The very sound of her voice was enough to make him hard with wanting her. Sitting with her at lunch had been an exquisite torment.

Her answering machine beeped, waiting for his message. When none came, it waited patiently for a few seconds, then not so patiently shut itself off.

But not completely. His phone trap blinked knowingly at him, telling him it was on and working. Listening, invading her apartment. Her privacy. Her.

"It was horrible, absolutely horrible." Angie stood in front of Paavo's desk and burst into tears.

He jumped to his feet. He'd rather face a murder suspect any day than Angie crying. "What is it?"

"Oh, God. They were so mean, so. . . so *evil!*" Her sobs grew louder. "He even called me a ptomaine pusher!"

The other detectives were watching. Even without looking their way, Paavo could feel their grins, their knowing glances at each other, their curiosity as to what Angie was involved with now.

He hustled her into an interview room, grabbing a handful of Kleenex from Inspector Mayfield's desk as he went by.

"Here." He handed Angie the tissues and shut the door. "Tell me what's wrong."

Angie wiped her eyes. "I'm sorry. I didn't mean to carry on like this, but I tried so hard. I wanted everything to be so perfect. I even cut my fingernails for the *gnocchi*, and now . . . "

He pulled one of the chairs out from the metal table and helped Angie sit. "Does this have anything to do with your audition this morning?" he asked, standing before her.

She nodded.

"It didn't go well, I take it."

She shook her head, wiping the tears that had started once more.

"Wasn't this your first audition, Miss Amalfi?" he said, keeping his expression serious, his tone professional.

She glanced at him. "Yes."

"Do you know how many times even the biggest TV stars had to audition before they got a show?"

"No."

"Well," his voice grew soft and gentle, "I have it on good authority that Leno went through dozens of auditions, and no one would touch Letterman for years. Julia Child wore out an oven before anyone would pick up her show."

She gave a half smile. "You're just saying that."

"Would I lie?" He sat in the chair beside her. "Nobody expected you to be perfect the very first time you tried it."

She used more Kleenex. "I did."

"I know." He covered her hand with his. "Did they tell you specific things they didn't like?"

"Just about everything."

"But some things more than others."

She had to think about this. "I guess so."

"Good. That's a place to start. Think about what they didn't like, what you can do to change or improve what you did, and then get out there and try again."

She dropped her gaze. "I couldn't do that. I feel like such a fool."

He lifted her chin and looked into her teary brown eyes, trying to gauge the extent of her disappointment. "You're no fool, Angie. You're clever and beautiful. If you want it enough, you'll probably be on TV some day, and then there'll be no stopping you. You can be anything you want."

Her arms circled his neck, and she pressed her cheek to his. "I wish I believed in myself half as much as you believe in me, Paavo." Then she raised her head again and sighed. "I know I try to talk big, but sometimes I feel like such a fraud."

He stroked her back. "You're no fraud, Angie. Not at all. The only problem you have is being impatient. Have patience, and believe me, you're going to do just fine."

"Do you really think so?"

"I know so."

She hugged him a long while, her eyes teary for another reason now. "What would I do without you?"

"Probably quite well."

"Never!"

He stood and helped her to her feet, then glanced at his watch. "Why don't we get out of here and have some lunch? I think a nice dessert in particular will make the world a much brighter place for you."

"Lunch? Oh . . . I . . . I can't. It's Lent."

"Forget the dessert, then."

"Well, I'd like to, but I'm . . . busy."

"Oh?" He frowned. "Something important?"

"No. I mean, yes. My . . . my mother. I promised Serefina I'd meet her. I'd better get going."

"I see."

"Maybe dinner?" she suggested.

He hesitated. He knew he could get away for a while now, but by tonight, he wasn't sure. "I'll know better later. I'll call."

"Hmm. Maybe you'll get some help in one of these cases soon," she said with a sudden cat-that-swallowed-the-canary smile.

"It would certainly help." Especially help us, he wanted to add.

"See you tonight." She gave him a kiss that scorched, then slipped from his arms, left the interview room, and headed out the door, waving a cheerful good-bye to the men in the office. He knew he was going to be in for a lot of ribbing about this little visit.

CHAPTER

THIRTY-FOUR

Paavo went to the computer center and asked for his printout. The new supervisor told him the job was still running.

"What do you mean, it's still running?" he asked. "There's never been this kind of delay before."

"It's a big job," she said huffily.

"Not that big."

She gazed pointedly at him. "You want us to be complete, don't you?"

"Where's Mr. Liu?"

"Myron has gone home." The supervisor picked up a stack of printouts and loudly rapped their edges against the desk top to straighten them. Also, Paavo figured, to let him know he was being dismissed. "I'll handle this," she said curtly.

"Can you get me the printout right now?"

"That's impossible."

"I want Liu here in twenty minutes."

"You can't order me around like that!"

He stared at her. He didn't bother to reply. Or to leave.

"All right." She sniffed. "I'll phone his house. But I'm not guaranteeing anything."

A half hour later, Myron Liu contacted Homicide.

"I'm at my computer, Inspector," he said to Paavo. "Tell me exactly what you need, and I'll get it for you right now."

"I want a list of any cases that Judge Lucas St. Clair and DA Lloyd Fletcher worked on together, in any capacity at all. Got it?"

"Yes. Give me ten minutes."

"I'll be right down," Paavo said.

Angie stood with Earl near the entrance to The Wings Of An Angel.

"Now, you sure you ain't gonna be alone wit' dis guy?" Earl asked again.

"I promise." She smiled. It was kind of cute seeing him act the Dutch uncle with her.

"I don't even like you doin' business wit' him."

"Shhhh! Here he comes."

Carter walked into the restaurant. A hard look flashed across his face when he saw Earl, but it softened immediately as his gaze met Angie's. In that instant, as she noted his quick cover-up, all her own misgivings about the man revived. She was glad she was meeting him here and nowhere less public.

This was a business transaction. Nothing more. And she wanted it over with.

They sat at a table, Earl hovering nearby.

"This piece needs to be hidden in the egg," Carter said, showing her a tiny round piece of metal. "Then you take this monitor"—he patted a black box with colored lights on it— "and it homes in on the pager. It blinks green as you get closer and red as you back away."

He carried the chip to one end of the restaurant and demonstrated how the monitor worked. Sure enough, the red and green lights blinked as he moved forward and back. She nodded sagely.

"Put the chip in the egg," Carter went on, "then take

the control home and hit this reset button. When—if—the egg starts to move, the control box will blink if it moves closer to or farther away from you."

"That seems easy enough," Angie said, deliberately giving a cool, businesslike edge to her voice.

"It is. But how about I come along to make sure it works."

"That won't be necessary. I've written a check for a hundred dollars. Who should I make it out to?"

"Oh . . . Carter Westin is the name."

She wrote out his name. "Here you are." She gave him the check and picked up the device. "Thank you."

"Shall we have some wine?" Carter suggested. "A little something to eat?"

"Miss Angie," Earl said, "Butch is waitin' for your lesson about da rigatoni."

"Thanks, Earl. I'm sorry, Carter. Good-bye." So saying, Angie turned and hurried to the kitchen, Earl bustling along right behind her.

The computer listing had fourteen names on it. They were all dated seven to fifteen years ago—covering the time Fletcher presented cases as an assistant district attorney for the city, up to St. Clair's retirement. Paavo glanced over the names, then handed the list to Yoshiwara.

"Let's see," Yosh said. "Darrin Alonzo, Percy Alexander, Dan Barrett, Peter Callahan, Wesley Carville, Manny Dain . . . lots of names here, pal. How do you want to handle this?"

Paavo frowned. None of the names meant anything to him. "Do you want the first half of the alphabet, or the last?"

Before pulling the criminal records for his half of the names on the list, Paavo drove over to the hospital and questioned Stan, still heavily medicated, but able to mumble a few words. Paavo could just make them out. Stan hadn't seen his attacker, but somehow he knew the man was muscular.

Paavo asked about the roses. Stan couldn't remember anything about them, not who had sent them or why. That was strange—how often did a man get flowers? He'd ask again later.

Back in Homicide, the files waited for him.

Alonzo and Hurley still in jail. Forget them.

Alexander, vehicular manslaughter, out six months.

Barrett, dealing heroin. Out for four years. Seemed to have gone straight.

Callahan, in and out a half dozen times for robbery, drugs, pimping. Latest release last December. Career criminal.

Carville, second-degree murder. Out since late February. Model prisoner, no priors.

Dain, in for rape, skipped out on parole three months earlier. Still not located.

Paavo moved Callahan and Alexander to his highly doubtful stack. Career criminals and drunk drivers rarely turned into sexual psychopathic killers. Barrett—four years straight. A maybe. That left Carville and Dain as probables. Dain would be his sole likely candidate if it wasn't for the timing of Carville's release. Carville got out just a short while before the first murder was committed.

Also, Carville was the only murderer on his list.

Paavo looked up at the city map hanging on the wall, on which Calderon had posted the Fabergé egg robberies. From the address in his file, Carville was living in a cheap hotel in the Tenderloin district. He probably didn't own a car yet.

What was he supposed to have done, ride the Muni to commit murder? Ride a smelly bus with food wrappings, undefinable crud and wads of gum all over the floor . . .

He jumped up and hurried to the map. Could it be? It was too simple, he thought. But on the other hand, why not?

The first robbery—the one during which Nathan Ellis had been killed—took place one block off the Geary bus line on Post Street. The next, farther west, a block off the bus line on O'Farrell. Number three was west again, this time on Sutter Street. The fourth jumped all the way to the Richmond district's Clement Street, a block off Geary, and very close to the city's Russian immigrant community, centered around a large, beautiful Russian Orthodox church . . . located on Geary Street.

In fact, if the pattern held up, then on Tuesday— today—the next robbery would be somewhere on the Geary bus line to the west of the spot where the last one occurred.

Paavo called the Holy Virgin Cathedral and asked when they held services. Daily, eight in the morning and six at night.

That meant morning service ended about nine. Since it took a city bus nearly an hour to get from Twenty-sixth and Geary through traffic down to the Sans Souci Jewelers, a bus-riding thief would arrive at 10:00 A.M., when the store first opened.

Two robberies had occurred between 10:00 and 11:00 A.M., and two between 4:00 and 5:00 P.M.

The idea of a church-going thief was too crazy. Paavo didn't know if he believed this idea of his or not.

Quickly, he opened the phone book, looked for gift shops and jewelers near the Orthodox church, and started phoning. One shop, the Volga Jewelers, between Eighteenth and Nineteenth Avenues, carried Fabergé replicas.

He tried to reach O'Rourke in Robbery, but O'Rourke was out on a bank holdup. He glanced at the clock. Three-forty-five. It was a long shot. But in case he was right, he didn't want to blow it.

He was almost out the door when he hurried back to his desk and made a call to Angie. There'd be no dinner date for him this evening.

"Hi! This is Angie. I can't answer your call right now . . ."

He nearly hung up. But then he remembered her irritation at the way he wouldn't leave her a message whenever he called. He might not have a chance to call back.

"Angie. It's me. I can't come by for dinner. Something came up. I want to see you, though. Maybe I can meet you later. Call anytime. I'll be here most of the night."

He hung up feeling like a tongue-tied teenager. The message probably made little sense. God, but he hated those machines.

"I can't do it tonight, Angie," Connie said.

"But I've got the paging device right here." Angie put her purse on the counter at Everyone's Fancy and pulled out the black box and the small chip. "I bought the egg from you, remember? In case it got stolen, and we couldn't retrieve it."

Connie frowned. "I'd like to help out. But . . . maybe we should give the police more time. I don't want to mess them up."

"This won't mess them up. It's between you and me."

"Well . . . the other thing is your cousin Buddy called me last night. He came over, and we . . . we hit it off really well. Tonight we're going out for dinner. I don't know what time, or if, well, what time, I'll get home."

Ah-ha! Angie thought. That explained Connie's languid, off-in-the-clouds demeanor today. She was acting like a woman in the throes of newfound passion. Despite her and Buddy both having had bitter experiences with love, and particularly with marriage in the past, they'd sought each other out and were ready to make a try at a having a good relationship this time. Angie added this bit of news to her marriage survey.

"I'm glad," Angie said. "Well, we can always try another day."

Connie looked relieved. "Here," she said, handing Angie the wooden box with the egg inside. "It's almost Easter. Why don't you take it home and enjoy it the way it was meant to be. The police will do okay with this one. Trust them."

"I do." Angie took the box. "But sometimes I think they need a little nudge, that's all."

Paavo drove down Geary Boulevard. He had just passed Eighteenth Avenue when he saw a small, bearded man slipped into the Volga Jewelers. He double-parked, flashers blinking, drew his gun, and hurried toward the shop.

Two women stepped out of a restaurant in front of Paavo. "Police! Stay back," he said. They ran back indoors.

He kept his body against the wall and slowly leaned forward to look into the shop from the big storefront window. The jeweler was lifting a Fabergé egg into a paper bag. The robber's gun was drawn.

Paavo waited until the thief had the paper bag, his gun no longer pointed at the owner, and then he stepped into the shop. "Police!" he shouted. "Drop the gun."

The thief didn't move. The jeweler froze.

"Drop it *now*. Raise your hands and turn around."

The gunman let go of the gun and it fell to the floor. He turned slowly and, facing Paavo, reached up and removed his beard, then peeled the short, black hair from his head.

When the wig was gone, shoulder-length brown hair, streaked with gray, bushed out around a ravaged, tear-stained face. The thief was a woman.

"It's not my fault," she said. The woman was of medium height, with a frail build. She looked in her early to mid-fifties.

Paavo pulled her arms behind her back and slipped handcuffs on her. As he did so, Officer McMahon from the Richmond Station showed up in response to Paavo's earlier request.

Paavo turned the thief over to the officer to read her her rights.

The jeweler, a thin, wiry little man, walked up to him,

his hand extended. "I'm Gregorovitch. Thank you for coming so quickly. When I got your call, I couldn't believe anyone would really want to steal such a thing. Then, when I saw the gun . . ." He shook his head.

"You did well," Paavo said, shaking his hand.

"I didn't want to hurt anyone," the thief cried. "I wouldn't have hurt him. I was just trying to help myself. Those eggs aren't worth much, you know. Just a little. This isn't even a felony, is it?"

"Armed robbery is a felony," Paavo replied. "And so is murder."

"Murder!"

"The murder of Nathan Ellis, the clerk at Sans Souci Jewelers. A young man with a wife, a future."

"But I didn't mean to—" She turned her head, her lower lip trembling.

"What's your name?" Paavo asked.

"Claudia Zelenin." Her voice was little more than a whisper.

"Address?"

"Ninety-three Presidio Terrace."

He glanced up at the posh address. "Do you live with anyone?"

"Alone. The house was once my parents'. It's mine now."

"Occupation?"

"I don't do anything," she replied. "The house is all I have left. It takes every bit of cash I can put my hands on just to pay property taxes."

"I see. It's tough." Paavo managed to keep a straight face. The house was probably worth a million, easy.

"That's why I needed the Fabergé eggs." Her hands were clasped, her eyes pleading. "I had a Fabergé once, you see, but it was stolen. It was a family heirloom, taken away from me."

"You had a real Fabergé egg?" He had read enough about them to know how impossible that was. They were museum pieces.

"Not an egg, but a ring box. It was very small and simple for Fabergé, but incredibly valuable nonetheless."

"Excuse me, Ms. Zelenin," he interrupted. "You might want to speak with your attorney before you say any more."

"I know," she said. "It's just that all this is so silly. So frustrating. I'm no criminal, to be handcuffed. I'm the victim." She spoke quickly, growing more impassioned with each word. "My grandfather brought the Fabergé with him when he left Russia, you see. But I was so stupid, I let someone come into my house, into my heart, and take it from me." Suddenly she began to sob. "I would have done anything for him! Anything! But he just wanted my money and valuables."

"And that's what drew you to the fake Fabergés?" Paavo asked.

"They're not fakes! I know they aren't worth much yet. But someday they might be. They are from Fabergé artisans, you see. No one thought, in the time of the tsars, that Fabergé pieces would become so valuable. These might be the same. It doesn't seem fair that I don't have any at all anymore. All I want is one good one—one to make up for that which love took away from me. Is that too much to ask?"

Paavo nodded to Officer McMahon to take the woman to City Jail and book her.

He had wanted to know why the thief had killed Nathan Ellis, why the eggs were so important that anyone would take a young man's life for one. It amazed him still, the foolish things people could do when caught up in the throes of newfound passion; and the even more foolish things they did afterward to make up for it.

He took a statement from the owner, then left the store and hurried to his car, which was still blocking traffic.

As he drove away, though, the thought of the foolish things we do for love reverberated in his mind. And suddenly he knew where he was heading.

* * *

"Smith! Who the hell do you think you are coming to my house? I told you already you're taking this thing too far," Fletcher said. The district attorney stood in the black-and-white marble foyer of his mansion, holding the carved solid oak door only halfway open.

Paavo put his hand against the door and pushed. Fletcher backed off and let him enter. "Where do you want to talk?" Paavo asked. "In the living room? Or, would you rather someplace private . . . away from your wife, for instance."

Fletcher's eyes narrowed. "I have nothing to hide. But I don't want to upset her by any crazy accusations. Let's go into the den."

They entered a room that was paneled in rosewood, lined with library shelves. An oversize desk with a leather top stood in the center of the room, a straight-backed chair behind it and two matching leather wing chairs in front.

Paavo dropped his files and mug shots on Fletcher's desk, then sat in one of the wing chairs. "This isn't a game, Fletcher. I want some straight answers, and to hell with your political ambition."

"I don't have to listen—"

"I've got a list of all the trials that involved you and Judge St. Clair. I'm going to go to the judge's house to see what he can remember. You can join us if you'd like, or we can go over the list right here."

Fletcher glanced at the printout. "I don't know what you're talking about."

Paavo paced. "I've been looking at a connection between two women—one involved with a judge, the other with a DA. What does that sound like to you, Fletcher? It sounds like a trial case, doesn't it?"

"What are you getting at?"

"I'm trying to find out if I'm on the right track with this, or if I'm 180 degrees off base. I need the truth about you and Tiffany Rogers."

"I've already answered that."

"I need your help, Fletcher. I need to find out who's

behind the killings, especially if I'm right about the motive. Think of it, Fletcher. Who else worked on this case? What other women is this guy after? And then, when he's done with the women, will he stop there? What if he decides this revenge isn't enough and goes after you next? To kill you the same way he did Tiffany Rogers."

Fletcher paled and sat down behind his desk. "You aren't making any sense."

"Come on, man. I've got to know for sure if you were seeing Tiffany Rogers, because if you weren't—if you *really* weren't—I could be heading down a blind alley that could be fatal to someone. You've got to tell me, Fletcher. Is hiding a liaison with Rogers worth the life of another woman? Is it worth your own life?"

"This doesn't concern me." His voice was unconvincing.

"It was your woman he got first. You might be the first man to get nailed by this guy," Paavo said.

Fletcher rubbed his forehead. "I love my wife, Smith."

"Then you'd better be telling the truth, because if you're not, and this psycho has something against you and those you love, your wife is in danger."

He gazed up at Smith, his eyes hooded. "All right. I was involved with Tiffany, but I'd better not hear a word about this anywhere."

"I can't guarantee that, Fletcher."

"Damn it, Smith. This could ruin me, and you know it."

"Is being mayor so important to you?"

"It's the only thing that's important"—he shut his eyes—"now that Tiffany's gone." He looked up at Paavo. "I did love her, damn it. It doesn't mean I feel anything less for my wife—Sally and I have had thirty-two years, wonderful years, and three fine sons." Tears filled his eyes. "But I also loved Tiffany. She made me feel young again. Important. She was the one who helped me decide to run for mayor, dammit!"

Paavo waited for Fletcher to gain control again.

The DA clenched his fist, his head bowed. "You're on

your own from here on out, Smith. Get the hell out of my life."

Paavo stood. "You should have told me about you and Rogers days ago, Fletcher. For your sake, it had better not be too late."

Despite the late hour, Julian Bosch agreed to meet Paavo at the Parole Office. Paavo had called several times that day, and every time was told Bosch was out or holding an interview and couldn't be disturbed. He'd never returned one call. Tonight, Paavo had reached him at home and insisted on a meeting.

Now, Bosch was waiting in his office when Paavo arrived. He was a small man with a florid complexion, heavy glasses, and a nervous tic at the corner of his eye. "I'm sorry I hadn't returned your calls, Inspector," he said. "But if it concerns Wesley Carville, I knew it couldn't be anything urgent."

Paavo went into the small, sterile office and sat in a high-backed government-issue chair. "Why do you say that?"

"Because Mr. Carville is one of my easiest cases. He's a well-educated man, Inspector. He'll do fine on the outside. I've already got a number of job interviews lined up. Just waiting for him to give me the word."

"Why hasn't he?"

"He's still got the money he earned while he was in prison. He's not ready to be tied down to a nine-to-five job yet. We see this all the time. Free at last, you know. But he'll come around. Why are you interested in him?"

"I'm investigating a murder."

"And you think Carville might be a witness?"

"I think he might be a suspect."

"Impossible."

"That's what I need to determine. May I see his file?"

"Of course. Here are his records. You'll see he was a model prisoner. No trouble at all. And he's the same with me. A joy to work with—and that's really rare, let me tell you." Bosch shuffled his papers and smiled proudly, as if to take credit for Carville's spotless record.

Paavo started at the back of the file. The write-ups were from wardens, for the most part, from the time Carville entered prison for second-degree murder. A twenty-year sentence—ten with good behavior. Paavo read through them. The man had worked hard, rarely spoke to anyone. Spent all his time in the electronics shop. No doubt about it. He was a model prisoner.

"What's this?" Paavo asked. At the bottom of a page, penciled in small letters, was the annotation, C53794.

"Another case number," Bosch said. "Probably somebody Carville knew in prison."

"Did you check it out?"

"Why should I? The page it's written on is dated eight years ago. I have enough trouble with the here and now."

Paavo nodded and kept going. He copied down Carville's current address—a cheap Tenderloin rooming house. "Is there anything at all strange or different, or in any way troubling, about this man?"

"Nothing. Absolutely nothing," Bosch stated emphatically. "I wish all my people were like him."

With a sweep of his arm he cleared the table in his Tenderloin hotel room of cockroaches and set up his tape recorder. Whistling softly to himself, he picked up his phone and tapped into Angie's answering machine. He hit the code for the machine to play its messages.

The first message was from her mother, asking how her baby daughter was doing. The second was from her sister, Bianca. Bossy bitch. Next came one from some producer, wondering if she'd like to try her audition again.

He shrugged. She wouldn't be around for it. Too bad.

Then he heard one from the cop. He sat forward in his chair, flipped on the record button of the tape recorder, and hit the replay code for the answering machine. This was even better than he'd hoped for.

Next, he dialed Homicide.

"Inspector Calderon here," came a gruff voice.

"Inspector Paavo Smith, please," he said.

"Just a minute." Calderon must have put his hand over the mouthpiece, but Wesley could hear the muffled conversation. "Paavo around? He's got a call . . . Be back soon? No? Not 'til late? Yeah, okay. I got it."

He didn't need to hear anything more. He hung up the phone.

CHAPTER

THIRTY-FIVE

"Seth and I used to fight all the time," Frannie said as she put an egg and some skim milk in a blender. Angie's fourth sister looked almost radiant as she awaited the birth of her first child.

"I remember your fights," Angie shouted over the loud whirring sound. "I think the whole neighborhood remembers. You two weren't exactly quiet about it."

Two years ago, Frannie had married Seth Levine, a young architect. One month after the wedding day, she was back home seeking special dispensation to divorce. Seth came seeking *her* two days later, and she went with him. Their truce lasted three weeks before they were at it again. Serefina threatened to put a revolving door in Francesca's bedroom.

"Ever since he found out about the baby, though," Frannie said, "he's been different. It's as if he finally realized that marriage means family and responsibility." She switched off the blender, dipped her finger in the mixture, and licked it experimentally. "It's as if he figured out what it's all about."

"Doesn't it worry him?" Angie asked, glad she could stop hollering. "You know, the commitment?"

Frannie poured the milk into a ten-ounce glass, then used it to force down a giant vitamin pill. "It does. There are times I think he gets scared by what's happening. I know I do."

"You do?"

"Look at me. I'm big as a house. I feel ugly, awkward, and sexy as an orange peel. I'm quite sure Seth's going to run off with the first halfway-decent-looking woman that smiles at him. But you know what?"

"What?"

"He says I look more beautiful to him now than ever. I guess it's not really beauty he's talking about, but something deeper, something that comes from the heart. Seth and I are closer than ever before. I guess that sounds weird."

"No, I understand."

"What about you and Paavo?"

"I don't know, Frannie. The more I learn, the more confused I am. He's no marrying man, that's for sure. I'm lousy at compromise, impatient, and sometimes a little too emotional. We have nothing in common, spend too much time apart, and rarely see eye to eye. Is that a recipe for a happy marriage?"

"Does it matter?"

Angie thought about Frannie's question a moment. Then, with a big smile, she jumped to her feet and gave her astonished sister a hug. "Obviously, not in the slightest."

CHAPTER

THIRTY-SIX

Paavo finally tracked down file C53794 in Oakland. At first, on being told by Criminal Records that the mysterious number found in Wesley Carville's file wasn't in San Francisco's numbering system, he thought he'd hit a dead end. But then he remembered reading that Carville had lived in the East Bay.

The file was waiting for him when he reached Oakland's Homicide Department. He sat down in an empty interview room and began to read the reports. Carville's parole officer was right about one thing—the case was old. But he was dead wrong about something else. It wasn't about Carville's fellow prisoners.

The case had begun twelve years before with a missing person report in Berkeley. A young woman named Heather Rose Fredrickson, a senior at the University of California, had disappeared.

Hundreds of people were questioned—everyone who had ever known the attractive, friendly coed. Wesley Carville, a graduate student in electrical engineering, was among them. Heather's friends had said she'd complained of someone following her, showing up wherever she went, but she never told them who he was. Or whether, in fact, she even knew. Wesley Carville never became a suspect in the disappearance.

Two years after Heather's disappearance, Carville was found guilty of electrocuting his landlord and sent to prison on second-degree murder. Two years after that, the widow sold the property—a badly run-down one-bedroom house in West Oakland—to some developers, who promptly tore it down. The wrecking crew found a human skeleton bricked into a wall. Dental records proved it to be the remains of Heather Rose Fredrickson.

No cause of death could be determined, and no evidence was found to prove that Carville had murdered her—except the obvious. The house had stood unoccupied over two years since he'd lived there, and, theoretically, anyone could have hidden Heather's remains there. But that was just legalistic maneuvering. It was clear from the way the reports were written, the homicide investigators knew who had killed Heather. Since the man was already locked up for murder, they didn't pursue another trial. But now, he was out.

Paavo shut the file. The coed had disappeared two years before Carville was imprisoned. If he murdered her, he had lived with a corpse buried in the wall of his house that entire time. Presumably, he'd become intrigued with her, stalked her, then killed her and kept her near him. It was a sick perversion of love.

A sudden chill gripped Paavo. Carville . . . an electrical engineering student at U.C. Berkeley. Something in that fact seemed to resonate for him. Something . . . from long ago.

Holding the door to the telephone closet open a tiny crack, he watched the white Ferrari pull into the parking space in the garage.

She got out of the car. His little one. His love. He longed to smother her with roses. She always liked roses.

He almost snatched her then and there, it was that tempting, that hard to watch her walk away from him once again after he'd waited so long. That painful to watch the elevator doors open and swallow her up inside them.

But too much could go wrong. Too many people down here. His original plan was a better one. Much better. In fact, brilliant.

She'd ultimately come to him—if not one way, then the other. He could be patient. After all, the longer the anticipation, the sweeter the fulfillment. Still, his heart pounded and he felt a sheen of perspiration on his forehead.

He waited until the elevator had time to reach the twelfth floor, then he dialed her number. He was a patient man.

Angie unlocked her door to the steady ringing of her telephone. This time of night it could be only one of two things—Paavo or a family emergency. She ran to catch it before the answering machine clicked on.

"Hello?"

"Angie."

It was a man's voice. Familiar. "Yes?"

"It's me. Carter."

She nearly hung up. "What are you doing calling me this time of night?"

"I hope I didn't wake you."

"No. What do you want?"

"I left out a part that belongs in the pager. It's an important part. The device won't work without it. I need to give it to you now. Tonight."

"No. I don't need it. My plans have changed. I have the egg here."

"There? That's even better. I'll come to your place. I charged you a hundred dollars for something that doesn't work."

He was making her nervous. "Forget it, Carter. You can give it to me at Wings. Or give it to Earl. He'll see that I get it."

"But I have to install it. It won't take long. Five minutes."

"I'm sorry. I'm going to bed."

There was a pause, and he spoke again. Very, very slowly. "I know where you live."

"No, stay away!" She slammed down the phone as hard as she could. Shaking, she stared at it, daring him to phone back. In her mind's eye she saw a face. But not *his* face. Not Carter's. It was the face of the man at the dance. Lee, his name was.

They were the same man.

No. She rubbed her forehead. Impossible. And yet . . .

A man sitting on the fender of a BMW at the college. A student, watching her . . .

He had the same broad-shouldered, muscular build. It had been hard to see his face, though, because of his dark glasses and baseball cap.

A baseball cap . . . glasses . . .

There was someone else . . .

Stop this nonsense, Angie! Stop it! She sat down, her knees suddenly too weak to hold her. Was she going mad, or was there really someone stalking her?

She had to call Paavo.

She was reaching for the phone when she noticed the blinking "1" on her answering machine. One message. She pressed Play.

"Angie. It's me." Warm relief eased over her and she felt better, safer, just hearing Paavo's voice. "I can't come by. Something came up." Static crackled over the connection making it difficult to hear his words as he continued speaking. "Another murder. I have"—the static suddenly cleared—"to see you. I can meet you"—static—"at Coit Tower." The static cleared once more. "I'll be here all night."

Coit Tower? At midnight? Why would he want her to come there, of all places? An image of the tower flashed across her mind. The beautiful shaft of white standing in lonely splendor at the top of Telegraph Hill. Sure, the area teemed with tourists by day and on summer evenings, but on cold, foggy nights like this one? There'd be no one there.

Why would Paavo want her to meet him at an investigation? He never had before. In fact, he'd tried to keep her away from his work. But he said he had to see her, that he'd be out all night. It didn't make sense.

She decided to call Homicide and see if anyone there knew what was going on. If not, maybe a dispatcher could locate Paavo for her.

She picked up the receiver and put it to her ear. There was no dial tone. She pushed the button several times and listened again. Nothing. A shiver went down her spine. Had Carter done this to her phone? He said he knew where she lived. And he knew electronics . . .

Suddenly, she wanted nothing more than to get out of her apartment. She should be safe. She had a dead bolt . . .

But with Stan in the hospital, she was alone on this floor of the building. Unable to call for help, unable to telephone the police.

That did it. There was no way she was staying here like a sitting duck, waiting to be scared to death by that man. She wasn't even going to take the time to change to something nicer than her Armani jeans and Cole Haan loafers, but grabbed her purse, a warm leather jacket, and ran out the door.

Coit Tower wasn't very far away. If Paavo wasn't there, she'd go straight to his house and track him down using his phone. That way, if Carter came to her place, he wouldn't find her. She'd tell Paavo about him. One meeting with an angry Paavo, and Carter wouldn't dare to frighten her again. He wouldn't dare to even *think* about her again.

Damn Carter for making her afraid to be alone in her own apartment. She wished she'd listened to Earl.

Back at the San Francisco Hall of Justice, Paavo decided to go down to the archives himself. The secretaries and file clerks had gone home long ago. But he was curious, and didn't want to wait until morning.

First he tracked down the report on Wesley Carville's arrest for the murder of his landlord ten years ago. Although the small, run-down house Carville rented in was in Oakland, the landlord lived in a mansion in San Francisco's Sea Cliff area.

Paavo opened the file and turned to the first incident report. The name of the reporting officer leaped out at him—Matt Kowalski. He knew that ragged scrawl well, almost as well as he knew his own handwriting. He stared at it a moment, then shut the folder. He rubbed his forehead, and then searched for a place to sit. He'd found more than he'd bargained for.

Matt and he had been rookies together, and then partners for a short while as patrol officers at the Richmond Station, which encompassed the Sea Cliff. Paavo was promoted first, and went to Northern, but Matt was right behind him. Eventually, they both wound up in Homicide and became partners again. More than partners, they were best friends. Last October, Matt had been killed in the line of duty.

As Paavo carefully read through the pages of the Carville arrest, he remembered a call he and Matt had taken about an accident at a house in Sea Cliff. The caller had said a man had been electrocuted while working on his house's wiring.

When he and Matt went out to the house, he noticed that the ground wire had been disconnected. They contacted Homicide. The next day, Paavo received word of his promotion, and in no time, he was at the new station. He hadn't learned, until now, what had come of the loose ground wire case.

Paavo put down the file. Fletcher, St. Clair, Matt. Fletcher's and St. Clair's women had received roses, and . . . Angie had received roses from an unnamed student. He felt his blood drumming in his ears, his breath quickening.

Stan, too, had received roses, but didn't know who they were from, or why. Apartments 1201 and 1202. Easy to confuse. Stan had told Angie something about a peculiar deliveryman.

He rubbed his temples. What he was thinking was impossible. Outlandish.

Hurrying back to his desk, he picked up the phone and called Matt's widow, Katie.

He apologized for the late hour. But she'd been a policeman's wife for eleven years. She understood. "Forget the apologies, honey," she said in the saucy, brusque manner she had. "What can I do for you?"

"By any chance did anyone send you roses recently?"

"Roses? Me?" She laughed, a rich, hearty laugh. Matt used to say he fell so hard for Katie because of her laugh. "I'm not ready to be courted yet, sweetheart. And everyone knows it. Why?"

"Just wondering if anyone strange has shown up at your door lately. That's all. It was a long shot on a case I'm working on. I don't even know why I called. I shouldn't have bothered you."

"It's no bother." Her voice turned serious. "But since you mention it, there was someone strange. He gave me the creeps, in fact."

"Tell me."

"It's nothing, I'm sure, but he was a *Chronicle* salesman. He had some sort of two-for-one offer. I told him I wasn't interested, but he insisted my *husband* would want the paper. Finally, I got so angry I told him my husband was dead, and I shut the door. He really upset me, though."

"What did he look like?"

"It was hard to tell because of his baseball cap and sunglasses. He had a mustache, dark brown hair, about six feet tall, muscular build. Like someone who worked out."

"If you see him again, keep away from him. Call for help. He's dangerous."

"Okay. I got it."

"Take care of yourself, Katie."

"You, too, Paavo. Love you, honey."

He hung up the phone. A *Chronicle* salesman asking about Matt.

The salesman that the judge had complained about.

The single, days-old copy of a *Chronicle* at Tiffany's.

And the copy of the *Chronicle* Angie left at his house one night.

"Good Christ," he whispered.

CHAPTER

THIRTY-SEVEN

No murder investigation going on here, Angie thought as she reached the circular parking area in front of Coit Tower. Just a couple of parked cars, and they stood empty. The thick fog made it hard to see into the bushes beyond the blacktop. Angie drove slowly along the edge of the parking area, trying to peer into the shrubs as she went by.

Near the road that led away from the tower and back down Telegraph Hill, she saw a tall, broad-shouldered man standing under a lamppost. The lights hit his jacket, a gray tweed—Paavo's favorite—but his face was in the shadow. She told herself it was Paavo, wanted to believe it was him, yet his stance, the angle of his shoulders, wasn't quite right. Was it someone else . . . or was something seriously wrong?

She rolled down the window. "Paavo?" He gestured for her to follow, then he turned and disappeared into the fog.

"Paavo!"

She agonized over what to do. Perhaps it was him, and it was just the fog refracting light from the lamp that made him appear different.

It had to be him. She'd heard him on the answering

machine, telling her to meet him here. And he'd just waved for her to follow.

The fog seemed thicker, making it more difficult to see. She rolled her car closer to the place where Paavo, or whoever it was, had stood, and tried to see where he'd gone. What exactly was back there in the trees. A thick mist covered her windshield, and the wipers only streaked it. She hesitated, then slowly lowered the window a bit so she could see better.

Suddenly, an arm reached in and pulled up the button to unlock her door. Startled, she turned, and in the instant it took for her to grasp what had happened, her door was yanked open. She stomped on the gas pedal, but felt the back of her jacket grabbed, felt herself being pulled from the car as it lurched forward. She landed hard on the pavement, and when she opened her mouth to scream, something smashed against the back of her head.

The world shattered, then went black.

Paavo hammered out Angie's phone number. The line was busy.

He slammed down the receiver and phoned the hospital. Expecting a nurse to answer, he was surprised when Stan picked up the phone.

"This is Inspector Smith. I didn't think you'd still be awake."

"The damn painkillers are wearing off," Stan complained. "I ache, but at least my head's not in a fog anymore."

"I'm trying to find Angie. Have you seen her or talked to her tonight?"

"She came by this afternoon. That was it, though."

"Did she say what she had planned for this evening?"

"No."

"Okay. Sorry to have disturbed your rest."

"Wait, Inspector. Didn't you ask earlier about some roses?"

"Yes."

"They weren't connected to the attack on me, were they?" Paavo heard a slight tremor in Stan's voice.

"I'm pretty sure they were. Why? Do you remember who sent them?"

"I thought *you* sent them."

"Me? What are you talking about?"

"I ran into the deliveryman down in the lobby and—stupidly—I diverted them. My God, man, you've got to do something!" Paavo's hand tightened on the receiver as he listened to the anguish in Stan's voice. "You see, the flowers weren't meant for me, Inspector. They were meant for Angie."

Angie felt her head being stroked and petted. She kept her eyes shut. Slowly, she began to sort out her perceptions. Her mouth was gagged and she was breathing deeply through her nose, the fear of her air being cut off causing her near panic. Her arms had been pulled back and her hands tied behind her back. And her whole head pounded mercilessly.

The gag cut cruelly into her flesh, preventing her from screaming. She trembled, terrified.

"Awake, my love?"

Carter!

"I didn't want to hurt you," he whispered, still stroking her hair. "You trusted me. You trusted my love. You should always trust me, Heather, and be true to me."

She realized her head lay in his lap, and that she was stretched across a short, upholstered bench of some kind. It smelled of stale tobacco, rotting food, a rancid, musty, dust-filled odor. He ran his thumb over her eyebrow, tracing it, gently at first, then harder and harder, as if he were trying to rub it from her face.

He was mad! Her heart beat so hard, she was sure her entire body was pulsating from it, but he didn't seem to notice. She ached to open her eyes, to try to get away from him. But as scared as she was, she was even more afraid of letting him know she was awake.

Suddenly, his tone changed. "Wake up, bitch! I don't have all night! I didn't hit you that—"

He broke off at the sound of an auto going past them. "Damn. We'll have to find someplace else. Someplace where we won't be interrupted. We need to have a long time together, don't we? It'll be like it used to be between us, Heather." He traced his finger over her ear, her jaw, her chin, then wrapped his hand around her neck. "Just like it used to be."

Paavo unlocked Angie's apartment door and went in. He could feel its emptiness surround him.

He'd phoned her immediately after his talk with Stan. When the line was still busy, he'd called the operator to break into the call, and was told the phone wasn't busy—it was out of order. He drove over here with his siren blaring, telling himself the whole way that she wasn't in any danger.

He'd prayed she'd be here. That when he knocked on her door she'd open it, her big, brown eyes widening in surprise. Then she'd smile and fling herself at him. He loved the way she did that. No one else had ever seemed half so happy to see him.

But her apartment was empty.

He saw a box on the coffee table and a strange metal device beside it. The box had the name Everyone's Fancy on it—Connie Rogers's shop. It was a Fabergé egg. Why would Angie have it? And the metal devices. What in the world were they?

What had she been up to?

He went through the kitchen, living room, bedroom, into the den, looking for a note or message that might give some clue to where she'd gone. Nothing.

Maybe she'd gone to her parents'? He picked up the phone to call. It was dead. Of course, what was he thinking? He put the receiver back on the hook.

He went back into the den, took Angie's appointment

calendar from her desk drawer, and opened it, flipping to today's date.

The page was empty. Where now?

He looked around her apartment again, feeling helpless, furious, and scared for her. It was eerie being here without her bubbling through the place, filling not only the rooms, but all the dark places of his soul. He had to find her.

Carter cranked the ignition switch.

Her eyes were open now. He had pushed her off his lap to the floor of the small, four-door car, and she lay on her side, wedged between the front and back seats, her legs bent. She was still gagged, her hands tied behind her back, and the throbbing of her head had grown worse.

Where did he plan to take her? The newspapers were full of stories about women driven to remote spots, raped, and murdered. Fear paralyzed her, tempting her to give in to whatever he planned in hopes of preventing more terror, more pain.

But something inside her wouldn't give up. Not yet.

As if some new thought had occurred to him, Carter suddenly reset the hand brake between the front bucket seats. She squeezed her eyes shut as she heard him shift in the seat.

"I'm making them pay, Heather. I'm making them all suffer like I did when they took me away from you. Separated us.

"You know what, Heather? Even our house is gone now, too. I know how unhappy you were, with the leaky roof, the heater that never worked. That goddamned landlord. I took care of him for you. I fixed him good."

She felt him grope for her, then his hand touched her hair and he began stroking it. "At least you're here with me again. Just like before." He shifted more, and the small car rocked. "Come here to me, Heather."

His hand gripped her hair and pulled upward. She couldn't stop her cry of pain, and her eyes flew open to see his face looming over her. He pulled harder, making her eyes smart as she scrambled as best she could into a kneeling position. "You're not Heather." He spit the words, letting go of her. "You're the one with the cop! Big shot, knew all about ground wires, electricity. No one would have investigated—they'd have accepted that it was an accident, except for him."

She shook her head, needing to convince him she was Heather. She'd be safe if he thought she was Heather. He loved Heather.

He leaned closer, his face only inches from hers. He smiled. "After I kill you, my vengeance will be over, Angelina. The men who hurt me, who took me from Heather, will have lost their women, too. Isn't that sad?" He chuckled.

Again, she tried to shake her head, to persuade him he was wrong. Despite trying to be brave, though, a tear formed at the corner of her eye. He lifted it onto his finger then put the finger in his mouth. "Heather did that, too," he murmured. "She cried when I told her she was going to die. But it was for her own good. She wanted to leave me. It wasn't safe out there, though. I found a place to keep her very, very safe." He ran his hand over Angie's face, touching the planes and angles of it. "You're so much like her. Like my Heather come back to me again. You were all I ever wanted."

His words devastated her. Even pretending to be Heather wouldn't save her.

Another car drove by, and he abruptly turned from her, released the brake, and sped down the twisting turns of Telegraph Hill.

She had to do something to stop him from going to that remote spot, wherever it was. She had to stay where there were people to help her. In the city. Her city—and Paavo's.

She moved so that she sat on the hump on the floorboard, her back to the console between the front seats.

She waited until he was past the twisting part of Telegraph Hill, where he couldn't drive very fast. Suddenly, the car tilted downward and she realized they were on one of the city's steepest hills. He stepped on the gas and all but flew down the first few yards.

This was her chance. She jutted out her bound hands behind her, grabbed hold of the hand brake, and pulled up on it as hard as she could. The back wheels locked and the car went into a tailspin. Carter screamed with rage.

Paavo noticed that her answering machine showed "zero" messages. He'd left one for her, so she must have played it. Maybe someone else had left a message, and that would explain where she'd gone?

He pressed the replay button.

"Angie. It's me."

He groaned at the thought of listening to his own awkward speech and looked for the fast forward button. He found it just as his words were nearly obliterated by static. A mercy, he thought.

". . . another murder. . . ."

A what? Had he said that? He pulled back his hand. Static erupted again at the words "Coit Tower."

Good Christ, he thought. It was *him*, his voice—except for those few, damnable words covered with static. Another murder. Coit Tower. Someone had tampered with his message, added words, someone who knew how to break into her answering machine, knew recordings, electronics . . . Carville.

How long ago had she played that message?

He ran out to the car and radioed Central Station to order an immediate all-points bulletin for Angie and Wesley Carville, giving the license number for a white Ferrari. They already had a bulletin out on a green Honda Civic. Fighting a sickening feeling at the pit of his stomach, he knew with an awful certainty that the Honda reported at Judge St. Clair's was, in fact, Carville's.

He gripped the dash, shouting into the radio at the dispatcher, who seemed too slow to act, too slow to comprehend, saying to start the search at Coit Tower and consider Wesley Carville armed and dangerous.

A lamppost stopped the Honda's mad spin. The car's front grille wrapped around it. The padded seats she had hurled herself between had protected Angie from being hurt, but crawling to her knees now, she saw the crack in the windshield where Carter's head had hit it. Blood streamed down his forehead and his eyes were shut. She wondered if he was dead.

She worked herself over to the door. With her back to it, she groped until she felt the door handle. She lifted it, then had to lean against it, pushing backwards, to get the door to open. As it opened, she had no way to keep her balance and tumbled onto the street.

Bruised and aching, without being able to use her hands to help her, she had to use the car for support to get back up onto her feet. She hobbled over to the driver's door and looked in the car. Carter certainly looked dead. His face was white and bloody. His knee must have hit the dash hard because his trousers were torn and the knee ripped open so deeply it looked like some bone was showing. Her stomach flipped over at the sight, and the world went a little tipsy.

She was surprised no one was out here yet to help. She'd wait. Someone would come soon.

Then she saw one of Carter's fingers twitch. She jerked back, terrified, and began to run up the steep hill, her only thought being that going uphill would be harder for him in his condition.

By the top of the hill, she was gasping hard for breath. The gag made it nearly impossible to pull in the deep lungfuls of air she needed. She rubbed her face against her shoulder in a vain attempt to ease the gag downward toward her chin. Running the way she'd just done had been silly, she told herself. No need. Carter wasn't coming after her. He wasn't going to be able to move in the condition he was in.

Somewhere, soon, she'd find a house light on, see someone out walking or a car go by. She'd find help and everything would be all right.

Through the fog, she saw the door on the driver's side of the Honda spring open.

CHAPTER

THIRTY-EIGHT

"Is that her Ferrari, Inspector?"

Paavo, standing by Angie's car in the dark parking lot, had been asked that question at least three times already—by each patrol car that cruised by. "Yes. Now find her!" The car, with a slight dent by the headlight, had been found up against a bench with the engine running.

Another officer walked up to him. "I don't see any sign of her."

"Of course not. She's not hanging around the tower. I can see that. She's got to be hiding somewhere on that hill. Look for her. Go through the bushes."

"What I'm saying, sir, is that she might not be anywhere around here. You said there was another car."

Paavo didn't want to think about that—about that bastard taking Angie to some place in his car. He wanted her hiding in the brush here, waiting for him to find her. He wanted her safe.

The policeman part of him, though, knew from bitter experience that if she was here, she was probably dead. He couldn't face finding her himself, but he couldn't bear to leave her out here in the cold, foggy night. He had nowhere else to search for her. No other leads to follow.

"Look a little longer, please," he whispered.

His car phone rang. He ran to it. "Smith."

"Officer Manning, Central. We found the Honda, Inspector. It's got a cheap coat of black paint, but the license matches."

His breath caught. "Yes?"

"It's been in a wreck. On Kearney near Chestnut."

His world tilted. "The occupants?" He could barely get out the words.

"The car's empty."

She saw a light in the upstairs window of a small house. Breathless, she stumbled toward the front door, but with her hands tied behind her, she could only kick it. Her arms and her wrists ached, her mouth burned where the tight gag pressed into her skin. She waited a moment, then kicked again, harder.

The light switched off. No! She wanted to cry out, but couldn't. Why was there no one to help her? From the corner of her eye she saw the black-and-white of an SFPD patrol car go by. She chased after it, but it had already disappeared into the fog.

She couldn't yell, couldn't wave her arms. Instead of coming to her aid, people seemed to shy away, to lock their doors instead of opening them. When had we come to this? Tears of frustration and fear filled her eyes. This was a big city, filled with people. But she felt completely alone.

A movement in the fog caught her attention. She stared at it, waiting, praying that it was someone who'd give her help. She took a step toward the person, then stopped, staring, not believing. He stumbled, his hand to his knee, but still he came forward, toward her, a figure in the mist. But she knew it was him. *Him.*

She turned and ran, praying that the fog had somehow shielded her. But since she saw him . . .

He could reach her easily. Grab her again. She ran.

Ss. Peter and Paul's was nearby. Maybe there . . .

Running down the steep Filbert Street hill, without the aid of her arms to steady herself and help keep her balance, she was forced to slow down, slipping and sliding, never actually falling, but coming perilously close. She expected Carter to catch up to her any moment.

Her lungs were ready to burst as she reached the ten-foot-high doors of the church. Locked. She fell against them, her cheek pressed against the ancient oak as choking, gasping sobs broke from her.

She forced herself to stop, to listen for the sound of Carter's running footsteps reverberating through the empty night.

She listened.

"Where is she, dammit?" Paavo pounded his fist onto the roof of the Honda, fear for her gnawing at him as he looked up at the rows and rows of flats and apartments surrounding them. Yoshiwara had shown up. Paavo wasn't sure from where, and now Yosh stood in the middle of the street directing the investigation. Yosh grabbed his arm. "Take it easy, partner," Yosh said. "We'll find her."

Paavo pushed himself away.

He peered into the fog, up and down the empty, silent street. He didn't know which way to turn, where to begin. He'd never felt so helpless.

The brick facades of some of the garages brought back memories of the Oakland police report of the way they'd found Heather.

"We've got to find her," he whispered. He alone heard his words.

The street was silent. Maybe it wasn't Carter that she'd seen in the fog after all? Or, maybe she'd lost him? Angie kicked at the church doors, but they were so large and solid, they didn't even rattle. She forced herself away from them, to go on, back down the broad church steps to the sidewalk, onward, expecting Carter to appear before her any second.

At the corner, she felt a burst of hope.

"Shhh! I t'ought I hoid somet'in'."

"I didn't hear nothin.'"

"I swear I did. Like a poundin'."

"You musta heard your brains poundin' in protest—from you tryin' to use 'em."

"Shut up, you two! We ain't got all night."

"Maybe it's da cops. You want I should go check?"

"Forget it, I said. Or I'll give you a real poundin'. Who's first?"

"Not me. I hate being foist."

"You never been first for nothin' in your whole life."

"Go on."

"No, you go on."

"No, you."

Angie kicked at the door to The Wings Of An Angel as loud as she could, but no one came to answer it. She was sure Earl, Butch, and Vinnie were down in their basement apartment fast asleep. They'd help her, if she could just reach them.

The door was old, with a large, single panel of glass in a wood frame. Probably not safety glass—probably not even up to code. The only way to get in would be to break the glass, reach inside the door, and unlock it. She tried kicking the glass, but she couldn't kick high enough to hit the sweet spot—the middle area—which she knew was the weakest part.

She'd have to use her elbow and shoulder. Even through the leather jacket, it would hurt, but not nearly as much as Carter if he ever caught up to her.

She rammed her elbow into the window, and fell back. Even her teeth vibrated at the blow. But nothing happened.

She tried again, smashing her shoulder into the center of the glass with as much force as she could muster. The glass shattered. Not bad!

Using her elbow again, she knocked away the glass near the doorknob, turned backwards, and reached in with her bound hands, flicked the dead bolt latch, then grabbed the doorknob and turned.

She ran in, slammed the door shut, looked through the shattered glass to the street—and nearly fainted.

Carter stood before her. Blood was smeared across his forehead and down his right cheek. The right lens of his glasses had a spiderweb crack in it. His stare was deathly cold.

He reached through the broken window for the lock. She brought her elbow down on his hand, grinding it into the jagged glass. He shrieked and pulled it free, scraping it across the broken shards and sending rivulets of blood streaming down the door.

She ran to the kitchen. Behind her, she heard his curses and the sound of more glass breaking.

At the back of the kitchen she found some steep stairs, apparently leading to the basement. Her three friends were surely down there sleeping. Once with them, she'd be safe.

She started down, but on the third step her feet slipped out from under her, and she slid all the way to the bottom.

Slightly dazed, she looked around. To her surprise, she wasn't in an apartment at all, but in an unfinished, bare-walled basement furnished with three old army cots.

Scattered about on the ground near the far wall were tools and a lit Coleman lantern. Directly above them was a huge hole in the wall.

And sticking their heads through the hole, staring intently at her, were Earl, Butch, and Vinnie.

"Miss Angie," Earl said. "What're you doin' here? What's dat t'ing over your mout'?"

She ran to them. Heavy footsteps and banging could now be heard overhead. Angie tried to tell them what had happened, but with the gag her words came out muffled and incoherent.

They asked no more questions. Three pairs of hands reached for her and half carried, half dragged her through the hole.

Earl removed the gag while Vinnie cut the ropes from her wrists.

"It's Carter," she panted. "He's insane. He wants to kill me."

"Good God!" Vinnie bellowed. "I'm too old for this stuff."

"Quick! Let's go up to the jewelry store," Butch said. "Maybe he won't know where to find us."

They ran across the basement and up the stairs to the ground floor. The door leading into the store was locked. Using a crowbar, Vinnie easily popped the lock, and they ran in.

The entire front of the store was windows. Outside, streetlights lit the interior for them.

"Let's get out of here," Angie cried. She ran to the front door of the jeweler's, turned the lock, and opened it, only to be stopped by a heavy metal gate that completely covered the front of the building—both windows and door. All four of them grabbed it and tried to force it open, but it wouldn't. It was padlocked from the outside.

Angie spun around. There was no back door, no back window.

They were trapped.

The streets were eerily empty. Through the fog, Paavo hadn't even spotted a *wrong* person to follow, hadn't even been allowed the faintest glimmer of false hope. He'd driven up and down Kearney and Grant. Now he was on Stockton. He turned off Stockton at Filbert to drive by Angie's church. Ss. Peter and Paul's.

The front of the church looked bare and empty. The doors, he was sure, were locked. God had closed up for the night, and only the godless remained here on the streets.

Angie's restaurant "find" was somewhere near here, he recalled. On Columbus. If she were near it—and able to—she might seek it out, a place where she'd been happy with people she'd liked. A sanctuary.

But at this time of night? Nobody would be there. Like the church, it'd be locked up tight. And besides that, he hadn't even bothered to ask her where it was. Why? Why hadn't he taken the time for her? What if—No! He couldn't, wouldn't, think that.

Gripping the steering wheel hard to rein in his rising panic, he gunned the engine and turned onto Columbus.

CHAPTER

∞∞∞

THIRTY-NINE

"Barricade the door," Angie shouted.

The three men began pushing anything they could find—a desk, a file cabinet, a chair—in front of the door that led to the basement.

She picked up the phone to call the police. It was dead. She dropped it and backed away. That explained why Carter was taking so long in the basement, why he hadn't run up the stairs immediately and tried to break in. But he was out there now, that was certain.

She ran to the back of the counter near the cash register and threw herself to the floor, searching for some kind of alarm. A loud thud hit the door, and the barricade moved back an inch or so.

The men threw their weight against the furniture, trying to keep the door from opening farther. But Carter was stronger. Angie knew they were four against one—but her friends were small, older men. And Carter didn't seem human.

The door inched open. Carter's fingers reached into the room and gripped the doorframe.

Earl, Butch, and Vinnie backed away, their eyes wide

and fearful. Earl grabbed a heavy ashtray, holding it high. Butch clenched his fists like a boxer, and Vinnie found a fake pearl rope necklace that the jeweler hadn't bothered to lock up for the night. He wrapped it around his fingers like brass knuckles.

Angie was in tears, frantic to find the alarm. She found a button on the floor, near the counter's edge. She pushed it. Nothing. It didn't feel as if it was connected to anything. Desperate, she pushed it again and again.

Carter must have cut those wires, too. He knew electronics, he'd said. Yes, he knew them.

He squeezed through the opening. A red, blood-filled bruise the size of an orange lifted from the center of his forehead, small, jagged cuts radiating from it. Strips of flesh dangled from the bloodied mess that once was his hand. His eyes were wild and staring. He took in the three small men, and then Angie. "Hail, the gang's all here," he said.

Angie scrambled to her feet and backed away.

"You ran away from me, Heather." He moved toward her, his voice low and growling. "To other . . . men. I don't like that."

"Get out of here, Carter," she cried. "The police are coming. They'll arrest you."

He pulled a long combat knife from his back pocket. "I don't think so," he said.

She cried out and bolted around the counter to her friends. Earl pushed her behind him.

Carter chuckled. "How noble."

He began to weave forward, making his way closer and closer to them, keeping between them and the door to the basement.

Suddenly, he lunged at Earl with his knife. Earl tried to step aside, out of the way, and at the same time swung the ashtray at Carter's head. The heavy object struck, but too late. The knife went into Earl's side and came out bloody.

"Earl! No!" Angie cried, trying to catch her friend as he fell. At the same time, Butch and Vinnie attacked Carter.

They barely reached his shoulders. Butch grabbed the arm that held the knife and tried to pry it from Carter's fingers. Vinnie, reaching up, pummeled his face with the pearl knuckles.

Angie couldn't get close enough to do anything to Carter, but she saw that the path to the basement door was now clear. She broke for it.

"No!" Carter roared. He threw off Vinnie with ease. Vinnie's head hit the wall, and he dropped, unconscious. Carter whirled and smashed a fist into Butch's face. Angie heard the crack of his nose and saw his blood splatter over the room. The little man went down.

Carter lunged toward her. She skidded to a halt, and spun away from the door just as he crashed against it.

A jeweler's stool had been pushed into a corner. She hurled herself at it and picked it up, holding the seat to her chest, its legs pointed outward.

"Keep away from me!" She screamed. "Keep back!"

"Heather, Heather, Heather." He shook his head, slowly brandishing the knife, as he stepped nearer. "Put the stool down, Heather."

She shook her head, perspiration dripping down her face, into her eyes, nearly blinding her.

He paced back and forth. "You're coming home with me. Again."

He reached for the stool and she swung it so that a leg hit his mangled hand.

"Bitch!" He grabbed the legs of the stool, tore it from her hands, and tossed it aside.

Gun drawn, Paavo stepped through the shattered glass of what had once been a door. The dining room was dark and empty. He ran through the swinging door to the equally empty kitchen.

In the back, stairs led down to the basement. Angie! His mind shouted. But what if his hunch about this restaurant was wrong? What if the broken glass was just some two-bit robbery—a coincidence—and Angie was still out on the street somewhere with Carville?

Could he chance it? Could he chance her life on no more than a guess? Did he believe in coincidence?

He moved swiftly, silently, fearful that if she was here with Carville, the sound of someone approaching might cause him to kill her.

As he descended the steps, he saw a large hole in the basement wall. A hole to the jeweler's next door? It all seemed so bizarre. But something, a vague feeling, told him to crawl through it.

That was when he heard a scuffling sound, a voice.

"Bitch!"

His heart nearly stopped. Silently, he hurried up the stairs.

A scream! Angie!

He burst into the room—in time to see Wesley Carville toss a stool out of the way.

Paavo saw the knife, saw Angie back into a corner, saw Carville slowly, menacingly step toward her.

"Drop it, Carville," he said.

Carville glanced his way, then smirked. "Forget it, Inspector. You can't stop me. No one can." He sprang at Angie.

Paavo fired. The force of the bullet caught Carville in mid-leap and knocked him sideways against the wall. The knife clattered to his feet. He slowly sank to the floor. Before he reached it, he was dead.

The room fell silent.

Angie crouched on the ground. Her eyes met Paavo's, and she tried to stand.

He reached her side in an instant and dropped to his knees. Her face crumbled as she looked at him. Gathering her up in his arms, he held her tight against his chest, rocking her, comforting her. Then he buried his face in her hair and didn't try to stop the tears that filled his eyes.

CHAPTER

―――∞∞∞∞――――

F O R T Y

Vinnie, standing tall in his black suit, greeted Angie and Paavo at the entrance to The Wings Of An Angel. "We saved a table for you an' the Inspector, Miss Angie."

The restaurant was filled to capacity. Three more tables had been added, and two couples sat by the entry waiting for the next available place.

Vinnie seated them, then hurried back to his station at the front door and the cash register.

"I can't believe this," Angie said, marveling at the crowd.

Earl walked up. "'Ey, Inspector, you made it. Awright!" He handed them each a menu. "Dey jus' came in today, Miss Angie."

On heavy, slick white paper, in gold foil lettering were the words: THE WINGS OF AN ANGEL. Below, Butch's specialties.

Angie jumped from her chair and kissed him on the cheek. "It's beautiful, Earl. Congratulations to all of you."

A blush started at the neck of Earl's white shirt and quickly traveled up his face to his shellacked hair. "T'anks, Miss Angie. You helped a lot, too."

She laughed as she sat down again. "How's the spaghetti and meatballs today?"

"Same as ever."

"All these people obviously think they're terrific," she said. "Of course, my article in *Haute Cuisine* praised this restaurant to the hilt, and—I know it's not very modest of me—but I'd say the recommendation of Angelina Amalfi carries some weight in this town." Facing Paavo, she beamed. "This is such a *find* for me."

"An' da food's okay, too," Earl said. "A lotta dese people say da place smells really good when dey pass by, so dey come in." He turned to Paavo. "Inspector, me and da boys wanna say t'anks for explainin' how dat hole in da wall was just 'cause we was tryin' to fix a leak in a water pipe. We didn't mean to go all da way t'rough to da jeweler's store. Honest."

Paavo fixed a steady gaze on Earl. "The guys at the Hall of Justice understood perfectly. I told them you three promised the next time you had a leak, you'd call a plumber. Right?"

"Sure t'ing, Inspector."

"Glad to see you're back on your feet."

"Yeah. It was jus' a nick. An' da swellin' on Butch's nose an' his black eyes is almost back to normal, too. I'll get your dinner."

Angie reached for Paavo's hand. He took hers and gave it a light squeeze. She looked beautiful tonight, with a cream-colored dress that dipped to a V in front and diamond earrings that sparkled with every turn of her head.

He'd taken her to his house that horrible night, and she'd stayed with him the past ten days. She was much better, almost over the nightmares that had awakened her every night for a week afterward.

Each time it happened, he'd held her until she fell asleep again. Held her so that he could pretend to be strong, so that he wouldn't need to talk about his own nightmare. The one that plagued him over and over; the one in which he was unable to find her no matter what he did, no matter where he looked. The one in which Wesley Carville won.

He looked at her small hand wrapped in his, at her well-cared-for nails. They were a soft, creamy white color tonight, to match her dress, he supposed. He must love her even more than he'd imagined if he even paid attention to her nail polish.

"I was thinking, Paavo, that after Easter dinner tomorrow at my mother's—oh, I did tell you all my sisters and their families were going to be there, didn't I?"

He grimaced. "You hadn't given me that good news yet."

"Well, anyway"—she drew in her breath—"after that I'm going back to my apartment."

He shouldn't have felt surprise. She had a beautiful apartment, a great view, while his place was just a simple cottage. But . . . on the other hand . . . so what?

She liked staying with him. He knew she did. She'd told him so often enough. "There's no need to rush," he replied.

"I was driven out of it by fear. I can't accept that any longer."

He nodded in understanding. "Keep in mind, Miss Amalfi," he said, "you can always come back."

"Oh, I'll keep that in mind all right, Inspector Smith."

"Good." He leaned back and smiled at her, his heart full.

"Very good." She leaned back, her eyes dancing.

"Here you go." Earl carried a tray with their meal and put their plates before them. "Enjoy."

"This is it, Paavo," Angie said excitedly. He picked up his fork. "These are the special meatballs and the wonderful spaghetti sauce I was telling you about. Butch won't tell me what the secret ingredient is. Whatever it is, though, he should package it. He'd make a fortune."

She watched expectantly as Paavo took a bite of the spaghetti.

Secret ingredient? he thought. What secret? He cut into the meatball and tasted it, then eyed the meat, then Angie, then the meat again, and nearly laughed aloud. No secret here. Not to him, anyway. To Angie, though, maybe. Yes, he could believe she might be puzzled by it.

"Paavo?"

He put down his fork.

"It's wonderful. Isn't it?"

He touched the napkin to his lips.

She gripped the tablecloth. "What's wrong?"

He looked at the plate of food. "Institutional memory, I'm afraid."

"Institutional what?" She clasped her hands. "I don't understand."

"You see, Angie, it's all of a piece."

She twisted her napkin. "You're talking in riddles," she cried. She hated it when he talked in riddles.

"Down at the Hall the other day, we were discussing Earl, Vinnie, and Butch. And Yosh, who knows all about old songs, remembered one from back in the thirties, with words something like 'if we had the wings of an angel, over these prison walls we would fly.'"

She felt her throat tighten. "Prison walls?"

He nodded. "Army vets, like me, and ex-cons have one thing in common. Unforgettable memories of institutional food. I remember. Butch *really* remembers."

She didn't want to hear any more. Visions of another assignment for *Haute Cuisine* flew away, just like those wings over prison walls. But she couldn't stop herself from saying, "Tell me, Paavo. What's the secret ingredient?"

"You really want to know?" he asked.

"I really want to know," she answered.

"Butch didn't use a whole lot of it," he said, as if that was some sort of consolation. "It's basically just to stretch the meat."

She groaned aloud. Gourmet restaurants did not *stretch* the meat. Barely able to speak, she whispered, "Out with it, Inspector."

"Don't say I didn't warn you," he said. And then, although he spoke in the lowest possible voice, his words seemed to reverberate throughout the entire restaurant. "The secret ingredient, Angie . . . is Spam."